Praise for The Women of Ivy Manor

BETTE

"Lyn Cote weaves a powerful story of love, secrets, betrayal, and passion during the tumultuous years of World War II. Her unique blend of storytelling and dynamic characters brings this era of history to life."

—DiAnn Mills, author of *When the Lion Roars*

"Lyn Cote lured me into realistic, gripping, and sometimes heart-wrenching encounters with an era that has left an indelible mark on both history and human hearts. BETTE is truly unforgettable."

—Kathy Herman, author of the Baxter series and
A Shred of Evidence

"Lyn Cote's craftsmanship shines in BETTE. Her beautiful plotting includes textured settings that jet you around the world into the lives of characters so real we think we know them. Add a heroine we can all admire, and once again the ladies of Ivy Manor grab hold of your heart and hang on."

—Lois Richer, author of *Shadowed Secrets*

CHLOE

"Will steal your heart . . . With her customary high-quality plotting, Lyn Cote has brought to life [a] long overlooked period of United States history. Appealing characterizations exemplify the pathos, despair, and courage of post–WWI America."

—Irene Brand, award-winning author of
Where Morning Dawns and *The Hills Are Calling*

more . . .

Book Three in
The Women of Ivy Manor

Leigh

A Novel

LYN COTE

WARNER
Faith®

NEW YORK BOSTON NASHVILLE

Warner Faith
Time Warner Book Group
1271 Avenue of the Americas, New York, NY 10020
Visit our Web site at www.warnerfaith.com

The Warner Faith name and logo are registered trademarks of the
Time Warner Book Group.

Printed in the United States of America
First Warner Books printing: January 2006

10 9 8 7 6 5 4 3 2 1

Library of Congress Cataloging-in-Publication Data

Cote, Lyn.
    Leigh / Lyn Cote.—1st ed.
        p. cm.—(The women of Ivy Manor ; bk. 3)
    Summary: "A young woman pursues her dreams of being a
journalist, immersing herself in the rights movement and antiwar
protests over Vietnam"—Provided by publisher.
    ISBN-13: 978-0-446-69437-7
    ISBN-10: 0-446-69437-1
  1. Young women—Fiction. 2. Women journalists—Fiction.
3. Nineteen sixties—Fiction.
I. Title.
    PS3553.O76378L45 2006
    813'.54—dc22   2005029158

*To my own college friends: Angie Greene Kuchenbecker,
Barb Ullrich Baumgartner, Jan Shortness Mottaz, and
Jeanne Mosher Craig.
Thanks for all the fun and great memories
from when we were all young and foolish—I mean,* idealistic.

*Also to Dar Listowski Holle, my traveling companion
to Europe and Hawaii.
When we were young and single and carefree.*

*And to Connie Brown Piper.
You've always been like a sister to me.*

"Amazing grace, how sweet the sound
That saved a wretch like me.
I once was lost, but now I'm found
Was blind, but now I see."
—*John Newton*

Leigh

The Carlyle Family

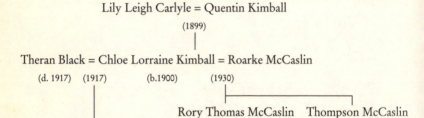

Lily Leigh Carlyle = Quentin Kimball
(1899)

Theran Black = Chloe Lorraine Kimball = Roarke McCaslin
(d. 1917) (1917)   (b.1900)   (1930)

Rory Thomas McCaslin   Thompson McCaslin
(b.1931)   (adopted 1931)

Curtis Sinclair = Elizabeth "Bette" Leigh Black = Ted Gaston
(d.1947) (1941)   (b.1918)   (1947)

Linda Leigh Sinclair   Dorothy "Dory" Lorraine Gaston
(b.1947)   (b.1958)

PROLOGUE

New York City, November 1983

Through two horrific days and one long night, Leigh Sinclair had held it together. Until an hour after she hugged her little girl and watched a doctor give the child a sedative at the hospital and finally, thankfully, brought her here—home to her own bed. Then Leigh had fallen apart.

All her self-control dissolved in an instant, and she started shaking and couldn't stop. Nate had led her from her sleeping child into the dark living room. He'd nudged her down onto her sofa. Murmuring, he'd sat down and laid her head against his shoulder. And slowly the trembling had ebbed.

Just a few weeks ago, Leigh had only known Nate Gallagher, NYPD detective, professionally. He'd made it clear she interested him, but she'd kept him at arm's length as she did every other man. Then she'd needed him and he'd come through for her. Now he stroked her long hair with steady hands, giving her wordless comfort.

"It's all my fault." The words flowed out of Leigh's

mouth a second time. Through the crisis, she'd fought voicing this admission, knowing it wouldn't help, knowing that guilt was natural and unavoidable. Yet all the while fearful that someone else—*everyone else*—would point accusing fingers at her.

Nate said nothing in reply, just continued stroking her hair. In her weakness, she felt the latent strength in his large rough hands.

"I've always carried so much guilt about Carly," she whispered. "Not just now. But always." *And I always will.*

Little Carly's face glowed in Leigh's mind. Grandma Chloe always said Leigh's little girl got her looks from Leigh's grandfather, who'd died in World War I. That was because Grandma Chloe had never seen Carly's father. Carly was the spitting image of her father with his fair skin, black hair, and gray eyes.

But Carly had never seen her father, either.

This fact never stopped gnawing at Leigh. She knew it had created an invisible barrier between her and Carly. Every time she looked at her, her daughter's sober little face—her silent little mouth, those somber eyes that hid every thought—haunted Leigh.

"Everything will be okay," Nate said at last.

Leigh gazed up at him. His face was guarded by shadow, but the moonlight illuminated the warmth of his auburn hair. She couldn't form words, her mouth paralyzed.

I've stood apart from my daughter since she was born. Secrets separate us. Secrets I can't divulge. Will I never break through to her, connect with her heart-to-heart?

Part One

CHAPTER ONE

Maryland, August 24, 1963

"I know why you're doing this," Leigh muttered beside her mother, Bette, in their Chevy Impala. Leigh kept her voice low, not wanting to upset her five-year-old sister, Dory, who sat in the backseat with a coloring book. "You think if you get me out of D.C., I won't be able to get to Dr. King's march."

Her mother made no reply.

Leigh snapped on the radio, knowing it would annoy Bette. The air between them vibrated with the top-of-the-charts "Heat Wave," the words blurred by the hot wind rushing through the wide open windows.

Still her mother made no response. "I don't know why you have to act like this," Leigh muttered louder.

That was enough to break her mother's silence. "This is not open for discussion," Bette said. "You have no idea what may happen this Wednesday. Have you forgotten mobs in Alabama clubbing Freedom Riders with baseball bats? *I haven't.*"

"This isn't Alabama," Leigh snapped. "And Mr. Pitney, the advisor to the school paper, doesn't think there'll be any violence."

"Mr. Pitney is very young and should have better sense, Linda Leigh," Bette answered back, her voice fierce but low.

"Don't call me that name. I hate it." *Hate you.* "I go by Leigh now."

Bette gave a sound of irritation. "Linda Leigh is a perfectly good name." She paused, obviously trying to control her temper. "You'll spend the last week before school starts at your grandmother's. And tomorrow, I'm going to call the school and tell the principal what I think of a teacher urging his students—my daughter—into harm's way."

"I will get back to Washington if I have to hitchhike there." Leigh stared straight ahead.

"Why can't I make you see sense? The march will be dangerous."

Martha and the Vandellas sang out husky and loud, "heat wave . . ." The raucous song evidently finally got to Bette. She snapped off the radio. "Why are we listening to that trash?"

"It's not trash, Mother. It's rock and roll."

Looking out the window at the lush green tobacco fields rolling by, Leigh realized they were almost there, almost to Ivy Manor. She folded her bare arms on the open window and set her chin on them, frustration roiling inside her.

"There it is," Dory piped up from the backseat, sounding the usual joy of coming to Grandmother's house. "There's Ivy Manor!"

As her mother drove up the lane to the large house with white pillars and green ivy, Leigh felt a lift in spite of her frustration. Until . . .

"Maybe Grandmother can make you see sense," Bette said as she parked and turned the key.

"No one—not even Grandma Chloe—is going to change my mind," Leigh kept her voice low as her little sister climbed out of the backseat.

Her mother ignored her, as usual. Now that they'd stopped and the wind no longer evaporated their perspiration, the humidity wrapped around Leigh, smothering her. She felt limp in the heat. Her mother, on the other hand, looked as fresh and collected as always. Of course, even when going to the country, her oh-so-proper mother wore a stylish red sundress and chiffon scarf, under which her bouffant style had every hair in place. In contrast, Leigh and Dory had dressed sensibly in one of their matching outfits that Dory loved so much—blue shorts and white sleeveless blouses with blue collars. The outfit now made Leigh feel childish in comparison to her mother.

Her insides still churning at highway speed, Leigh got out and slammed the car door, eliciting a world-weary sigh from Bette, who scolded her with a look for slamming the door. Leigh felt like going back and slamming it again. But she couldn't give in to childish anger. Instead, her ponytail swishing against her shoulders, she ran ahead, overtaking her sister, calling for her grandmother. Then Leigh heard the voice she loved best, summoning them to the shaded and screened summer house on the back lawn.

With Dory right at her heels, Leigh whipped inside the summer house and flew straight into Grandma Chloe's arms. Dory was right beside her, and they hugged Chloe together. Chloe wasn't overweight and she didn't rinse her gray hair blue or tease it like other grandmothers did. And she always smelled subtly of roses. The fragrance enveloped Leigh, giving her a sudden feeling of ease. Grandma Chloe would set everything right.

"Leigh, Dory, how wonderful to see you." Chloe kissed

their foreheads and cheeks before releasing them. She rose then and reached for their mother. The two older women hugged. "Bette, honey, of course I'm happy to see you, but what's come up so suddenly?" Dressed in a cool, sleeveless lavender-print sundress, Chloe eased back onto the wicker rocker. Dory took her usual place, perching on one of its wide, curved arms.

With another sigh, Bette sat down on a white Adirondack chair. "I hope you can put up with these two girls for the rest of the week."

"No!" Leigh fired up, vaguely aware of her grandmother's surprised look. "Grandma, Mr. Pitney, my journalism teacher, said that the one of us who writes the best first-person account of the march on Washington will be the new editor of the *Scribe* this year."

"Your safety is more important than an article in a school paper," Bette snapped.

"Grandma, she's treating me like a baby again." Leigh pictured Mr. Pitney's face in her mind. He'd said the newspaper staff could call him Lance when they were working on the school paper. Mr. Pitney looked like a Lance—tall, young, with golden hair and a cool mustache. "I'm old enough to go to a public place alone. I've been to Lincoln's Memorial a zillion times."

"Mother," Bette raised her voice, "would you please talk some sense into this girl's head? President Kennedy tried to persuade Martin Luther King Jr. to cancel—"

"Nothing's going to happen!" Leigh's hands tightened into fists. Her mother never took her seriously. Lance did. He didn't treat her like she was just another teenager. "It's going to be a peaceful demonstration. Dr. King believes in nonviolent protest—"

"Well, the KKK doesn't," Bette declared flatly. "The police in Washington and the surrounding counties in Virginia have had all leaves cancelled. The Justice Department and the army are practicing riot control—"

"Stop it," Leigh snapped, imagining the appreciative look on Lance's face when he read her account of the march. "Nothing's going to happen."

Chloe looked back and forth between her daughter and granddaughter with a look of growing distress.

"That's enough, young lady," Bette ordered.

"But," Leigh began. Dory hid her face against Chloe's slender shoulder, bringing Leigh's words to an abrupt stop. She sighed.

"Sorry, ladybug," she apologized to her little sister with her favorite endearment.

"I don't like arguments, and don't speak disrespectfully to your mother, Leigh," Chloe scolded gently, rocking while patting Dory's head.

Leigh flushed, feeling warmth suffuse her face and neck. "Sorry." Her little sister looked upset, but their mother had involved her in this. Leigh hadn't.

"The KKK will not let this go by without reacting," Bette continued in a calmer voice. "They gunned down Medgar Evers on his *own* front porch just two months ago. What if one of them decides to shoot Dr. King right in the middle of the march? It would be chaos. Leigh could be trampled—"

"This is Washington, D.C., *not* Mississippi." Leigh felt her tenuous hold on her temper begin to fray. She could not lose this battle. She'd die if Mary Beth Hunninger got the editor's job. Mary Beth was "the girl" on campus at St. Agnes Girls Academy—runner on the track team, National Honor Society president last year, and now she wanted to horn in on the *Scribe*.

"Why does everybody got to be so mad?" Dory's small

voice asked. "Make them stop fighting, Grandma." Again, Dory buried her face in their grandmother's shoulder.

"I'll do what I can, ladybug." Chloe smoothed back Dory's dark bangs and then tightened the little girl's ponytail. "Now, if I have this correct, Bette, you want me to keep your girls here at Ivy Manor this last week before school starts so that they will be out of Washington, away from Dr. King's march, right? And Leigh, you want to go to the march and write an article about it for school?"

Leigh stood in the center of the screened octagonal room, tension zinging through her.

Chloe sighed. "I hate being put into the middle like this, Bette."

Leigh stood her ground. Surely Grandma Chloe wouldn't side with her mother. She couldn't.

Bette rubbed her forehead. "I know, but for some reason whatever I say, my daughter always does the opposite."

That wasn't true. Leigh folded her arms and glared at her mother.

"What does Ted say?" Chloe asked.

Bette humphed. "He says he won't get into it."

Chloe nodded and continued to stroke Dory's hair. "Well, only because you asked me, I'll tell you what I think. You're both right. Dr. King plans this to be a non-violent protest. But there's always a possibility of violence whenever any very large group of people gets together."

Bette nodded and murmured a satisfied, "I know."

Leigh frowned at her grandmother.

"They're preparing for at least one hundred thousand," Bette declared. "Apart from the KKK barging in with baseball bats, just a crowd of that size . . . Anything could happen to Leigh."

Sensing defeat, Leigh flung herself down into a wicker chair with a sound of disgust.

"Why is reporting on this march so important to you, Leigh?" Chloe asked.

Leigh frowned. That was easy. She couldn't bear to think of having to take direction from *Mary Beth*, her rival ever since Leigh had started at St. Agnes in the ninth grade. "Grandma, I've worked hard on the *Scribe* the last two years. I can't let . . . someone else get the editor job." *I'm going no matter what you say or do, Mother.*

"Your mother's fears about possible violence aren't exaggerated." Chloe rocked back and forth gently. She picked up a strand of Dory's ponytail and tickled the little girl's nose with its end, making her smile. "Even Dr. King is afraid that they may be met with resistance from white supremacists."

Leigh looked down at her lap, fisting her hands. *No. No.*

Bette sat up, looking relieved. "So you'll keep Dory and Leigh for the rest of the week?"

Leigh could defy her mother, but not her grandmother. She recognized this, but couldn't explain it. She blinked back frustrated tears. Defeat tasted bitter. *This can't be happening.*

"Bette, while I agree to some extent with what you've said," Chloe continued, "I can't do what you want me to do."

Leigh's head snapped up to see her grandmother's face.

Bette leaned forward. "Why not?"

Chloe met their eyes. "Because I'm going to attend the march myself."

Chapter Two

Shocked silence reigned in the summer house. Then Leigh squealed, "Grandma, we can go together! This is so cool!" She leaped to her feet and ran to hug Chloe.

"*Mother*," Bette opened her mouth and babbled, "have you lost your mind?"

"Bette, I didn't tell you because I didn't want to worry you." Chloe let Leigh hug her and then pushed her to go back to her seat. "But your stepfather and I discussed it, and we've decided to go and show our support for civil rights. You know we've been hoping and praying for the end of Jim Crow since before you were born."

"But to actually attend a march, *Mother*." Bette stared at her, her mouth still open.

"You can't stop me from going now," Leigh declared. "Not if Grandma and Grandpa are going."

Bette's gaze went from her mother to her daughter's, and then sharpened. "You are still my daughter," she stated firmly. "And you will not—"

The sound of a car horn blaring from the drive interrupted the conversation.

Chloe stood up, joy flashing over her face. "They're here!" She hurried out of the summer house, nearly running toward the front of the house, calling, "Minnie! Minnie!"

With open arms, an older Negro woman met Chloe in the drive. They crashed together—hugging, laughing, weeping. Leigh stood back, wondering who this woman was and why she was so special to her grandmother. And did any of this have anything to do with Wednesday's march?

Leigh couldn't take it all in. That evening, the white-linen-covered dining room table at Ivy Manor was crowded with family—her own, including her stepfather (who'd arrived just as they sat down), her grandparents, and three strangers. At least strangers Leigh had heard of but never met. These were Mrs. Minnie Dawson (whose stage name was Mimi Carlyle), her husband, Frank Dawson, and their grandson, Frank Dawson III, who had been away in college. In her late eighties, Minnie's frail mother, Jerusha—who'd still been the housekeeper at Ivy Manor when Leigh was a little girl—had also joined them.

Minnie was very attractive for her age—she had a nice figure and was well-dressed, with only a touch of gray in her hair. Her husband matched her in good looks and fashionable clothing, as did their grandson.

While this wasn't the first time Leigh had seen Negroes sit at her grandmother's table, Leigh sensed these strangers were different . . . special. Chloe and Minnie kept touching hands, grinning at each other and wiping away tears with embroidered hankies. From their conversation, Leigh understood this wasn't a reunion of two friends long separated. Her grandmother and Minnie talked of visits over the years. But the visits had apparently been in New York City rather than at Ivy Manor. The tears, the auspicious quality of the moment, came from Minnie's long-awaited homecoming—after having spent nearly fifty years away.

Leigh listened with avid interest to Chloe's explanation that Minnie and she had grown up together at Ivy Manor and had gone off to New York City in 1917. Minnie had ended up as an actress there. It sounded like a story from a book, but the truth was sitting here right in front of her.

Delighting in the history lesson, Leigh asked several questions. After a while, though, she noticed Minnie's grandson, whom they called "Frank Three," glancing her way a few times, looking amused. Something about his looks made her feel very young and even gawky. Embarrassed, she curtailed her comments, answering just yes and no to questions sent her way. This was not like herself at all, especially here at Ivy Manor.

After a dinner that passed with laughter and much banter (some of which Leigh didn't fully understand), she was sent upstairs to put Dory to bed. She kept the door to the hallway open as she tucked her sister into the trundle bed for the night. Snatches of conversation floated up to her.

"I'll never forget the first time we saw you on the stage." That from her grandfather Roarke, she assumed, to Minnie.

"Oh Bette, I loved picking out your prom dress." That from Minnie. *Why did Minnie pick my mother's prom dress?*

"I can't believe I'm really here." That from Minnie, repeated one more time. "And sitting at the dining room table." She chuckled. "Chloe, what would your parents say if they could see us now?"

Leigh heard her grandmother laugh amid the sounds of everyone rising to go sit out in the summer house. But she missed the rest of Chloe's response because Dory interrupted Leigh's eavesdropping, reminding her primly she hadn't said her prayers. Leigh performed the nightly ritual, concluded with hugs and kisses, and then left her sister. She knew the younger girl would get right up and sit at the window watching and listening to the night sounds and the conversation below. She didn't blame her. The day had turned out so much differently than Leigh could have predicted.

She walked down the front hallway stairs. With everyone outside, the house felt empty and silent. Leigh decided to use the front door and strolled outside, somehow hesitant to join the adults. Although she'd enjoyed the dinner conversation, hearing facts she'd never known about her grandmother's life and from strangers had struck her as . . . odd. It pressed her to change how she'd thought of her grandmother, as a woman without a past. *Why hadn't I ever thought of Grandma Chloe as young?*

Outside, twilight had taken over the sky in blazing pink and bronze layers and a watermelon-red sun hung suspended just behind the silhouetted tree tops. As she walked down the side of the house, she glimpsed Frank Three standing near the line of poplars along the drive. His skin was the color of coffee with cream; he was tall, lean, and good-looking. He'd shed his sports coat, and his starched white shirt glowed in the dusky light. Her own casual shorts and blouse made her feel at a disadvantage. Wishing she were wearing something more elegant, like his grandmother's white Chanel sheath, she halted, uncertain of approaching him, uncertain of her welcome.

With a nod, he acknowledged her. In fact, he appeared to have been waiting for her and now he motioned her to come to him.

She sucked in a breath. Anywhere but here at Ivy Manor, a conversation between Frank and her would be dangerous, especially to him. But here he was, the grandson of her grandmother's oldest friend, a welcomed guest. Leigh considered this, gathering her courage. Then she tossed her head, shaking off her fears. This wasn't 1917. Her hands clasped behind her, through the growing shadows, she sauntered toward him and onto shaky ground. "Hi," she murmured with what she hoped was the right amount of friendliness.

"Hi." He grinned. Then he nodded toward the summer house, where conversation and light laughter continued. "I don't feel up to any more 'do-you-remembers.' Why don't we take a walk? There's a river near here, isn't there?"

Leigh tingled with uneasiness. In spite of the twin protections here of privacy and family, speaking to Frank challenged her to cross more than one line. He was older than she, and she'd never talked to a Negro boy before and certainly never alone. But then, attending an all-girls school meant that she rarely spoke to white boys either, and also never alone. It was his color, though, that heightened her reaction to him, to the situation. She felt awkward and yet she also felt daring. Speaking to a Negro boy carried many possible consequences. Or was she just prejudiced?

This thought struck her then with blinding force. She'd wanted to go to Dr. King's march on Wednesday, but she realized now she'd intended to go only as an observer, not a participant. Until this moment, civil rights had been abstract to her. It hadn't been to her grandmother. She and Minnie had grown up here together; they'd helped each other break away from Ivy Manor. And now they were planning to march together on Wednesday as they had back in 1917.

What did this Negro college boy think of the reunion between their grandmothers? Why was he daring her to step out of her place and his?

"Meeting you, your family . . . This is really weird," he

murmured. "Isn't it?" He glanced in the direction of the voices. "Maybe we should just go to the summer house?"

His uncertainty matching hers made the difference. She felt the tension inside her loosen. She straightened. "You got that right," she whispered and gave him a smile. "The creek's this way." She led him down the rutted dirt lane toward the nearby wide creek that fed the Patuxent River farther downstream. As they walked, she realized that until that moment she'd thought of him as just a boy. But he wasn't like the other boys she met. For the first time, she realized, she was alone in the company of a young *man*. This was unusual enough without anything else added. Waves of reaction to his alien masculinity flowed through her. She hoped she wouldn't do or say anything stupid and embarrass herself.

"I had planned to attend King's civil rights march with a couple of college buddies," Frank spoke casually as if they weren't really strangers, "but then my grandmother said no, to come with them. And then one buddy got drafted and the other got a job."

Frank's easy conversation helped Leigh get a feel for him, helped her relax more. "You're in college?" she asked.

"Just graduated. I completed a B.S. in mechanical engineering from NYU."

Frank was even older than she'd thought. "Congratulations," she said automatically.

"Where are you drudging away?" Frank kicked a stone with the polished toe of his brown shoe.

Leigh hated to admit to still being in high school, but he'd know she was younger than he. "I'm a junior at St. Agnes, a girl's school in the D.C. area."

"Really? I thought you'd be starting college by now."

Leigh flushed with pleasure.

"So you want to go to the march, but your parents, especially your mother, don't want you to?" he asked lightly.

"How did you guess that?" Leigh stared up at him as they passed under the tall, tangled oaks, stretching over the lane. The argument over the march had not been referred to at the dinner table.

"Your mother has a very *expressive* face." He chuckled. "Every time the march was mentioned she frowned—usually at you."

"Oh." Leigh didn't want him to get the wrong impression. "Mother isn't against civil rights. She just doesn't—"

"Doesn't want her daughter in a march," Frank cut in. "My father was the same way when I decided to go south and join a sit-in at a lunch counter in South Carolina."

Leigh took in her next breath sharply. Stark black-and-white newspaper photographs of the incidents flooded her. "You did that?" *How did you have the courage?*

"Yeah, two summers ago, right after my sophomore year. My father, Frank Two, was afraid I'd get arrested and have that blot on my record to dog me the rest of my life."

As they neared the creek, she picked her way over the ruts, patches of grass, and tree roots with care and chose her words the same way. "Did you get arrested?"

"Yes, twice." He shrugged. "But it was just a misdemeanor charge, like a parking ticket. No big deal."

He must think the controversy over whether I can go to the march is lame. Although she was impressed by his courage, Leigh didn't think she should remark about it. His casual attitude had set up the way he expected her to react. "You're lucky," she said. "You're older and male. You can get away with . . . going against your parents. I'm afraid I'm going to miss the march."

With one hand, Frank batted a floating swarm of gnats

away from his face. "Maybe your grandparents can persuade your mother to let you go with them."

"Maybe," she replied without conviction.

They arrived at the stream, which was edged by weeping willows, maples, and brush. Frogs bellowed back and forth. The stream rippled in the twilight, reflecting the gold, pink, and red sinking sun behind them.

Frank took one of the weeping-willow whips in his hand, running it through his palm. "My grandmother has never been back here since she left in 1917. I've heard about Ivy Manor all my life, but I never thought I'd be here." He glanced over his shoulder at the distant lights from the house.

"Really? I love it." Leigh mimicked Frank and tugged at a willow whip, feeling the long slender leaves and smooth bark rasp across her palm. "Grandma Chloe and my other grandmother, who lives nearby, always have us—Dory and me—stay for most of the summer. And we visit often."

"You don't know, do you?" Frank asked, releasing the willow branch, which snapped back into place. He turned to face her. The low light illuminated his face, making his large black eyes glimmer. She nearly took a step backward.

"Know what?"

"Know that Minnie was your grandmother's maid?"

"Well, I suppose that makes sense." She tickled the underside of her chin with the end of the willow, wondering why he'd brought this up. "I mean, it was the World War I era, wasn't it?"

"And did you know that my great-great-grandmother was your grandmother's *mammy*?" He said the final word with a disdainful twist, like a taunt.

Leigh tried to follow the connection through what she knew of Ivy Manor and her grandmother. Was he trying to make her uncomfortable? "You mean Aunt Jerusha's mother?"

"Yes." He gave a sudden twitch and batted away a mosquito.

She looked down at her open-toed sandals, at the white pearl Maybelline nail polish her mom hated. What was he trying to get from her? She challenged him with a grin. "When I was a little girl, Aunt Jerusha made the best sticky buns."

Allowing the moment to lighten, Frank laughed. "She did. She made them for us when she came up to New York to visit us. But it's interesting you called her Aunt Jerusha. That form of address goes back to slavery, too, you know."

Finally, Leigh processed the other part of his original statement. She cocked her head toward him. "A mammy? You mean like in *Gone with the Wind*?" She'd seen this 1939 film classic in 1960 when it had re-released in theaters.

"Well, I hate to give any credibility to a movie that portrayed Negroes as preferring slavery to freedom, but yes. Haven't you ever realized that the Carlyle family, your mother's family, owned slaves? In fact, owned my ancestors?"

Leigh felt her mouth open but no words came. The willow whip slid from her fingers, bouncing away from her. Finally, she said, "But Grandmother's not like that." *I'm not like that.*

"Well, I'm not talking about your grandmother. I'm talking about your ancestors. Maryland wasn't in the Confederacy, but it was a slave state." Frank's tone was merely conversational. He wasn't giving her any hint of what he might think about this.

"I know that." *I just never thought of my family as slaveholders.* "Are you sure?" For something to do with her hands, she tightened her ponytail by pulling on its ends.

"Both *my* grandmother's family name and *your* grandmother's family name was Carlyle. That tells the story." He took a few steps and leaned a shoulder against a venerable wide oak. "Slaves usually took the name of their masters at the time of emancipation. It also means that we're probably related by blood, too."

Leigh couldn't believe that this young Negro man was standing here telling her these things as if it were common knowledge. Did everyone else know these things about her family history? Was she the only ignorant one? *What else don't I know?*

"Have I shocked you?" he teased, grinning.

"I think you wanted to shock me." The words came out without forethought. "I've never had a conversation like this before."

He chuckled. "You're not a kid. Though I think you have a mother who overprotects you. The next time you're alone with your grandmother, ask her. I'm sure she'll tell you the truth."

His affirmation that she wasn't a kid and could be trusted to hear such things heartened her. But was he telling her the truth? "Why didn't Aunt Jerusha ever say anything to me?"

"Probably for the reason you gave earlier—you're a young white girl and must be protected from the harsh realities of life and history." Turning, he rested his head against the trunk, facing her fully.

The same irritation that she'd felt on the way there that day flushed hot in her stomach. "I don't want to be protected."

"Ah, you may say that—" He lifted one eyebrow in the lowering light. "—but I've been unprotected, and it's not fun."

When had he been unprotected? She thought over his

words and he gave her time, just watching her. "You mean when you were sitting-in?" she asked finally, hesitantly.

"I do indeed. You see, I hadn't realized how much I'd always been hedged in by money, my professional-level family, and living up north where discrimination is more subtle. But two minutes sitting at an all-white lunch counter in South Carolina stripped all that away from me." His voice firmed, hardened. "People bumped me, struck me from behind, cursed me, aimed catsup down my collar. And then I was dragged, and I do mean *dragged*, off to jail. If that doesn't humble you, nothing in this world will."

Leigh felt as well as heard the passion seeping into and through his words. Before they'd just been talking about history. Now this young man was revealing himself to her. It was almost as if he were warning her. But of what? "But you went back?"

"Yes, I went back the next day and the next." His voice had a fierce edge now. "It both humbled me and gave me a hint of what my ancestors had endured for centuries—what I'd been shielded from—and *that* made me angry. *That* made me determined. I'm going to live life on my terms or not at all."

Leigh felt his last words burn through her, searing her deep inside. "That's what I want," she murmured.

He chuckled gruffly. "Well, don't we all?"

Why was he telling her all this? Was there a secret or hidden message, or was he just telling her things he wouldn't reveal to someone in his everyday life? She'd experienced that before, often when riding the bus in Washington, when strangers, often tourists, had for some unknown reason told her their life stories. Was this a case of that? "I want the same thing. I want to live life on my own terms."

"You come by it honest." He moved to stand in front of

her. "Your grandmother ran away with my grandmother to the big bad city. If you think you're overprotected, just think how your grandmother lived."

She sensed his nearness in two ways. Physically, she tingled with awareness of him. In her heart, she thought he might be wondering why'd he talked so much, why he'd opened himself to her, too. But Leigh didn't put any of this into words. Again, he'd set the tone. They were two adults speaking. So she skimmed over everything and made the expected reply. "You're right. And if she can do it, I can, too."

"And remember, you're not alone. I don't do what my parents want, either." He grinned suddenly. "They all think they know what's best for us. My parents are upset that I haven't enrolled in law school or graduate school yet. They're afraid I'll get drafted if I'm not a full-time student. But I don't want to get my masters' degree now or even a law degree. I haven't decided—"

"Leigh!" her stepfather called through the falling night. "Leigh, are you with young Frank? Your Uncle Thompson and his family are here."

"Yes," Frank answered for them, "we're coming." Frank leaned close. "Let's go back. We should have remembered," he taunted, "that even here at Ivy Manor we'd need a chaperone."

She made a sound of irritation. Maybe that's what had really nudged her into sharing this private time. She didn't doubt that her mother had sent her stepfather to find her, to keep her within her mother's bounds.

He leaned close to her ear. "I'll do what I can to see that you get to the march."

Leigh didn't have a chance to respond because suddenly her stepfather was there, holding out his hand to her. She and Frank obediently joined their families in the summer house.

But Leigh barely paid attention to what was being said. Frank's conversation kept going around and around in her mind. What did he mean about helping her? What could he do to get her to Washington on Wednesday?

Wednesday, August 28, 1963

*I*t was barely morning, and Leigh couldn't believe her eyes or ears. On Sunday evening, her parents had driven home to jobs in northern Virginia. Leigh and Dory had been moved—with Chloe's apologies—from Ivy Manor to their Grandmother Sinclair's home . . . for safekeeping. Chloe would not go against Bette, so Grandma Sinclair would take them for the week. Last night, Leigh had nearly burst into tears with frustration. How could she get away from Grandma Sinclair's home? It was impossible.

Then today's dawn had seeped in through the sheer yellow curtains and Leigh had heard something at her second-story window—pebbles hitting the glass. She looked down to see Frank, who was motioning her to come. She leaned over the sill and heard his murmur, "Get dressed, write a note so you don't worry everyone, and come on. We have to get going."

It hit her then. Frank was keeping his promise. He was going to take her to D.C. Equal amounts of guilt and excitement overwhelmed her momentarily. Then she nodded vigorously and pulled back inside. Within minutes, thinking of the heat but also of the possibility of sunburn, she dressed in blue pedal pushers and a blue-and-white sailor blouse. She scratched a hasty note to Grandmother Sinclair, slipped her small white pocketbook into her pocket, and tiptoed down the stairs.

Outside the day was bright and pleasant, but with a heavy feeling, promising to be another sweltering day. Her heart did flip-flops in her chest. Immediately, she glimpsed Frank's grandparents' silver Buick up the road, partially concealed by a knot of pines. She ran down the drive straight to the car.

Standing by the car, Frank put out a cigarette, mashing it underfoot. He was wearing a summer-weight suit of tan. He smiled at her and opened the car door. "Ready?"

"You're taking me? You mean it?" Delicious freedom swelled inside her.

"Get in." He ushered her into the passenger seat, then started the car and drove off, quiet and slow.

"How did you manage it?" Leigh asked, irresistible excitement bubbling up inside her.

"I told my grandparents that I wanted to go ahead. I had a friend I'd promised to pick up. They're all taking the train in. But you and I are going to drive to the outskirts of D.C., park, and take the bus or subway to the Lincoln Memorial."

"Cool. This is so cool." Leigh almost bounced on the seat.

Frank laughed out loud. "This day is all about freedom, and I decided you shouldn't be cheated out of yours. Besides, this year is the centennial of the Emancipation Proclamation, and I decided that our attending the march together is too symbolic to miss."

"You mean because my family owned your family in 1863?" These words still made her feel strange. It was hard to say them aloud.

"Exactly. Our grandmothers made their escape from Ivy Manor forty-six years ago, and it changed their lives. Maybe our running away together today will have a similar effect on our own lives."

Leigh turned and studied him. He was treating her like an

equal—like she wasn't just a sixteen-year-old girl. She thought suddenly about Mr. Pitney—Lance—and compared the two men. The contrast was easy to detect. Frank had a confidence that seemed limitless, but he didn't preen or call attention to himself like Lance did, always running his fingers through his bangs. She wanted to tell Frank this, but thought it might sound too silly and was too involved to explain.

"So what do you think?" he asked.

"I think you're wonderful," she blurted out and then blushed hot crimson.

Frank roared with laughter. "You're easily impressed. And I like that." He grinned at her. "How about some music?" he switched on the radio and Bobby Vinton crooned, "Bluuue vel—vet." "I don't think so. Let's have some rhythm and blues." He punched another station in and The Chiffons sang out, "One fine daaaaay."

Leigh let the lilting music flow through her, lifting her spirits and making her even more aware of Frank sitting so close, driving them to the march so effortlessly. He'd helped her find a way; he'd done the impossible, and this was her "One Fine Day."

But the Chiffons singing about how someday he'd want her for his girl left her suddenly tongue tied. This wasn't a date in any way, but it felt odd being alone with Frank. *It's just because I never talk to guys. That's why I feel funny.*

Determined to keep any evidence of this immaturity undercover, she settled back and watched the green fields, houses, and lush trees pass by.

"You're uncomfortable with me, aren't you?"

How did he always know what she was thinking? "No," she said quickly, too quickly. Then, more slowly, "Yes."

He nodded. "I had to make myself come and get you today."

"You did?" She wondered if he would tell her why. But why bring it up if he wasn't going to?

"Yes. I know your grandparents won't be shocked at your going with me, but I don't think your mother would like you to spend the day with me." He went on before she could comment on this, "And I didn't like telling my grandparents a half truth. I mean, I consider you a friend, but—"

"Me, too," she interrupted him. "I just never had a friend who was a guy." She blushed.

"Or one that wasn't white?" Again he went on, not letting her speak. "I'm glad you noticed I wasn't wearing a skirt." He smiled again. "What I mean is when I told them I was meeting a friend, they had no inkling that you were the friend. That's why I feel guilty."

She was relieved that he hadn't pressed her on whether she'd ever had a friend who wasn't white. Because, of course, she hadn't. But again she followed his lead and responded to his concern over deceiving their parents. "I understand. My parents will be unhappy with me—"

"Right. I wondered if I should encourage, actually enable, you to defy your parents. But I finally decided that this day is history-in-the-making and that you shouldn't be shut out. And if there is any violence, I'll make sure you get out safely."

"I don't think there's going to be any violence," she said, trying to match his confidence. She sat up straighter.

He gave her a sidelong glance. "And your basis for that statement is what, Miss Sinclair?"

She chewed her lip, thinking. The radio began playing, "Blueberry Hill." Frank didn't hurry her; he just drove on one-handed, humming to the melody. "I think it's the numbers," she said at last. "And the fact that it's taking place in Washington, D.C., and there will be TV stations covering it. Does that make sense?"

"I'm impressed. Very perceptive. Leigh Sinclair, you're nobody's fool."

Leigh sizzled from head to toe with pleasure and a touch of embarrassment. "Well, I gave the KKK a lot of thought. But I don't think the Klan will do anything today. They always operate at night and with their members masked. They don't want the light of day and the light of a television camera to expose their . . . hatred and evil. They try to make it sound and look like segregation is good for the south."

"Did you know that the Klan once burned a cross on your grandmother's lawn?" Frank turned onto the highway to D.C. and merged into heavy traffic.

"What?" Why did no one tell her the good stuff about her own family? "When?"

"It happened before World War II."

"Why?" Even as she asked, she tried to come up with a reason.

"Your grandparents took in a German immigrant girl who was Jewish—"

"You mean Aunt Gretel?"

Frank chuckled again. "You have an interesting variety of relatives. *Aunt* Jerusha and *Aunt* Gretel?" He swung into the passing lane and sped around a smelly, groaning eighteen-wheeler.

Leigh hadn't considered this before. "Aunt Gretel sends me gifts from time to time, and I know she and Mother still correspond regularly. Aunt Gretel wants my parents to visit her in Israel."

"Well, it was because of your Aunt Gretel that the cross was burned on their lawn."

"Why?" She edged forward, turning toward him on the seat.

"Because the KKK hates Jews and Roman Catholics almost as much as they hate Negroes."

"That's right." Leigh folded one leg under the other, wondering about her mother. "Do you think that's why Mom's so afraid of my attending the march?"

He nodded. "But I think your assessment of the chances of the KKK or violence is more accurate." He muttered under his breath as a red Corvette cut in front of him. "But like I said, I'll make sure you don't get hurt."

His words gave her a wonderful, breathless feeling. *Frank wants to protect me.*

Finally, in spite of several traffic jams, they reached the outskirts of Washington. Frank parked the car in an already crowded public parking lot and led her to the nearby subway station. She noticed that the crowd was unusual—the dark faces overwhelmingly outnumbered the white ones. For the first time, she felt like the minority, an uneasy sensation.

Soon they reached the gathering point for the marchers. It was still early, though the yellow sun was high now and beginning to blaze down. But the march wasn't to begin until noon.

Pulling a red triangular kerchief from her pocket to shield her from the sun, she tied the ends under her ponytail. Frank picked up signs for them to carry and they smiled and greeted other marchers. Leigh's sign read: "We Demand Equal Rights Now" and Frank's announced: "We March for Jobs for All Now." Leigh tried to become a human camera, recording the sights and sounds to be written down later in her report of this day. She hadn't felt that bringing along a notepad fit the occasion somehow, so her memory would have to suffice.

Then Leigh heard a woman's voice calling, "Frank! Frank!"

For just a second, Leigh's heart sank. Were they going to be joined by a girlfriend Frank hadn't mentioned? Then she chastised herself silently. *What, are you crazy, Leigh? He's a college boy and a Negro. This is all about the march. Not about you and him. He's off limits, and you know it. Plus he'd never be interested in you in a million years.*

Frank turned toward the voice and waved his arm in a wide arc as an attractive redheaded white woman in a pale blue linen dress and jacket hurried toward them. She was far too old to be Frank's girlfriend, and Leigh tried not to have a reaction to this. *You're letting yourself get carried away. Frank's just a nice guy who doesn't treat you like a baby.*

The redhead threw her arms around Frank, and they hugged. Then Frank turned to Leigh. "I'd like you to meet my mother."

CHAPTER THREE

Staring at Frank's mother, Leigh couldn't speak for a few moments. But even in her shock, she managed to keep her mouth closed. And she was able to shake hands with the woman, who looked her over very thoroughly as Frank explained who she was and why they were together.

"Wonderful, Frank," his mother finally enthused. "I'm glad you didn't let the girl miss this. Leigh, you'll tell your grandchildren about today."

"Did you have far to come, Mrs. Dawson?" Leigh asked and then realized that she was "making polite conversation," just like her mother would. This threw her.

"I live in the Village, dear, and please call me Lila. I don't go by Mrs. Dawson much anymore."

Leigh tried to decipher all of this. "The Village" must mean Greenwich Village, which she had seen on a trip to New York City, but what about the name thing?

Lila turned to get herself a pre-printed sign.

Frank whispered into Leigh's ear, "My parents divorced when I was twelve."

"Oh." Leigh couldn't think of anything else to say. "Oh."

Frank grinned. "You are a sweet kid."

She blushed again, blood warming her cheeks and neck in response to her own naiveté. She silently scolded herself, *Stop acting like a kid.*

"You are very pretty," Lila said, returning. "But then Frank has a very good eye for that kind of thing. Just like his father."

"Mom, we're not a couple," Frank said with a shake of his head.

His mother looked more amused than convinced.

Since Leigh couldn't think of a thing to say, she decided a smile would have to be her response.

Then private conversation stopped as a contingent of grim-looking, silent policemen appeared and some of the march organizers began speaking over megaphones to the marchers. Like a man-made forest, the placard signs held high blocked Leigh's vision. The press of people grew and grew until the marchers could no longer be contained. The march began of its own accord.

Frank drew her along with him, his free hand gripping her elbow as the marchers began their trek to the Lincoln Memorial earlier than expected. As they marched forward, policemen walked along with them at the edges of the procession, which filled the street, curb to curb.

After some time, they arrived at the Lincoln Memorial and the marchers spread out, filling the area around the Reflecting Pool in front of the Washington Monument. That towering obelisk would begin to cast its shadow, shimmering on the pool as the sun lowered in the sky.

"Do you think we'll run into our grandparents?" Leigh said into Frank's ear.

"In this crowd?" He shook his head. "We only met my mom because I told her I'd be early at the staging area. And what if we do? They can't make us go home, and I doubt they'd try."

They'd lost his mother in the crowd earlier. "Should we look for your mother?"

"No, she can take care of herself. She isn't your average mother."

She looked into his face, trying to understand what he meant.

He grinned. "She's not like your mother. She doesn't worry about me, or at least she never shows that she does. She guards her freedom and leaves me to mine."

Again, Leigh tried to analyze his tone and his words along with his expression. He was revealing himself to her again, but indirectly, and she felt out of her depth.

"Don't mind me," he said. "I'm in a strange mood today."

She gave him a smile, and then he helped her settle onto a small spot of well-baked concrete. The golden sun was nearly at high noon now and the heat and humidity were suffocating within the mass of warm bodies. Her red scarf soaked up the heat of the sun, uncomfortably, but kept it from burning her scalp. She was fortunate to be right beside the Reflecting Pool. Dipping her fingers into the tepid water, she then sprinkled her face and Frank's with the drops.

"Thank you." Frank grinned.

The public address system started up with metallic squawking and screeching. They all rose when requested. And at the front, the famous Marian Anderson stood above them with Abraham Lincoln's somber statue behind her and began singing the national anthem. The words, somewhat indistinct, warbled over them with sound-system distortion. However, the echo of her strong, richly textured voice hovered above their heads and touched Leigh's emotions. She felt a welling up of pride that she lived in the "land of the free" and the "home of the brave."

A Negro man stepped to the bank of microphones, the first of several who would speak before Dr. King. Leigh tried to keep her focus on the faces above the microphones, but other marchers—both black and white—kept turning to look at her as she sat beside Frank. It made her uncomfortable and irritated at the same time. Finally, she lifted her eyes to look over the crowd, blocking out their curiosity and even censure. Today was history, and she wouldn't be bothered by petty human emotions.

Speakers stepped up to the microphone one after the other. Leigh kept sprinkling Frank and herself with water as she felt the two of them baking and melting on the concrete. She finally ripped the cardboard placard off its wooden handle, alternately shading and fanning herself with it.

At long last, Martin Luther King Jr. took the podium. He looked down at his notes as he began his speech. Leigh felt a jolt of electricity shiver through the mass around her and then the distinctive voice spoke and the shiver went through her, too. She'd heard the cliché "a magnetic speaker," and Dr. King fit this. His rich voice carried his intense passion clearly across the huge crowd, which began to sway and react to his message. The hair on the back of Leigh's neck prickled as the contagious response swallowed her up in its power. She leaned forward as if that would help her catch every word, every nuance.

When Dr. King looked up from his notes, Leigh felt as if he were looking right at her—though she knew that was ridiculous. The sea of faces before him must be impersonal and indistinct. But she couldn't shake the impression that all of this was meant just for her, that he would have said the same words if she were the only one who'd arrived to hear him. "I have a dream," he repeated and embellished, gesturing with his hands. Each phrase built on the last until she rose with the rest of the crowd to echo, "Free at last! Thank God Almighty! Free at last!"

Leigh felt tears streaming down her cheeks. Frank pulled her under his arm and hugged her close. Her ear pressed against his chest, and she felt his heart beating against her cheek. She turned into him and hugged him back, too moved to speak. Her scarf slipped back and she felt him kiss her hair. Then the crowd was applauding, shouting, screaming with fervent joy, giving voice to Leigh's wildly cascading, ricocheting emotions.

Driving home was anticlimactic. Night had fallen by the time they edged their way out of the march area, onto the crowded subway, and finally to their car. As Frank drove, they remained silent, listening to Motown over the radio and news reports about the march. Leigh couldn't have explained in words what she was feeling for a million dollars or a Pulitzer Prize in journalism. Frank's silence didn't make her feel rejected. She felt he must be struggling with the same intense reaction to a once-in-a-lifetime experience.

Finally, as they drove down the darkened roads near Ivy Manor, Frank turned to her. "Which grandmother's house do you want to go to?"

"I wish," she said, her voice feeling rusty in her throat, "that I didn't have to go to any place where I have to talk to anyone."

Frank drove off the road and shifted into park. He stared straight ahead for several long moments. "I know what you mean. I feel like I've been on a trek to some faraway place and I don't feel like sharing my photographs back at home."

She appreciated his attempt at humor. He understood. He did share the same emotions she did. It was a heady feeling.

Until now, only Grandma Chloe had ever appeared to understand how Leigh felt about anything. "Thank you for taking me. You gave me a gift today. You took me a long way from home."

He rested his slender, dark hand over hers on the seat between them. "As odd as this might sound—since we only met a few days ago—I'm glad you went with me. I saw it all for myself and also I saw the reflection of everything, all of today, in your eyes. It made the experience richer, deeper . . ." He fell silent.

Words failed her. Tears clogged her throat. She squeezed his hand.

And then he drove her to Grandma Sinclair's and walked her to the door. He apologized to her grandmother for stealing her for the day. Then he drove away, leaving her half listening to Grandmother Sinclair scolding her as she dialed Leigh's parents to report her safe return. Leigh felt as if she'd left her old, her former, self here this morning and a new Leigh had walked back inside this familiar place tonight. She felt the pull of Dr. King's stirring words again and then Frank's tender lips kissing her hair.

The next morning, Leigh sat at the small desk in the room she always used when visiting Grandmother Sinclair. Leigh had been grounded for a month, and her mother was livid at her disobedience. But Leigh and Dory would spend the remainder of the week with Grandma Sinclair. This was a relief to Leigh because her mother's anger and disapproval were easier to bear at a distance. And she wasn't forced to explain anything.

Leigh stared down at the open spiral notebook where she intended to write her account of the march. She couldn't even pick up her special just-for-writing cartridge pen with the turquoise ink she preferred. She closed her eyes, trying to come up with an opening sentence. "My life will never be the same." Too trite even to jot on paper. "I met a boy . . . a man I'll never forget." Too true, too dangerous to reveal. If she wrote that, people would misunderstand it. Frank was the first person who'd taken her seriously, made her feel grown up. And she didn't want people twisting their friendship into something it wasn't. *I can't write about it. I can't.*

She pushed herself up. Maybe she could settle down tomorrow and write something, but not today. She wanted to go to Grandma Chloe and talk about what she was feeling. But the Dawsons were still staying at Ivy Manor, and Leigh didn't want to see Frank again. Somehow that would spoil the way Frank had left her. And to see him again would dilute what they'd shared. Did that make sense? *It doesn't matter. It's how I feel.*

Washington, D.C., September 1963

At the start of the first day of classes, Leigh sat at a table in the St. Agnes lunchroom where study halls were held. She stared at the first issue of this year's *Scribe*. Voices and shrill laughter bounced off the walls, but faded into the background as she looked for the byline of the lead story. She had not written an account of the march. And she'd prepared herself to see the byline read: "Mary Beth Hunninger." But that wasn't the name she read on page one. *Who is Cherise Langford?*

"Why did you do it?" Mary Beth demanded, appearing suddenly. She stood over Leigh, looking ready to spit.

Both of them were dressed in the St. Agnes uniform—a white blouse with red kerchief and navy-blue pleated skirt. Leigh studied the other girl's reddened face. "What are you talking about? I didn't do anything."

"That's right. You didn't. I could stand it if I'd lost out to you. At least *you'd* have done a good job with the article on the march."

"Who's Cherise Langford?" Leigh read the byline name out loud.

Mary Beth plumped down beside Leigh with a huff. "You didn't even come to the meeting last Friday."

"I was staying with my grandmother in Maryland." Leigh didn't go into any further detail.

"Oh, so you didn't get to the march?" Mary Beth's voice was a curious combination of sympathetic smugness.

Leigh felt no inclination to agree or deny this question. "What did I miss at the meeting?"

Mary Beth looked as if Leigh's nonchalance had taken her by surprise. Her words confirmed this, "I thought you *wanted* to be the *Scribe* editor this year."

Leigh shrugged. *So did I. But that changed and I don't know why really.* "Who's Langford?" she repeated.

"Haven't you seen her?" Mary Beth asked. "She's our new Negro student." Mary Beth tried to sound matter of fact, but ended up sounding disgruntled. "St. Agnes is now integrated—with her."

Leigh took this in. *Ah.* "I see." And she thought she did.

"Have you read her article yet?"

"No, I just started—"

"Well, go ahead. I'll wait," Mary Beth said, looking like a teacher about to write out a detention slip.

Leigh thought this was a strange request, but didn't see why she should argue since reading the article had been her intent anyway. She read the brief article and frowned. *Lackluster* was the word that suggested itself to her. How had Cherise missed all the emotion, the eloquence, the impact? But Leigh merely shrugged again. "You think your article was better?"

"I know it was better," Mary Beth barked. "I was trying to top *you*. I worked on it practically nonstop from the moment I got home. My dad and mom both proofread it, and they were impressed."

Mary Beth's father was an archeology professor and his wife an English professor, so they should know, Leigh thought. "I'm sorry," was all she said.

"It's not fair. My article was better, but Lance chose hers because she's Negro. And now she's the editor," Mary Beth ended up with a whine.

"I'm sorry," Leigh repeated and she realized that she was sorry for Mary Beth. Leigh realized she didn't feel the same rivalry toward Mary Beth as before. *How could I change this much in just one week?* She had no answer.

"I wouldn't mind just having Lance choose her article, but to have her as editor . . ." Mary Beth shook her head.

"Hi." A Negro girl, also in school uniform, walked up behind Mary Beth. "Someone pointed the two of you out to me. You both wanted to be editor of the *Scribe*, right?"

"You must be Cherise. I'm Leigh Sinclair." Leigh held out her hand, grinning secretly over Mary Beth's rigid expression. "Welcome to St. Agnes."

Not looking Cherise in the eye, Mary Beth muttered, "Hi."

"Thanks." Cherise studied both Leigh and Mary Beth in turn. "I wanted to speak to you two before we got off on the wrong foot. Someone told me that both of you wanted to head up the school paper this year. And I want to make it clear—I do not want to be the editor of the *Scribe*."

Mary Beth's mouth dropped open.

"You don't?" Leigh asked, somehow amused.

"Yes, I'm going to tell Mr. Pitney today. I dropped in on the Friday *Scribe* meeting because I was finalizing my registration that day and the principal suggested I stop by and meet Mr. Pitney."

Leigh couldn't help herself. She chuckled.

Cherise smiled. "I mean, I'm just a sophomore and I haven't worked on a school paper before. Why would I make a good editor?"

Mary Beth stared at the new girl. "Then why did you write the article?"

Cherise grinned. "I only wrote it because Mr. Pitney asked me personally to do so. I mean, I only watched the march on TV—"

Leigh laughed out loud and then covered her mouth with her hand. "Sorry. It's not you. I'm laughing about—" She stopped because she couldn't bring herself to say she was laughing at Mr. Pitney.

Interrupting their conversation, the teacher at the front of the room began to take roll. Mary Beth walked quickly to her appointed seat. At the teacher's direction, Cherise sat down on the bench beside Leigh. They grinned at each other and Leigh wondered what Mr. Pitney—Lance—would have to say when Cherise gave him the news.

After school that afternoon, Leigh walked into Mr. Pitney's classroom. She knew it was naughty of her, but she was eager to hear what he had to say about the editorship of the *Scribe*. He was sitting at his desk, marking papers. "Hi," she said softly in the quiet room.

He looked up, blond, young, handsome. Leigh drew up

Frank's image—dark curly hair, smooth *café au lait* skin, and large, black eyes. *Why am I comparing them? They have nothing to do with each other.*

"I'm glad you stopped in, Leigh." Lance pushed back his chair and stood up. "Why didn't you submit an account of King's march?"

Why ask me that? You wouldn't have published it anyway. I'm white. Leigh shrugged. "So you chose the new girl's article?"

"Yes, well, I didn't think it would look right if I chose an account by a white student over a Negro student's."

Leigh nodded. So he'd done it for appearance's sake just as she'd guessed. Why did she feel like she was on the outside looking into St. Agnes as if she weren't a part of it? She watched him finger back the thick blond hair that always dipped over his forehead, a gesture he repeated several times an hour. It reminded her of a few guys in surfer movies. It was like he was always calling attention to his hair, himself. Didn't he realize how that gesture revealed his self-absorption?

"I know Mary Beth is upset, but I'll find a way to reward her for her cooperation." He walked up the aisle between the desks toward her, the sun at his back, his face in shadow. "And I know both of you will help Cherise as she heads up the *Scribe*."

So he didn't know yet.

At that moment, Cherise walked in. "Hi. Mr. Pitney, I don't have—"

"I told you to call me Lance." Beaming, the teacher hurried around the desks to Cherise.

"I came to tell you," Cherise said, sounding apologetic, "I don't want to be editor of the *Scribe*."

"You what?" Lance gaped at Cherise.

As Cherise continued, Leigh turned to leave, hiding a

smile. In her mind, she started to describe all this to Frank. But she wouldn't be seeing Frank again. He was back in New York City with his family, his life, and he'd probably forgotten all about the silly teenager he'd taken pity on.

But Leigh recalled what he'd said when he'd decided to take her with him to the march. He'd said something about their grandmothers running away together and that it changed their lives. What he'd said next she remembered word for word: "Maybe our running away together today will have a similar effect on our own lives." Well, that had been true for her. Their day together had changed the way she saw people, Lance, for instance. But she wondered if it had affected Frank in the same way, to the same extent. After all, he was older, and he had more experience. Wasn't it just wishful thinking that the shared day had forged a tie between them? Make that dangerous, wishful thinking.

Four days later, Leigh stared at the return address on an envelope from the mail she'd just brought in after school. Dory already sat in front of the TV watching a noisy cartoon and Leigh was about to go into the kitchen to make her little sister a snack. But the letter halted her. It was from Frank.

He wrote to me. Why? What did it mean? Her hands trembled slightly as she held the unassuming-looking envelope. With the letter opener on the hall table, she slit open the flap, drew out a single sheet of paper, and read:

Dear Leigh,

I just wanted to drop you a line or two since I think you may be the only person who will hear my news and not begin squawking. I applied for Officer's Candidate School with the army yesterday.

Yes, your eyes are not deceiving you. I "enlisted" yesterday. I don't have to tell you what attending the march did to me. You were there. I know you were moved and changed by it, too.

He'd sensed that about me. The words made Leigh's heart pound. She read on.

Anyway, I thought over my options. I don't want to be a lawyer like Frank Dawson One and Two. I also don't want to get my master's degree in engineering. I want to go out and live life on the front lines, so to speak. I decided that I was already about to be drafted for my two years of military service and that I would prefer to be an officer.

The U.S. Army is technically integrated, but Negro officers are scarce. I hope I can change that. I also hope that merit and not my skin color will be what I'm judged by. Signing up for Officer's Candidate School, of course, means that I had to take qualifying tests and then sign up for four years. But that will give me time to see if I like the military or not. Maybe by the time I'm out, I'll want to be a lawyer like Dad and Grandad.

Well, my family is angry with me. Shocked. You name it. Though they should have realized I might do something like this since I was active in ROTC in high school and college. Anyway, I thought of you and knew you'd understand. If you have a kind word to send to a soldier, here is my military address. I leave for camp in three days.

Yours, Frank Three

Leigh reread the letter, feeling something inside her expand. *He doesn't think I'm just a kid.*

"I'm hungry," Dory called from the couch.

Leigh folded the letter and slipped it into her pleated skirt pocket and headed for the kitchen. Her mind was already composing the first sentence of her reply. But should she even send him an answer? Suddenly she wished Grandma Chloe were here to talk to. Something warned her that her mother would not want her writing to Frank. Maybe she'd be allowed to visit Ivy Manor this weekend without Dory and she could show Grandma Frank's letter.

Or would her mother's anger keep her at home?

Sunday afternoon, September 15, 1963

Call me when you want me to pick you up," Ted, her stepdad, said as he parked his gray Mercedes sedan to let her off at the curb in front of Cherise's house.

"Thanks, Dad." Leigh leaned over and kissed his cheek. Internally, she sighed. Why couldn't her mother be more like her stepdad, who was fun, easygoing, and didn't freak out over every little thing. Her mother hadn't liked her coming here today—it was like she wanted civil rights to succeed, but some form of separation to continue—but her stepdad had persuaded her to let Leigh go.

Frank's letter, concealed in Leigh's purse, had remained unanswered. What was she going to do about it?

She'd hoped Grandma Chloe could help her decide. Last weekend, her stepdad had persuaded her mom to let her take the train and stay at Ivy Manor. Sitting in the summer house with her grandmother, Leigh had asked why her mother liked

Aunt Jerusha, seemed to admire Minnie Dawson, but wanted to keep her distance from them. Why hadn't she wanted Leigh to go to the march? Why was she so angry at Frank for taking her? There hadn't been any violence, and Frank had been a perfect gentleman.

Her grandmother had been vague at best—she'd told her to discuss it with Bette, not her.

A red Volkswagen Beetle pulled up near their bumper as Leigh got out and shut the door behind her. She had been a bit surprised when Cherise had invited Leigh's former rival to her home along with Leigh. But the three of them did share a French class, and Mary Beth was very good at languages. Now, Mary Beth met her on the sidewalk and they walked together up to the strange house in a newer Negro neighborhood in northern Virginia.

"Do you feel weird about this?" Mary Beth whispered.

Leigh glanced at her. And then raised one eyebrow. Did Mary Beth mean about getting together with her or visiting Cherise?

"I've never been in a Negro person's house before," Mary Beth admitted, as if embarrassed about revealing this private information, but unable to stop herself.

Ah, it was Cherise's being different. Leigh thought of Aunt Jerusha, whom she and Grandma Chloe had visited last weekend. In her late eighties, Aunt Jerusha, Frank's great-grandmother, lived in a neat little cottage behind Ivy Manor, close enough for Grandma Chloe to check on her every day. What would Mary Beth say if Leigh told her that?

Mary Beth nudged Leigh's arm, bringing Leigh back to the present.

"This isn't my first time," Leigh said, leading Mary Beth up the steps.

"You probably think I'm dumb for feeling odd," Mary Beth muttered.

"No, feelings are feelings. I wouldn't try to deny yours or tell you not to feel them." *Like my mother always tries to make me feel what I should, not what I really feel.* "Maybe Cherise," Leigh suggested, "will feel funny having us over."

"I didn't think about that." The other girl brightened.

Leigh and Mary Beth reached the door of the white-frame bungalow on a quiet street of small neat homes and lawns. Leigh knocked. A pretty Negro woman opened the door. "You must be Leigh and Mary Beth."

"Hello, Mrs. Langford." Leigh held out her hand.

Eying them thoroughly, Cherise's mother welcomed them inside and sent them upstairs, after calling out, "Cherise, your classmates are here!"

Leigh's mind went back to Ivy Manor again. The afternoon spent with Aunt Jerusha had brought back what Frank had said about how their two families were related. *Frank.* She resisted the urge to trace the outline of his letter within her purse. Over the past few days, she'd changed it from purse to drawer and back again—it was crumpled and finger-smudged, worn from her touching it over and over. But she still couldn't decide whether or not to reply.

Obviously still in her church outfit, Cherise met them at the top of the stairs and led them to her room. "Have you listened to the news?" Cherise motioned toward a small black-and-white TV with rabbit ears in the corner of her pink-and-white Early American bedroom.

"Wow," Mary Beth breathed, "you've got a TV in your room."

Cherise chuckled. "Mom and Dad got a new color set in the living room, and I got the old, small one for here. I had to promise it wouldn't interfere with my homework." Cherise gave them a look to show how silly parents could be.

On the small black-and-white, slightly fuzzy screen, Walter Cronkite was talking to some NAACP officer about a tragedy that had just occurred in Alabama. Leigh perched on the side of the sheer-white canopied bed, folding one leg under. In green pedal pushers and matching blouse, she felt as if she'd dressed too casually for the very feminine setting. "What happened?"

Smoothing her straight skirt carefully as if not wanting to wrinkle it, Cherise sat down beside Leigh. "The KKK blew up part of the Sixteenth Street Baptist Church and killed four little girls."

Leigh took it in. "They blew up a church?" The news was unreal, like saying the Martians had landed. A bomb set in secret. A cowardly act of intimidation, of violence. The Klan didn't want to be photographed doing their dirty work, but didn't they realize that its results were just as overwhelming? It caught in Leigh's craw, especially knowing that Frank would hear about it at boot camp, probably on someone's transistor radio. He'd be angry.

"That's creepy," Mary Beth commented, staring at the TV while settling herself on Cherise's other side. Even though Mary Beth wasn't wearing her school uniform, the top button of her plain blouse, the one most girls left undone, was buttoned up tight at her neck.

"I guess the KKK still thinks they can hold back integration with violence," Cherise said. "You'd think they'd get the message. The day has come for the end of segregation."

"Well, in the past, violence and intimidation served them—before nationwide news coverage," Leigh pointed out. She remembered Frank's bitter tone when he'd told her about sitting in at the lunch counter. "The KKK burned a cross on my grandparents' lawn back before World War II." The words just slipped out.

"Why'd they do that?" Mary Beth wanted to know.

Leigh wished she'd kept her mouth shut. But she couldn't refuse to answer. "My grandparents took in a Jewish immigrant."

Both girls stared at her. Walter Cronkite began repeating the story of the day, the four little girls who'd died at church this morning, another day of tragedy in Alabama. Leigh shifted her attention to him, but it was just a cover. She studied the other two girls on the bed surreptitiously.

Cherise was very pretty, light skinned, and dressed in a very feminine pink blouse with a Peter Pan collar and a black straight skirt, hose, and black flats. Somehow she wore the clothing as if it were finer than it was. Cherise had an air about her that drew attention—favorable attention—to herself. Leigh had observed her over the past two weeks at St. Agnes and she'd noted that about her. Cherise was very good at getting people to like her. She'd bowed out of the *Scribe* editorship and Mary Beth had gotten the job. And in the process, Cherise had won quite a bit of good press for herself.

Leigh wondered why she was studying and analyzing the new girl's every move, every word. Was it prejudice? Or did it have anything to do with her friendship with Frank?

Mary Beth wore brown plastic glasses, a very plain white blouse, a pleated black skirt, white bobby socks, and white tennies. Her hair was a nondescript brown, and her eyes were lost behind thick lenses. Mary Beth was the epitome of *dogged*. She staked out her goal, and heaven help the person who got in her way or wanted the same plum. Last month this had irritated Leigh; now it amused her. And she didn't know why she'd changed.

And what would Cherise and Mary Beth say about her?

A commercial for Pepsodent came on. Cherise got up and switched off the TV. "It's depressing, and we've got homework to do. I need help with my French. I thought it would be good to practice the conversation we're supposed to memorize and recite."

Leigh decided suddenly to take a chance, to upset the apple cart and see what popped out. "What do you two think about interracial dating?"

Chapter Four

Both Mary Beth and Cherise stared at her, wide-eyed. Through the open window, sounds from outside—someone raking grass clippings, rasping the ground and then sidewalk with a rake, little children giggling and calling to each other in a game of tag, cars passing—filled the silence in Cherise's bedroom. Leigh fought a blush, but it took over her face anyway.

"Are you dating?" Mary Beth asked, sounding dumbfounded. "Who?"

"I'm not dating anyone." Leigh primed her lips. *I should never have asked them.*

"You mean you're just asking in general?" Cherise probed.

Leigh looked straight into Cherise's dark, very pretty eyes and nodded. She'd begun to like Mary Beth and Cherise. When she'd transferred to St. Agnes two years ago, she hadn't really tried to make any close friends. After going to public school for elementary and junior high, she'd felt odd at an all-girl's Catholic school where everyone had known each other since kindergarten. She'd been unhappy that her mother had insisted she go there, and resentment had tied her tongue.

Also, the atmosphere had been so competitive and so repressive—the strict nuns in their white wimples and black habits—that Leigh had not made any overtures of friendship and few had come her way. Now, as her public-school friends drifted away, she realized she'd become very lonely.

But in the past weeks, Mary Beth had done a turnaround from treating Leigh as a hostile rival to treating her as a friend. Evidently beating Leigh out of the editorship had satisfied Mary Beth in some way. And Cherise often sought her out, to walk to classes together and eat lunch together. But no confidences had been shared—yet.

"Yes, just in general," Leigh replied, unwilling to expose herself to either girl. *But then why did I ask them?*

Mary Beth twisted a short lock of her brown hair around her forefinger and stared at the gray carpet. Cherise studied Leigh. "I don't think I would ever date any white boys."

Leigh tried not to look away from the girl's scrutiny, so she would seem to be just asking this in general.

"Why?" Mary Beth asked, saving Leigh breath.

Avoiding eye contact, Cherise smoothed her dark skirt again. "I think it would upset my family."

"Really?" Mary Beth considered this with an intent expression. Finally, she contributed, "My mom and dad are NAACP members, so I don't think my family would be too upset. But I don't think any guy will ever ask me out anyway. I'm not pretty like you two."

"What does that have to do with it?" Leigh asked.

"Guys don't date plain girls who read all the time. 'Boys don't make passes at girls who wear glasses,'" Mary Beth recited.

Leigh found this hilarious. "Then how come so many married women wear glasses?" She burst out in laughter.

"And anyway," Mary Beth continued grumbling, "when

do we ever get to meet any guys at St. Agnes? Whenever we have those dances with the guys from St. Ignatius, I always end up serving punch." Mary Beth glared at Leigh. "You always get asked to dance."

" 'Gentlemen prefer blondes,' " Leigh couldn't resist saying. She flipped her ponytail at Mary Beth. "One cliché deserves another," she added, teasing a smile from Mary Beth.

"If the only time you see guys is at a school dance," Cherise said with a grin, "then, girlfriend, *you* need to get out more."

Leigh felt her spirits lift. Teasing with friends or girls who might become her friends lightened her mood. But she still couldn't bring herself to share Frank with them. He was too personal, too special a friend.

And then she had her answer. Frank had become an unexpected friend, just like the two girls across from her. Just because she and Frank had spent such an emotion-packed day didn't mean they were more than friends. Writing to Frank wasn't *dating* him. He would never date her anyway. Why was she making such a big deal about his letter? She was six years younger than him, and he wasn't interested in her like that. The kiss on her hair had just been because of the special moment they'd shared. Maybe that was why he'd written her. They had shared an experience like no other.

But she couldn't forget his kiss or his covering her hand with his in the car that evening. No man had ever touched her like that. Like she was a woman.

"Are you girls studying French or discussing boys?" Cherise's mother's voice floated up the stairs.

All three of them smothered giggles. And then Leigh opened her French conversation textbook. "*Bonjour, Mademoiselle,*" she began, lifting her voice so Mrs. Langford would hear her. *I'll write Frank tonight.*

Then another thought stopped her in her tracks. What if her mother found out? And wasn't that what had really been stopping her from replying? The truth wound itself around her lungs, tightening like a boa constrictor.

Well, it wouldn't be the first time she'd disobeyed her mother. But something told Leigh that this might elicit more than the usual scolding. However, her mother was wrong. Leigh shouldn't have to be afraid of having Frank as a friend. Right was right.

That evening, Leigh sat at the desk in her pale blue room and began to write.

> *September 15, 1963*
> *Dear Frank,*
>
> *I'm so sorry it has taken me a few weeks to reply. Starting a new school year has kept me busy, and Mom's been piling on the chores.*
>
> *How are you? How's Officer's Candidate School?*
>
> *I'm sure you've heard about the four little girls and the explosion at the church in Alabama. I felt awful for their families. How sick can you get—blowing up a church with children in it?*
>
> *I didn't write the article about the march in Washington after all. Is that crazy or what? I just couldn't get it down on paper. However, I'm still writing for the school paper. I do love to write.*
>
> *Well, that's all the news that's fit to print!*
> *Yours,*
> *Leigh*

She folded the sheet of lavender stationery and put it into the matching envelope. She'd mail it on the way to school tomorrow—after Bette had gone to work.

In his crowded barracks, Frank sat hunched on his bunk, writing on a book on his knee. Fluorescent tubes glared down on the blank white page. The guys nearest him were arguing about this year's World Series.

September 20, 1963
Dear Leigh,

Thanks for writing. I know what you mean about keeping busy. I barely have time to think. Officer's Candidate School is a combination of college and a little like boot camp. Discipline is the main goal, of course. Intellectually, I can understand that, but it's hard to be on the receiving end. It's just like what I described to you about how I felt when I took part in sit-ins. Again, I feel stripped of all my family's protection, my identity as part of that family. In the army, it's just me and what I am. The challenge is learning enough to be able to lead a fighting group of men and at the same time submitting to the authority of others here and now. Very intense at times, and at times . . . irritating.

Some of the other candidates are good ole boys from the South. They don't like it that I'm "edji-cated." But I ignore them for the most part. And I make sure that they know I can take care of myself so they don't try anything.

I try not to take satisfaction that in the future, I

*may command some "good ole boys." But I'm human
enough to look forward to the experience.*

*I think I understand why you couldn't write
about the march. I have trouble talking about it myself. Some experiences are too deep to share with
strangers.*

Yours,
Frank

"Lights out!" the loud voice announced, and darkness
filled the room. Frank folded and then tucked the letter under
his pillow. He'd mail it tomorrow after evening chow. He
wished he had a picture of Leigh.

Leigh sat at the back of her journalism class. Mr. Pitney was
lecturing them on journalistic sources and court cases up-
holding the free press's rights to keep sources confidential.
She began writing as if she were taking notes.

October 2, 1963
Dear Frank,

*I'm so glad I wrote you. Or, should I say, that
you wrote me? (Sorry for the delay in replying but too
much homework.) Anyway, you understand what I
mean. Sometimes I feel like I must be very strange or
something because until I met you, only Grandma
Chloe ever understood me. I wonder why that is. Do
you feel like your parents don't understand you, or is
this something I'll outgrow? I get so sick of hearing
that, or words to that effect, from my mother. Will I
outgrow being me? Did you?*

Leigh

The bell rang, ending class. Closing her notebook, Leigh rose and in the crowded and noisy hallway caught up with Cherise on their way to their next class. She wished she had a photo of Frank. She still kept Frank's letters hidden in her room. And since she always brought in the mail, Bette was no wiser about the secret correspondence.

It was Sunday afternoon, and Frank was enjoying a few hours relaxing outside in the autumn sunshine and rereading Leigh's letters. He settled himself on a bench in a small grassy area on base and began writing.

October 20, 1963
Dear Leigh,

I'm getting near the end of OCS. I'll have no regrets when graduation comes! Can't wait to be done with this grind.

Now to address your question—no, I don't think you'll outgrow being yourself. And I know what you mean. I never seem to live up to my father's expectations. My mother is a different story. She accepts everything I do with the same bland approval. Now that I look at those words, I see that they leave a lot to be desired. But one demanding parent and one who is completely laissez-faire is hard to take sometimes. Of all my family, I think my grandfather and I are the closest.

But still, I feel a distance from him. Our times are so different. I mean, they didn't have the atomic bomb when he was growing up. Sometimes, I wonder if the president will ever press that button and launch a nuclear strike. And what would our world

be like? Would it, would we survive? Would we want to?
Frank

He pictured her fresh young face, long golden hair. He wished she could always stay as idealistic and honest as she was. Not for the first time, an inner voice chided him, "Stop writing her. You're liable to mislead her. Negro men and white girls can't be friends."

In the hushed, busy silence, Leigh sat in the library at school and started to write.

November 15, 1963
Dear Frank,
  What you said about nuclear war—I've thought that so many times myself. Nuclear war seems to hang over us—unseen and not to be spoken of—but there. Always there. Sometimes I almost feel stupid planning for my future. I don't have any control over what is going to happen on the world stage. Who does? One man in Washington, D.C. and one in Moscow. I was so scared during the Cuban Missile Crisis. I don't understand how anyone could even think of using nuclear weapons. Where would it all stop? Who would win in such a war?
  Did you see the movie On the Beach? *Very scary at the end, just newspapers blowing around empty streets in Australia. Chilling.*
  What do they teach you about this in the military?
  Leigh

She'd never expressed this before to anyone, but she had felt it so many times. Once she'd tried to discuss it with her mother, but her fears had been dismissed as unimportant. Just because Bette was a secretary at the CIA, she evidently thought she was an expert on foreign affairs and especially the Cold War. But what human being knew the future? There were nuclear weapons—and they'd been made to be used, hadn't they?

November 21, 1963

*L*eigh stuck her key into the backdoor keyhole, and then the door swung open on its own. Her mother stood in the doorway, glowering at Leigh.

"Oh, oh," Dory said. Her little sister, whom she'd walked home from her school as usual, stood just beside Leigh.

Bette looked at Dory and gave her a tight, tiny smile. "Your after-school snack is on the coffee table."

Obviously recognizing another storm about to hit, Dory gave Leigh a questioning, worried look and then hurried away, vanishing into the living room.

Leigh pushed her way past her mother and laid down her books on the kitchen table. "You're home early," she commented, unwilling to give in to apprehension. Bette was always upset about something.

"I wasn't feeling well today and came home before lunch." Her mother followed Leigh to the refrigerator, where Leigh pulled out the glass jug of milk. The jug was cold and heavy in her hand as she turned to carry it to the counter. She felt tension radiating from Bette. But she refused to ask what was wrong. She wouldn't give her mother the satisfaction.

"I brought in the mail." Bette folded her arms in front of herself and stared into Leigh's face.

A sinking feeling started in the pit of Leigh's stomach. But she didn't let it show. "Oh?"

Bette waved a letter from her pocket in front of Leigh. "How long have you been writing to Frank Dawson?"

Leigh refused to react, but hot acid singed her stomach. She poured herself a tall glass of milk and went to the kitchen table and sat down. She shrugged as if this were nothing of importance. "A few months."

"So you admit it?"

Leigh looked up, keeping her expression nonchalant. But she felt the buzz of adrenaline start inside. "Of course. Why should I deny it? Frank is an old family friend, isn't he?" Leigh was proud of the way she was handling this. *Just play it cool.*

"That's not the point and you know it." Bette reached over to the counter and then tossed all of Leigh's letters from Frank onto the table.

Jolted, Leigh felt anger flame through her. "You went through my things!"

"Yes, I knew something was going on. You've been acting strange . . . different. And then when I found that letter from Frank today, I decided I'd better find out how serious this was."

Leigh surged to her feet, her pulse pounding at her temples. "You had no right to go through my things—read *my* letters! No right—"

"Yes, I did." Bette propped her hands on her hips. "You're a minor, my daughter, and I'm supposed to protect you—"

"You don't have to protect me from Frank." Leigh

clutched the cold glass in her hand. "What kind of person do you think he is?"

"I think he's the kind of person who helps you defy your parents and go to a march against their wishes. That's the kind of person I think he is."

Containing her rage nearly made Leigh weak in her knees. "Frank felt bad about deceiving his grandparents that day. But he wouldn't let me miss the march. You had no right keeping me from experiencing an historic occasion."

"Frank is only twenty-two and he isn't my judge, young lady. Now, I will write Frank and tell him not to write to you anymore. And I want you—"

Shaking with outrage, Leigh set down the milk glass, sloshing some on the tabletop. "I will go on writing to Frank if I want to. This is none of your business."

Bette slapped her.

Her cheek stinging, Leigh gasped. Bette had never struck her before.

"You are too young to know what this can lead to. But I know, and it scares me to death. I won't have you beginning a relationship that could end in tragedy—for both of you."

"You're making a big deal out of nothing." Leigh rubbed her tingling cheek with the back of her hand.

"No, I'm not. I know just how impressionable a young girl can be and how making the wrong decision about a man can ruin her life. Your father . . ." Bette stopped and pressed her lips so tightly together that they turned white.

"What about my father?" Leigh asked, taking a step forward. Bette never spoke about Leigh's father if she could help it. Almost everything she knew about her father, she'd learned from Grandma Sinclair and Grandma Chloe. "Why don't you ever want to talk about my father? What did he do that was so wrong that you never—"

Bette turned away. "Go to your room."

Leigh said, "No, I—"

"*Now.*"

Leigh burned. She wanted to break something, to slap her mother back, to scream. Instead, she shoved the chair out of her way and stalked from the room. Her only hope was her stepfather. He knew how to get around her mother's unreasonable, stubborn streak. But an inner voice whispered, "You knew she'd react like this. You knew what you were doing when you wrote to Frank."

Early the next morning, Leigh dressed in black Capri pants and a thick heather-blue cardigan and packed a small, gray, zippered bag. Just after dawn, she slipped out of the house and hurried to the nearest bus stop. After arguing most of the evening with her mother, Leigh felt bruised and battered. Her eyes were swollen from weeping and gritty from lack of sleep, and Ivy Manor summoned her with an irresistible call. Her stepfather had tried to intervene, but for once, he'd been unable to sway Bette to see sense. Bette had been implacable, immovable. Leigh would not be allowed to write Frank again.

The city bus pulled up and Leigh got on. Grandma Chloe would understand. Somehow she would make her mother see she was overreacting. Not for the first time, Leigh wished she could live at Ivy Manor. Her mom hovered over her like Nemesis. She was never satisfied. No matter what Leigh did it was never perfect enough, good enough, to suit her. And yet, she seemed to want to keep Leigh a little girl on a level with Dory. *Why do I even try?*

Late that afternoon, Leigh finally trudged up the quiet lane to Ivy Manor. Sparrows twittered overhead and crows cawed in a raucous chorus. She'd missed the last morning express and had to take the local train from Washington that stopped at every little town. And then, after arriving in Croftown, the streets were unusually deserted. And the bank was unaccountably closed. She'd not seen anyone she knew. So she'd had to walk all the way to Ivy Manor.

She finally went up the lane and around to the backdoor. Feeling victorious, rebellious, and fearful, she stepped inside and set down her bag in the back hallway. "Grandma? Grandpa? Rose?" she called out the names. Rose was a grand-niece of Aunt Jerusha's and the present housekeeper of Ivy Manor.

No reply. Leigh walked through the quiet house. It was empty. She'd never suspected that when she got there, no one would be at Ivy Manor. Where had everyone gone? She wasn't surprised that the doors had been left unlocked. They always were.

Leigh wandered outside to the deserted summer house where all the outdoor furniture was covered with dark green tarps. The sound of a TV reminded Leigh of Aunt Jerusha in the little cottage. She hurried there. The sound of the TV increased as she approached the little house. She knocked on the back door and then let herself in. Aunt Jerusha was unsteady on her feet and expected everyone just to come on in.

Leigh found Aunt Jerusha in the small front room filled with knickknacks in front of the TV with rabbit ears. "Aunt Jerusha?"

"*Child*." The old woman looked up, startled. "What are you doin' here? I know nobody's spectin' you."

Leigh came over and leaned down to kiss the old

woman's forehead. "I needed to see Grandma Chloe. Where is everyone?"

"Child, your grandparents gone to your house. Miss Chloe said she had to be with you all in Virginia. She wants to go and view the president's body when it lies in state."

"The president's body?" Leigh's mouth stayed open.

"Don't you know, child?" With a man's white handkerchief, Aunt Jerusha mopped tears from her wrinkled mahogany cheeks. "They gone and shot our president—that good man."

A wave of emotion weakened Leigh. She sat down in the nearest chair. "I didn't know." She remembered now. People had been talking, but she had been too wrapped up in her own misery and hadn't tried to understand what they were talking about. "I've been on the train and then I walked here. I haven't been near a radio or TV." She glanced at the screen. David Brinkley was questioning someone about the whereabouts of Lyndon Johnson, the vice president.

"Around noon, Mr. Kennedy was ridin' in a open car in Dallas and someone shot him. They're huntin' for the murderer—the FBI. Maybe your stepfather gone there, too."

Leigh closed her eyes. She couldn't ever remember feeling what she was experiencing now. It was as if someone had hit her head with a heavy object and at the same time punched the air out of her. The president . . . dead. Impossible.

"You're lookin' white. Bend down your head, child. Right now," Aunt Jerusha ordered, reaching over and pushing Leigh's face down to her knees. "Take a deep breath. You gone to faint if you don't."

Squeezing her eyes tight against the vertigo, Leigh obeyed and drew in air deeply. Her head cleared but then tears welled up. "I can't believe it. How?"

"I remember when that bad man shot McKinley." Leaning on her cane, Aunt Jerusha rose, hobbled to the TV, and turned down the volume knob. "I was already a mother then. But that isn't like this. This time I *cared* about the president. He was for us. Things are changin'. I was thinkin' of registerin' so I could vote for him. That would have been my first time. I wouldn't put it past the Klan to gone and done this. They hated him."

Leigh couldn't speak. The wind still felt knocked out of her. She glanced at the muted TV. They were playing a newsreel of the president's cavalcade in Dallas earlier. She looked away.

"He's got two little children—those poor babies." The older woman shook her white head and looked grim as she inched back to her chair. "And their mama, that sweet woman."

Leigh struggled to hold back surging emotions. How could it affect her so? She'd only seen the president a few times in his motorcade in D.C., but this felt so personal—as if she'd known him.

"What are you doin' here without your family?" Aunt Jerusha eased her arthritic joints back down into her chair.

Leigh looked up. "I needed to talk to Grandma Chloe. My mother..." Leigh felt her face flushing with recalled anger. "My mother is being unreasonable and I wanted Grandma Chloe to talk to her."

Aunt Jerusha frowned and shook her head. "You should have stayed at home and went to school. Your grandma isn't gone to argue with your mother over you. That's not right."

"It's about Frank, about your great-grandson." Leigh plunged on, wanting Jerusha's approval, her understanding. "He's been writing to me from the army and I've been writing him back. My mom says she won't let me write him anymore." Leigh made a face. "It's not her business who I have as a friend."

"A friend?" Aunt Jerusha said in a mocking tone. "You're a young white girl and Frank Three's a young Negro man. The two don't become friends."

Her tone startled Leigh. "That's old-fashioned, Auntie."

"No, it isn't." Jerusha shook her head decidedly and let a frown drag all her wrinkles down. "What is Frank thinkin'? He should know what kind of trouble he can get into messin' with a white girl."

"He's not messing with me." Leigh moved forward on her chair. "He's just writing me letters."

The older woman snorted in reply.

In the house in Arlington, Chloe watched Bette go to the kitchen to start supper and then followed her. Everyone was in an odd mood. The news of the assassination had kept Bette restless and she'd paced so long she looked worn out. Even now, she switched on the kitchen radio and listened to the low murmur of voices discussing when LBJ would take the oath of office.

As if that hadn't been enough to contend with, Bette had explained how she'd found a note left by Leigh, announcing she'd gone to Ivy Manor on her own. But the girl hadn't called to say she'd arrived there and when Chloe had called, no one had answered. Rose must have gone to her own place. Chloe didn't blame her. She'd felt the same need to be with family during this national tragedy.

But why had Leigh gone to Ivy Manor? Chloe had waited to ask this touchy question. Until now.

"Do you think Leigh has finally gotten to Ivy Manor?"

Bette turned and stared at her mother. "I'll call Rose and

ask." She dialed the familiar number, but soon she hung up. "No answer."

Chloe suppressed the fear that something could have happened to Leigh between there and Ivy Manor.

"Why don't you call Rose's home? She can check on Jerusha and find out if Leigh has arrived," Bette suggested in a wary voice, washing her hands at the sink.

Chloe made the call but got no answer. She faced her daughter. "We've been so caught up in the assassination that I haven't had time to ask you why Leigh has run away. Don't you think it's time you told me?"

Donning a floral apron, Bette passed the back of her hand over her forehead. "Mother, I don't understand Linda Leigh. She does crazy things that I would never have thought of doing. Running off with Frank that day and going to the march when I'd forbidden it. Now I find out she's been writing Frank secretly over the past three months. It's as if she hasn't any common sense."

Chloe gazed at her daughter, considering this revelation. "She was writing him secretly?" *I'm not surprised, Bette. Why are you?*

"Yes, and both you and I know that nothing good can come of a friendship between them. Leigh's so young and idealistic she doesn't understand what she'd be getting herself into. Look what happened to Frank's parents' marriage." Bette unwrapped a cut chicken from white butcher's paper.

"Were these love letters?"

"No, but writing Frank *secretly*," Bette said, getting out flour and oil. "You know how impressionable young girls are. Frank's good-looking, older—"

"And forbidden," Chloe cut in. "Forbidden fruit is always the sweetest." *How could you be so foolish, Bette?*

Bette continued, heedless, "I was never like that when I

was in my teens. It's just one thing after another with Leigh. Ted and I have given her every advantage—"

Chloe stepped closer. "Bette, times are different now."

"What has that got to do with anything?" Bette added salt and pepper to the flour, then stirred everything with a fork. "You can't mean that you approve of Leigh and Frank becoming involved?"

CHAPTER FIVE

"I'm more worried about you and Leigh than Frank and Leigh," Chloe declared.

"What does that mean?" Bette put down her fork with a snap.

"Leigh is living in different times than you did. The Depression and then the war coming on—you had to knuckle under, put aside your private feelings, private wants. But Leigh is living in a time of fast change and prosperity like I did. My life in 1917 was like night and day compared to my life in 1921. Women got to vote. We cut our hair. We shortened our skirts and went dancing at speakeasy nightclubs."

The radio announcer fielded discussions of possible funeral arrangements for the president.

"What has this got to do with Leigh?" Bette clattered the skillet onto the burner.

"Leigh's time is going to be like mine, not like yours. It's another boom time, and now the Negroes are going to get the vote back for the first time since the Reconstruction. It seems like in America, we have these times that come through like gangbusters, ripping things apart, and what's been accepted for decades and decades changes overnight. Leigh suits her time."

Bette stared at her for a moment and then deposited a large scoop of Crisco into the pan. "I can't disagree with you about prosperity and things changing, but life is the same generation to generation. You fell in love and got married—"

"And you fell in love with Curt, who hurt you dreadfully. That's what drives you to be so overprotective with Leigh, isn't it? That's why you sent her to that strict girl's school." Chloe had wanted to say this for a long time. She'd held her peace, but no more. Leigh was in danger. "You thought you'd control what boys she came into contact with and that they'd be very few. You're afraid she'll fall in love with someone who will end up hurting her."

"Why shouldn't I be concerned?" Bette countered. "She's much too young to be writing to a young man *six years* older than she is."

"I'll have to agree with you there. But what other young men has she met? You've shut her off from the natural way of things."

Bette swirled the pan, making sure the melting shortening coated in the skillet. "She will have plenty of time for boys after she finishes high school."

Chloe went on as if Bette hadn't spoken. "I agree Frank is much too old for her. But you can't stop young men from coming into your daughter's life. Leigh is lovely, and she will be stunning in just a few more years. Frank would have to be made out of stone not to find her attractive."

Bette tapped the spoon on the side of the skillet. "So you agree that he's trying to fix his interest with Leigh?"

"I don't think he has any intention of marrying or even dating Leigh."

Bette frowned at her. "You can't mean that."

*　　*　　*

"I thought *you'd* understand," Leigh said.

"I understand a lot," Aunt Jerusha replied. "I'm almost ninety years old. I didn't go through those years with my eyes shut tight. I know that many a Negro man has gotten lynched for doin' less than writin' a white girl a letter."

The TV screen beckoned to Leigh. They were replaying Robert Frost reading a poem at JFK's inauguration. She turned back to Aunt Jerusha. "But lynching is a thing of the past."

"Only nine years past." Jerusha pointed her cane at Leigh. "1954—that poor Chicago boy got lynched for just sassin' a white woman in Mississippi."

"Why does everyone try to make this something it isn't?" Leigh extended her hands, palms up, pleading her case. "I'm not in love with Frank. We're just writing letters."

"Peddle your papers somewhere else, young lady." Jerusha's mouth puckered up. "Frank is a man, not a boy. You're a pretty girl, and he's got eyes in his head. There's a touch of wildness in him. He come by it honest with that mother of his."

"You don't like his mother because she's white?"

"You know that?" Aunt Jerusha frowned.

Leigh nodded. "I met her at the start of Dr. King's march. Frank said his parents divorced when he was twelve."

"That's right." Jerusha began rocking her chair, creaking on the wood floor. "Frank Two never should have married her. Not just because a mixed marriage sets a man and woman up for extra pain and some real nastiness. I never liked Lila. I've always thought she married Frank Two just to shock people—not because she really cared about him as a person. And when she divorced him, she was happy to leave Frank Three with our family. She didn't want to raise a mixed child. Oh, no."

Saddened, Leigh worried her lower lip. Maybe, just maybe, Jerusha would give her some information. She began tentatively, feeling her way. "Frank told me things that first night when I met him and we walked to the creek."

Cocking her head, Jerusha studied Leigh's face. "What things?"

"He said our families are related by blood."

Jerusha's face became grim. "He should never have talked about such things to you. You're a young, innocent girl."

Leigh felt no surprise. Frank wouldn't have misled her. "It's true then?"

"It was different times. Slavery times." Aunt Jerusha looked out the window as if seeing something besides the barren trees outside. "My parents were slaves, you know. And I grew up when the fear of lynchin' was always there, always waitin'."

"Why did your family stay here after the Civil War then?" The TV announcer now discussed plans to transport the president's body back to Washington, D.C. by air.

"This was our home. And moving north doesn't change the color of your skin. The Carlyles weren't as bad as some, and my family was house slaves. It was better than workin' in the tobacco fields. But nothing was easy in those days. No matter what color you were born, life was hard. No electricity, no hot runnin' water, no indoor plumbin', no radio, no phones, no cars or tractors or washin' machines. Men and women—white, black—worked themselves into early graves. And after the Civil War, money was scarce, and the KKK was ridin' high."

Leigh sat down. Sometimes her grandmother would talk about the Carlyle family, her grandmother's family, the ones who built Ivy Manor, but never about this side of the family history. "It's true then? We are related?"

"I do mean it. Frank will never date Leigh." Chloe edged closer to Bette. "Frank suffered when his parents got divorced and his mom left him to be raised by his father's family. Do you think he'd do the same thing to his own children?"

Bette looked away and began dredging the chicken through the flour mixture. "Then why is he writing to my six-teen-year-old daughter?"

Chloe looked down at the highly polished, gray-speckled linoleum floor, praying for wise words. "It's hard for Frank. He has an edge to him because of who he is. Minnie wrote me, he recently went against his family and entered the military. I think he's done that because he wants to find someplace where he'll be judged for himself alone—not because of who he's related to, not because of his race. I don't know if he will find that in the army or not. I hope—for his peace of mind— that he does."

Bette slipped the first piece of chicken into the hot oil, and it began to sizzle and spit. "What has this got to do with Leigh?"

Chloe drew back from the stove. "Leigh is special. She doesn't look at people with any prejudice. She's open and ac-cepting. And the two of them shared a special experience, going to the march together. You're the one who forced that to happen."

"You mean because I was concerned about my daughter's safety?" Bette asked in a snippy tone, continuing to add chicken to the skillet.

"If your stepfather and I thought it was safe to go, you should have backed down and let Leigh go with us." Another thing Chloe had held back from saying. "Then it wouldn't have been Leigh and Frank alone. It wouldn't have been Frank becoming Leigh's hero for taking her to be a part of an historic event. *You* are going to have to learn when to bend, or your relationship with your daughter will be damaged forever."

"So it's my fault Leigh is attracted to Frank, and I should just let them go on writing letters." Bette bristled in concert with the snapping oil.

"Yes, that is exactly what I'd prescribe for this situation." *Listen to me, Bette.* "The more you try to control Leigh, the more she'll pull away from you and the more rebellious she'll become until she finds herself making terrible choices just because she's so busy fighting you." Chloe took hold of one of her daughter's arms. "Stop it now, Bette, before you cause real harm to your daughter and your family."

"Yes, we share blood relatives. Another thing they didn't have in slave days was that new-fangled birth-control pill," Aunt Jerusha said dryly.

Leigh was shocked in spite of herself. The nuns at school had lectured them all repeatedly about the sin of birth control—but without any reference to human biology, and without ever mentioning the word *sex*. And sex was a subject her mother wouldn't discuss, either. When Leigh was eleven, Grandma Chloe—not her mother—had explained to her about her monthly flow and all about how babies were made. "Do you know how we're related?"

"I don't know everything. After all, we were slaves here for almost a century before emancipation." Jerusha kept rocking. "But I know for sure my father was an illegitimate son of your . . . let's see . . . great-great grandfather, the daddy of your grandmother's mother, Miss Lily Leigh. You're named for her."

Leigh let this sink in as she recalled framed photos and tintypes of her ancestors that sat on the mantels and decorated the walls of Ivy Manor. "Does Grandma Chloe know about this?"

"I think so, but we never talked about it." Jerusha gazed at the TV screen.

"You haven't? Why not?"

The older woman shrugged. "Why? Can we do anythin' about who we're related to? Your grandmother is a good woman. And she had a rough childhood with those two fightin', good-for-nothin' parents of hers." Jerusha looked grimly satisfied, as if she'd wanted to say that for a very long time. "What saved Miss Chloe was she was raised by my mother, Patty, and your great-grandma Raney, two good women. Miss Chloe had a few years where she lost her way, but when the Depression happened, she come home and made sure no one was turned off the land."

This didn't interest Leigh. The announcer murmured that they'd have a retrospective on JFK's life later. Leigh was sick of her mother always telling her how hard life had been during the Depression. Was being poor as hard as living with the atom bomb hanging over everyone's heads?

"Now I think you should do my grandson right. Stop writin' him. You're a very pretty girl and sweet like your grandmother. It's easy to see why Frank would take a shine to you. But it's not gone to do him any good. You could make him a target of bad things, real bad things."

"What things?" Leigh folded one leg under her and suddenly the sting of hunger hooked her.

"I already mentioned lynchin', but even if it didn't come

to that . . . people can be plenty nasty and they'd go after him not you."

"But—"

"Enough talkin'. Have you called to let your family know you're here?"

"No." Leigh felt weighed down. Her mother prying and now the assassination. What an awful day. She'd heard about carrying the weight of the world, but this was the first time it had been real to her.

"Go, then." Aunt Jerusha waved Leigh toward the back-door. "Use the phone in the kitchen up at the house and then make us a snack. I'm hungry."

"How can I let her go on corresponding with Frank?" Bette demanded.

"She's going to do it anyway. You may think you've put a stop to it, but she'll find a way. Unless you want to quit work and follow her around every day of the week, she can still go on writing to him without your finding out." Chloe didn't want to say that Bette was reminding her of her own mother, who had burned Chloe's letters from her first love— a futile gesture that had pushed Chloe into rebellion. "You know I ended up running away from my parents."

Bette looked uncertain for the first time. "I thought that your running away was just because you and my father wanted to marry before he left for the war."

Chloe made a sound of irritation. "That and the fact that my parents didn't want me to marry someone they hadn't chosen for me. They wanted to control me, keep me theirs alone."

"I don't want to do that." Bette worried her lower lip. "I just don't want her to make a disastrous mistake."

"Bette, we liked Curt," Chloe appealed to her. "He was a good man. How could you or your father and I have predicted how your marriage would turn out? No one but God knows the future. No matter what precautions you take, your daughter will grow up and she'll make her own choices, her own mistakes. I'm just worried that you will push her into such a state of rebellion she will do things she ordinarily would not do."

"Thank you, Chloe," Ted said, entering the kitchen. "That's been my point all along. Leigh is pretty, smart, and has so much personality. Whatever she decides to do, she'll be a success. Bette, you try to control her too much. You've got to let go. Or you will bear a bitter load of guilt."

Bette threw her hands upward. "All right. She can write Frank. I'm just trying . . ." She burst into tears and Ted folded her into his arms.

The phone rang.

Chloe walked to the wall phone and picked up. "This is the Gaston residence."

"Grandma?" Leigh's voice came over the line—tentative.

"*Leigh*, where are you?" Chloe felt a rush of relief.

"I'm calling from Ivy Manor. I got here about an hour ago."

"You shouldn't have left home like that, Leigh," Chloe scolded. "No matter what your mother said or did. Carlyles don't run. They stand and fight."

"I'm tired of fighting, Grandma. Aunt Jerusha told me to call you," Leigh sounded defeated. "If it's all right, I think I'd like to stay here with her for the night. And I think she would like me to stay, too."

"You'll have to ask your mother." Chloe handed the phone to Bette. "Your daughter wants permission to stay the night with Jerusha."

Bette took the phone as if it were a cobra. "Leigh, honey, are you all right?"

Leigh felt relieved her mother didn't sound angry. She just didn't have the energy to face any more of her mother's displeasure. "I'm fine. I'm sorry I cut school today."

"You know the president's been killed?" Bette's voice was gentle.

Had the assassination overshadowed everything else—even her mother's anger? "Yes. Please, may I stay with Aunt Jerusha tonight? I don't want to have to walk back to town."

"That's fine," Bette agreed. "Call tomorrow and we'll make plans for you to come home."

"Okay." Leigh paused and then guilt made her say, "I love you, Mom." Then she waited for more scolding. Whenever she showed any contrition, her mother always followed it with the "you are such an ungrateful daughter" lecture.

"I love you, too, honey."

Surprised that the lecture didn't come, Leigh hung up and walked into the large country kitchen. She opened the refrigerator door and the phone rang. *Oh, great. What now?* She hurried back into the hall and picked up. "Hello?"

"Hello, this is Frank Three. Is that you, Mrs. McCaslin? Could someone ask my great-grandmother to—"

Leigh heart stuttered. "Frank, it's me, Leigh."

"Leigh. *Leigh?* What are you doing there?"

"I ran away today and came here." Leigh held onto the phone as if it were an extension of Frank. "My mother found your letters to me."

"And you've been forbidden to write me again." He sounded disgusted but not at all surprised. "I knew that would happen. I've been waiting for it to happen. I'm sorry for putting you—"

"It was my decision to write you." Leigh made her shaky voice firm. She recalled his large black eyes and thick black lashes. "I could have just kept your first letter and left it at that. I wanted to write to you. I still do."

"I'm too old for you, and you're white and I'm black," Frank spoke the words like a familiar litany, "even if this is the *1960s*, not the *1860s*."

Fear nearly choked her. "Frank, we can't let . . . nonsense like that spoil our friendship."

"This isn't friendship. We know that. You're so sweet, so innocent, so passionate about life. You attract me like no other girl ever has."

His words went through Leigh like a lightning bolt.

"And I shouldn't have said that, either." Frank sounded disgusted. "I won't write you again, Leigh. I'm . . . sorry."

"Frank," Leigh clung to hope, "isn't it possible for a white girl and a black man to be friends?"

"No, I don't think so."

She felt her throat tightening. "Frank, I—"

"Please tell my great-grandmother," he interrupted, "that I called to see how she was in light of the president's assassination and tell her I'll write her soon. Good-bye, Leigh." The line went dead.

Shaken, stinging, yet faintly relieved, Leigh returned the receiver to its cradle and made her way back into the kitchen to get on with making Aunt Jerusha a snack. As she worked and pondered the days' events, a line from a Langston Hughes poem about hope came to mind: "What happens to a dream deferred? Does it dry up like a raisin in the sun?"

Leigh felt hemmed in on all sides, trapped, smothered. *My mother's spoiled it all.*

*   *   *

A week later, Leigh sat on the bed in Mary Beth's large turquoise-blue room. It was raining outside, and the leaves and branches from an old oak outside the window kept dragging over the glass, adding a creepy haunted-house quality to the atmosphere of the sleepover.

"So what's wrong, Leigh?" Cherise asked. She sat near Leigh on the bed in a pink-flowered flannel nightgown.

Leigh's spirits had been at low ebb since President Kennedy's assassination and Frank's good-bye call. "What?"

"You've been miserable all this week." Mary Beth chipped in from where she sat cross-legged in blue pajamas on the floor. "Is it because of the assassination?"

Leigh—to her horror—burst into tears.

Mary Beth leaped up and perched beside Leigh. "What is it?"

"You can trust us," Cherise said, patting Leigh's shoulder. "We won't tell anything to anyone."

Leigh wiped her wet face with her fingers. She had held it all in. Now, evidently, she wasn't going to be able to go on without trusting someone. "You promise?"

Mary Beth raised her hand as if she were taking an oath. "On my honor."

Cherise nodded. "Come on. Is it a boy?"

"It's a man. His name is Frank Dawson III." Each word dragged at Leigh's mood. "He's in Officer's Candidate School."

"He's in the army?" Mary Beth breathed in, looking excited.

Leigh again wished she'd been strong enough to hold it all in.

"How'd you meet him?" Cherise asked, looking wary.

"At my grandmother's this summer. Our grandmothers

grew up together." She looked into Cherise's pensive face. "He's Negro."

"Negro?" Mary Beth echoed. "That's why you asked us what we thought of interracial dating." She nearly bounced with excitement.

Leigh frowned. "We're not dating." *We'll never have the chance.* "We're just friends, but I knew what my mother would say if I let her know we were writing to each other."

"You've been forbidden to write him ever again," Cherise inserted, nodding knowingly.

Leigh gave a half smile. "At first, but then it got weird and my mom said I could write him. But when I told him this, he said he shouldn't have written me and that he wouldn't anymore. That we couldn't be just friends."

"Ah." Cherise raised her chin.

"Well, if you understand this, explain it to me," Leigh said, feeling out of sorts.

"He's older than you, isn't he? He'd have to be in order to be in service."

Leigh nodded. "He's twenty-two."

"He's twenty-two," Mary Beth repeated reverently.

"He's trying to protect you," Cherise said. "He knows that no one will believe a man and girl can just be friends—especially not when one is white and one is black."

"What are they protecting me from?" Leigh asked, knowing she wasn't being completely honest.

Cherise looked down her nose at Leigh. "Don't give me the naïve act. You know exactly what kind of trouble. He might not be lynched these days, but if you went out with him . . ." Cherise shook her head and gave Leigh another knowing look.

"So that means you think I shouldn't write him again."

Leigh lifted her chin. "We should just bow to prejudice and I should just let it . . . him go?"

Cherise looked as if she were mulling this over. She propped her chin on one hand. Mary Beth sat like a hopeful puppy, waiting for a treat. With her forefinger, Leigh traced the fancy stitching on Mary Beth's turquoise satin quilt.

"Why couldn't we all three write him a letter together?" Cherise grinned suddenly. "I mean, then it's not just a two-some. It's three girls writing a soldier who will someday defend our country."

"That's right." Mary Beth's head bobbed. "It would be patriotic."

Leigh did not like this suggestion, but what could she say? "I want Frank all to myself"? Impossible. "Okay," she agreed reluctantly.

Mary Beth jumped up, went to her desk, and snatched up a clipboard and a sheet of stationery. "What's his name?"

"Frank," Leigh said.

"Dear Frank," Mary Beth began writing, "I'm one of Leigh's friends, Mary Beth." She proceeded to explain who she was and what they'd decided and then handed the clipboard to Cherise who took it and wrote her own introduction. Finally, the clipboard came to Leigh. There was much she wanted to say, but she limited herself to an explanation of why the three would be writing him: "So that no one can say it's a boy-girl thing." Leigh wrote a few more lines and then Mary Beth folded the letter and asked Leigh to address the envelope.

"This is so cool," Mary Beth said.

Leigh tried not to look unhappy. She glanced at Cherise, wondering why the other girl had proposed this. Of course, no one would be upset with Cherise for writing to Frank. But then Leigh felt small for thinking that. A pretty girl like

Cherise wouldn't have any trouble finding guys to date. And her idea would make it possible for Leigh to keep somewhat in touch with Frank.

Leigh didn't want to examine how desperately she wanted to keep this channel open. Neither did she want to delve into exactly what her feelings for Frank were. *We can only be friends. That's what he wants.* Once again, she thought of Aunt Jerusha and how she'd said Frank's mother had married Frank Two just to be . . . what? Different? And that she'd left Frank Three to be raised by Minnie. *No wonder he doesn't trust me. I'm white.*

St. Agnes Catholic Girls School, May 1965

The organist played "Pomp and Circumstance." In a black cap and gown, Leigh walked very straight down the aisle and up to the row of seats on the platform reserved for the graduates. In the crowd, she glimpsed the top of Frank's head among the proud parents and relatives. *He came.*

Chapter Six

$\mathcal{L}$eigh made herself continue marching as the nuns had rehearsed them to do over and over on the day before. But her heart had begun singing and she couldn't stop it. Maybe today she'd be able to reconnect with Frank, get back to the way they were that night he'd driven her home from Dr. King's march two years ago.

She joined the two rows of black-garbed graduates on the platform. Mary Beth sat in the row ahead of Leigh, but Cherise sat opposite them among the audience. She wouldn't graduate until next year, but she'd come to see her friends cross the stage.

The three of them had decided to take a chance and invite Frank. Over the past two years, the trio had continued to correspond with Frank, but only three or four times a year. Frank always took his time replying to their letters.

Leigh wondered if he stretched out the intervals between letters so she would believe he'd lost interest in her. Still, she'd treasured the words he blurted out that awful day she'd run away to Ivy Manor and President Kennedy had been assassinated. Frank had said, "You attract me like no other girl ever has." But then he'd said he wouldn't write anymore and had hung up.

In the intervening years since the last time she'd seen Frank, Leigh had begun dating on and off. Her mother had backed off, for some unexplained reason. As long as Leigh got good grades and introduced the young man to the family before going out, Leigh had her freedom. But it was a hollow victory. She'd won her liberty on November 22, 1963, but she'd lost the reason she'd wanted that independence.

The principal, Sister Maria, was peering through thick lenses, reading her welcome to the assembled friends and families. Leigh was so happy that her days at St. Agnes were ending today and that everything, anything seemed possible. Today, Leigh would find a way to let Frank know she still cared about him, but that she would never do anything that would cause him harm. Somehow it seemed very important to tell him this, to put it into words so that the awful gulf between them could be bridged. It felt like a debt she owed him.

At the end of the welcome, the organist switched to Bach's "Ode to Joy" and Leigh felt the awesome significance of the day. Today, childhood ended and adult life began.

Now, the black-and-red-robed monsignor stepped to the front of the platform and bowed his head to give the invocation. Leigh started to lower her head, but then she decided to take the opportunity to look over the bent heads and scan the audience. Minnie and Frank were the only dark faces in the crowd except for Cherise and her mother, of course, who sat nearer the front. In dress uniform, Frank was sitting beside his grandmother Minnie. Grandma Chloe sat on Minnie's other side. Beside Grandma Chloe, Grandpa Roarke, her parents, and then Dory sat in the row along with Grandma Sinclair—all in their Sunday best. Her mother kept frowning at

Frank. But Leigh refused to let her mother spoil this, her graduation day.

The graduation ceremony took over an hour and then finally Leigh, along with the rest, rose and moved the tassels on their caps from one side to the other. The symbolic act released all Leigh's tension. She nearly leaped into the air, but contented herself with a broad smile. Everyone applauded and the graduates marched out to the closing recessional to the reception area.

Leigh worked her way through the milling crowd of families and graduates until she reached her family. Her stepfather hugged her first. In this moment of dawning adulthood, she recognized how much she adored this laughing man who'd always loved her as his own. She hugged him back and whispered, "I love you." He murmured the same phrase to her and then passed her to her mother.

Bette leaned forward and kissed Leigh's cheek. "We're so proud of you, honey."

Leigh noticed that her mother had tears in her eyes. She hugged her mom; in that moment forgiving all the fights they'd had over the past four years.

Then each of her grandparents hugged her tight and both grandmothers cried. And Dory wrapped her small arms around Leigh's waist and held on as if Leigh were leaving her that very day.

Finally, Leigh turned to Minnie, very aware of Frank, standing tall and handsome beside her. "Mrs. Dawson, I'm so glad you were able to come." Then, clearing her throat, Leigh looked up at Frank. "And you, too."

Before Leigh could say another word, Mary Beth crowded close, holding her mortarboard on with one hand. "Frank," she squealed, "you came!" Then Cherise appeared at his elbow, smiling shyly.

Leigh introduced everyone while Frank stood back, smiling and responding to Mary Beth, who was doing her eager-puppy imitation. Then he focused on Cherise, who looked very pretty in her new royal-blue shirtwaist. Frank must have agreed because he kept studying her until Cherise's cheeks turned a dusky pink. Leigh pushed away a trace of irritation that buzzed through her.

It seemed to Leigh that people flowed around her, cutting her off from reaching Frank, from being close enough to speak. But they wouldn't be in the crowd much longer, and with this thought, she relaxed. At the end of the public graduation, Frank and Minnie would be coming to Leigh's home where her mother was having an open house for friends and family. There Leigh would snatch a private word with Frank.

At last, Leigh's family and their friends left the high school grounds and arrived at home. The caterers had everything ready in the backyard under a clear, true-blue, happy-days sky. Flowers decorated tables of finger foods, cake, and punch. Leigh finally slipped off her black graduation gown and showed off her new coral dress, whose short skirt instantly brought her mother's disapproval. "Your skirt wasn't that short when we bought it."

Leigh gave her mother an innocent smile, admitting nothing. This was not the moment to thank her Grandmother Sinclair for teaching her how to put in a professional-looking hem. Instead, Leigh turned to greet longtime neighbors and accept their felicitations. Then Minnie was at her elbow.

"That Cherise seems very nice."

Remembering all that Aunt Jerusha had said on the day JFK died—about Minnie raising Frank after his parent's divorce, Leigh's nerves tightened another notch. "Yes, Cherise is a good friend." Leigh chose her words with care. "She graduates next year."

Minnie nodded. "Frank tells me the three of you have been writing him."

Leigh tried to analyze Minnie's tone. She couldn't, so she just nodded.

"I hope you have given up any thought that Frank will pursue you," Minnie murmured under the cover of all the other voices. "Or maybe I should say, I hope *you've* given up any idea of pursuing him?"

Leigh was blindsided. She'd never expected Frank's grandmother to bring this up. Frantically, she weighed different responses before finally saying, "Frank has made it clear that he isn't interested in me as a girlfriend."

Minnie searched Leigh's face as if somehow matching her words against her intentions. "Frank is doing well in the military. I think he will go far."

"I'm glad for him." Leigh's heart sped up as if she were lying.

Then Mary Beth called out, "Come on. Someone take a picture of the three of us with our soldier before we have to leave." She claimed one of Frank's arms. Smiling, Cherise took the other and Leigh stepped in front of Frank a little to one side. Mary Beth's father, whose hair had begun to grow longer over the past year, clicked away with the fancy Canon that hung around his neck.

When he was done, Leigh turned and smiled at Frank. "I'm so glad you were able to make it. I hope we can have time to talk in this crowd."

"Oh, I wouldn't want to monopolize the graduate," he sidestepped her adroitly.

Leigh tried not to be put off by the rebuff. She wanted to touch his arm, but she sensed his grandmother's hostile stare searing her back. Regardless, Leigh went on in a low tone, "Frank, I don't want to put any pressure on you. I just want you to know that I still treasure our friendship—"

"As do I." His set expression, his terse words warned her away.

It was a stern warning she found she couldn't ignore. Frustrated, she retreated to safer ground. "So you decided to re-up?"

"Yes." He gave her an easy smile. "After my promotion to first lieutenant, I decided to stay in for another hitch. I'll be heading to Nam soon."

His news made her tingle with uneasiness. "Viet Nam? Oh, Frank—"

"Now, don't worry about me," he said dismissively. "I've already been through the wringer with my mother, the peacenik. I'll just be there as an advisor."

Leigh pursed her lips. Viet Nam seemed a very long way away. But before she could say any more, Frank had turned slightly to be introduced to Cherise's mother. He smiled down at Cherise, answering a question Leigh didn't hear.

Leigh noted his special expression as he gazed down at Cherise and she froze. The expression was one of attraction and pleasure, and Cherise studied Frank with something like wonder.

Frank had come to see Leigh, but he'd come as a soldier protected by impenetrable armor. A shield to keep her from reaching him. But he'd lowered his mask for Cherise, who teased him with a nothing bunch of words, flirting effortlessly. He grinned and looked entranced.

Watching this, Leigh's heart squeezed together, nearly making her gasp. Frank had made his decision to shut her out, and there didn't seem to be any appeal left open to her.

Columbia University, October 1966

With the door open to the hall, Leigh paced the floor of the small dorm room she shared with Mary Beth. Uneasy, she glanced at her wristwatch again. Mary Beth had been fixed up with a hippie or surfer from California who was visiting a guy in her psych class. Earlier, downstairs in the dormitory parlor, Leigh had glimpsed the stranger when he'd picked up her roommate. He was Mary Beth's dream date, having shoulder-length blond hair, ragged jeans, and a tie-dyed shirt with beads around his neck. Upon seeing him, Leigh had nearly hummed, "When You Come to San Francisco, Be Sure to Wear Flowers in Your Hair." In contrast, Mary Beth—with her long, flyaway hair, blue jeans, and love beads—had looked like it was Christmas morning again. But at least Mary Beth and her hippie had gone with a group.

A half hour ago, Leigh had gotten in early from a Saturday night party. Her date had been another in a string of guys who liked blondes. On their walk home from his frat house, when he'd tried to put the moves on her in a secluded area, she'd claimed a headache. She didn't like being groped on the first date—or any other date. *Jerk*.

Now she heard giggling swelling outside her door and a rush of footsteps over the linoleum hall, the signals that curfew had come. Outside, the necking couples who'd gathered around the entrance had separated to let the girls come in before lockup, and everyone was rushing past her door to their rooms. Opening it, Leigh stood at the door, hoping to see Mary Beth. *Why am I so worried?*

But she hadn't liked something about the Californian. Now the girls on the floor all waved to her or wished her good night, and after a spate of late-night showers, the floor grew quiet and the lights in the hallways were dimmed. Still no Mary Beth.

Leigh realized she needed to shut the door to the hall before the resident assistant on the floor noticed that Mary Beth hadn't returned. Mary Beth had been fine as a freshman, working hard not to flunk out. But now, a month into her sophomore year, she'd already gotten two demerits for staying out after curfew and a third could mean social probation. And their RA didn't like Mary Beth.

With the lights switched off, Leigh paced the tiny patch of linoleum in their room, trying not to make a sound. The glow-in-the-dark clock on the desk stated the time as well after midnight. Just as Leigh was about to give up and dress for bed, she heard muffled giggling outside their first-story window. She looked out and there was Mary Beth and the blond Californian. Leigh opened the window and leaned out. "Mary Beth," she hissed, "what are you doing? It's after curfew."

The Californian gave Leigh the peace sign and then in a sort of wobble, motioned to Mary Beth. He cupped his hands together and Mary Beth, still giggling softly, put her foot in them and let him hoist her up to the window. Shocked, and terrified of their being seen from a window of the neighboring dorm, Leigh hauled the giggle princess into the room. Mary Beth's weight almost took Leigh to the floor, but she stayed on her feet long enough to shove Mary Beth onto her nearby twin bed. Then she shut the window and turned, ready to read Mary Beth the riot act.

"I don't feel very good," Mary Beth moaned. "I'm gonna be sick."

Leigh shoved the wastebasket under her roommate's chin just in time. She held Mary Beth's head there until the fit of retching passed. A sour, sick odor competed with Mary

Beth's alcohol breath. "How much did you drink?" Leigh snapped.

"Not much," Mary Beth mumbled, then she giggled. "Chance had weed."

Leigh nearly shook Mary Beth, but didn't want her to start throwing up again. "Are you insane?" she hissed next to Mary Beth's ear. "Drugs on campus? Do you want to get expelled?"

"Aw, lighten up. What's a little weed between friends?"

Nothing, just a felony and expulsion. "You don't have any on you, do you?"

Mary Beth looked at her as if this were an unknown collection of words.

"If you have any on you, give it to me. We've got to throw it out the window. What if they do a bed check?"

Mary Beth shook her head. "Didn't bring any—"

Light streamed in around the door to the hall. "Bed check!" the resident assistant announced in a loud voice. Their door flew open first. Leigh glared at the RA. "We're here. What's your problem?"

"She better not have brought any alcohol—" the RA began.

"I'm clean," Mary Beth crowed. "Just a little happy." And then she began humming the Beatles, "Love, Love Me Do."

The RA looked Mary Beth over and then shook her head. "You're going to end up flunking out if this doesn't stop."

"Peace." Mary Beth held up her hand in the two-fingered peace sign. And then passed out on the bed.

Leigh wanted to shake Mary Beth until her teeth rattled out onto the floor. Mary Beth had begun by going to drinking bashes at the different frat houses. And now a hippie and marijuana . . . She had to find a way to turn Mary Beth around. Otherwise, where would it all end?

Chicago, August 28, 1968

Outside Leigh's hotel, the Conrad Hilton, police sirens sounded in the distance, releasing another spurt of adrenaline in Leigh. Where was Mary Beth? Was she safe? Her friend had promised to steer clear of trouble this week, but so many opportunities presented themselves. And she'd already been picked up by the Chicago police once. Leigh stared down from the high window of the room she shared with other girls attending the convention. Mary Beth had chosen instead to camp out in Grant Park with Chance, her hippie boyfriend from California. Fretting, Leigh stared down at the yellow police barricades below near the hotel entrance, and at the line of helmeted, blue-uniformed cops along it. From the transistor radio, Martha and the Vandellas sang "Nowhere to Run, Baby . . ."

The sense of a world spinning out of control, of a beast waiting to be unleashed, ate at Leigh's peace. And why not? The International Amphitheatre where the Democratic Convention was being held was surrounded by steel-wire fences and ugly yellow barricades and armed riot police. How crazy did the world have to become? When had it grown dangerous to be a politician, dangerous to be near politicians?

But of course, it had all started with the assassination of President Kennedy five years ago. That thought took her mind back to that dark day. Another unhappy thought. Frank was in Viet Nam for his second tour of duty, and thousands of U.S. soldiers were dying there. At home, the Viet Nam War had ignited a blaze of nationwide protest and forced LBJ not to run again.

She rubbed her tight neck muscles and turned to get ready for this evening. *Mary Beth, please come now. Please.*

Leigh had come to Chicago in the entourage of the Maryland delegation. It had been set up through her college and with her grandmother's influence. Leigh hadn't taken much interest in her great-grandfather before, but evidently he had been a politician. And Grandma Chloe still knew people in the Democratic Party, people who could arrange for her granddaughter to have a plum job at a convention.

Both Leigh and Mary Beth had come to write articles about the convention experience for college papers. But where was her friend? Mary Beth was supposed to be here to go to this evening's session with Leigh, who'd finally gotten her a visitor's pass.

Leigh glanced at her watch. She couldn't wait any longer for Mary Beth or she'd miss this evening's limo to the Amphitheatre. In front of the closet door mirror, she glanced at herself. She wore a shades-of-pink paisley miniskirt and matching vest over a pink blouse with a large ruffled collar. She adjusted her pantyhose. Then she refreshed her pale-pink lipstick and combed her waist-length blonde hair, swinging around to catch the ends and comb them, too.

Tonight, the delegates would cast their votes and all the excitement, craziness should end. "Please hurry, Mary Beth. It's dangerous out there."

Leigh tried not to worry, but 1968 had been a year for worrying. The Tet Offensive at the end of January had heated up the Viet Nam War, sending two hundred thousand U.S. troops there. Then in April, Martin Luther King Jr. had been assassinated in Memphis. Race riots had burst cities all over America into flames and funerals. Then at the end of March,

LBJ had dropped out of the race for a second term. Finally, in June, Robert Kennedy had been killed in California while campaigning for president, and another rage had boiled over into the streets.

From the transistor radio came Simon and Garfunkel singing, "Feelin' Groovy." Leigh did not feel groovy. She switched off the radio.

"What a bloody year," Leigh murmured to the universe. Each disaster had hit her as another wave of hopelessness. Soldiers were dying in a war the generals had bungled and misrepresented even to the powers that be. The world had careened off its axis. But all her mother wanted from her was good grades and to know whether Leigh was dating anyone "nice."

Leigh glanced at her watch again. "Mary Beth, I can't wait any longer," she said aloud in disgust. She headed down the stairs, her footsteps echoing in the concrete stairwell. She walked out the entrance into the sunshine and looked around for the limo, for Mary Beth, for others in the Maryland delegation. A nearby crowd of demonstrators with long hair, bare feet, and homemade signs was yelling but that wasn't new. Chicago might have been "the city of big shoulders" to Sandburg, but it was the city of loud mouths to Leigh.

Bottles and toilet paper were raining down from the Hilton. She caught the yippie chant, "Hey, Hey, Go Away!" The worry that Mary Beth might be out there among the protestors again pinched Leigh. She shaded her eyes with her hand. *But what can I do about that?*

The long black limo was farther away than usual—too near the line of police for comfort. Leigh hurried forward, waving to the driver.

Then there were screams, shrieking police whistles, people running toward Grant Park, toward the Hilton. Blue-uniformed police chased the fleeing demonstrators—billy clubs flailing. Leigh felt, but couldn't hear herself screaming. Just yards ahead, a policeman was clubbing a hippie sprawled on the pavement already bleeding. In a sickening moment of terror Leigh recognized the man on the ground—it was Mary Beth's boyfriend, Chance. Horrified, Leigh ran—full tilt—toward the cop. "Stop! Stop it!" *He's down! Leave him alone!*

The policeman turned on her and swung his billy club wide. Leigh ducked and charged under his arm, butting into his chest. The two of them went down and landed on top of Chance. People surged forward, tripping over them, cursing, yelling. Leigh felt her skirt rip at the waistband. The policeman pushed her away and rolled to his feet. He kicked her in the side and then ran back into the fray.

Pressing her arm against the pain in her side where she'd been kicked, Leigh rolled off Chance. "Are you okay?" Panting, she bent over him, trying to protect his head as people jostled over and around them.

He moaned as she mopped the blood that leaked from a gash on his forehead with the tail of her blouse. Blood also flowed into his long blond hair—and more from his nose.

Quiet came suddenly. Leigh stood and helped him up. Numbed by the bedlam she'd just witnessed, she looked around for assistance and located a yippie aid station on the north side of the street. She staggered there, hauling him with her.

"The revolution has started," was the exultant greeting she got there. For a moment, a scene from *Dr. Zhivago* flashed in her mind—a wintry street in Moscow, the red-coated Cossacks riding down a silent march of poor people. And for a moment, the unreality of being attacked on an American street by a policeman surged through her, weakening her knees. She slumped down on the curb, shaking with the residual terror of what she'd just seen, just been caught up in. But around her—obviously exhilarated—the protestors exclaimed, "Power to the people!"

"Hey, you're my old lady's friend," Chance said, eyeing her from under the new bandage over his eye.

"Where is Mary Beth?" Leigh asked.

Before he could answer, out of nowhere—the next wave launched. Bottles flew over their heads. Trash barrels rolled and careened toward the re-formed line of police and National Guard. And the sound of booted feet and chanting swelled all around. Voices shouted, *"Sieg Heil! Sieg Heil!"* Tear-gas grenades exploded.

Chance dragged Leigh off the curb and behind the shelter of a large blue mailbox. She huddled with him behind it, watching several policemen pick up a yellow traffic barricade that had been pushed over. The police, using it as a battering ram, charged the crowd in front of them. More screaming, cursing. Blood spattered on the street.

Leigh gagged with the shock and horror. Choking on the tear gas, she clung to Chance's T-shirt, trying to make herself the smallest target possible. She wanted to scream, "Stop it! Stop it!" But she shrank down farther. Chaos raged all around them. Who would hear her, obey her?

Another chant started, loud and strident. "The whole world is watching! The whole world is watching!" Then Leigh glimpsed Mary Beth in the crowd. A cop had her by the hair. "Mary Beth!" Leigh screamed, rising.

First Chance, then Leigh leaped from the shelter and plunged into the fray, trying to reach Mary Beth. A policeman knocked Chance to the ground. Leigh screamed at the cop. Then he swung his billy club.

Leigh saw it coming, felt it, heard it crack against her

head. Stars burst before her eyes and she felt herself falling, falling into darkness.

She opened her eyes and blinked. Her eyes were full of sleep-dust and stung from something. At first, she didn't move. She couldn't move. Her fuzzy mind groped for information. *Where am I?* She moaned and the sound rolled through her throat and mouth, sounding loud and fuzzy in her ears. She felt around with her hands. She was lying on cool concrete and people were nearby, talking and laughing. Laughing?

Slowly she sat up. Looking around, blinking in the stark light, blinking to rid herself of the sandy feeling in her eyes, she was met by a motley circle of amused faces—black, white, and tan. Some were hippies; the rest looked like prostitutes or street people, junkies.

"Cinderella finally woke up," said a long, lean black woman with very red lipstick. She wore a tiny red miniskirt.

A younger woman, a hippie, came to Leigh and helped her up onto a bench. "We're in a holding cell. I was afraid when you didn't wake up. They should have taken you to an emergency room. You've got a nasty bump on your head."

That wasn't surprising news. Leigh felt nauseated and her head pounded. "Why am I here?" she mumbled.

"You got in the way of a billy club," the woman with the red lipstick answered with a smirk. "You college girls don't know when to duck."

"What time is it?" Leigh asked. She'd lost her wristwatch somewhere.

"We don't know," the hippie said. "They come and get us one at a time. But we can't call anyone because of the phone strike." The girl cursed AT&T, Mayor Daley, and the whole city of Chicago from top to bottom. The other women chuckled with appreciation.

Footsteps. A burly cop appeared and barked, "Leigh Sinclair."

Leigh held up her hand a few inches.

"Come on." He unlocked the cell and waved at her. "Come on, come on, girlie. I ain't got all night."

Leigh looked around uncertainly but finally limped to the door. She looked down and noticed she'd lost the heel to her right pump. She followed him, swaying slightly as he led her down corridor after corridor. Her head pounded with what must be a migraine.

Finally, the cop opened a door and said, "In here. Wait."

She staggered into a small room and just made it into a chair. She'd never felt so weak, battered, nauseated.

The door opened and a familiar face came in. Her splitting headache and vague disorientation slowed her recognition, but then she placed him. The man was Dane Hanley, an FBI agent, a friend of her stepfather's. His thick dark hair looked a bit too long to please the FBI and his too-serious dark brown eyes bore into her. The white of his shirt contrasted with his tanned neck and face. He looked like a man from a Marlboro ad who'd been forced off his horse and into a suit.

For the first time in hours, she felt safe. Dane would protect her. And she fought the urge to throw herself into his arms. Without a word, he handed over a small, tan shoulder bag that the police must have taken from her.

She recalled then that this was her second trip to a Chicago police station and her memory of yesterday returned. She'd met Dane yesterday when he'd come to help her bail out Mary Beth. In another ancient-looking police station, she'd stuck close to the protection of Dane's side, searching for Mary Beth's face among the hippies lining the walls and sitting on chairs and the floor. Dane had shown his FBI badge and ushered Leigh with him down several poorly lit, cramped corridors. Finally, a door was opened and Mary Beth had leaped into Leigh's arms—laughing—as if being picked up by the police were a joke.

Now, Leigh recalled seeing her friend tonight in the second wave of trouble. She squinted up at Dane and murmured, "Mary Beth."

"What?"

She cleared her raw throat. "Is Mary Beth here?"

"No. Come on," Dane said. "Let's get out of here."

"I'm not steady on my feet." She put a hand to her brow. "My head . . . pounding." Then she burst into hot, embarrassing tears.

Dane put an arm around her and helped her up and out the door, his strength a balm for her frazzled nerves. "You're bruised over one eye. I'm taking you straight to the emergency room."

Soon she was aware that they were riding in the back of an air-conditioned taxi through the city and then she was in a wheelchair being pushed into a hospital—swarming, buzzing with yippies, hippies, doctors, cops, and nurses. In a daze, she tried to find Mary Beth's face. Then the motion of being pushed along made her sicker and she felt herself sliding down . . . The soft darkness took her again, blotting out everything.

Leigh opened her eyes. The effort was almost too much for her. Pain seared her consciousness, stunning her once again. She heard a moan and realized it was hers.

"Is she coming around?" a man asked.

Lost in a clammy gray mist, Leigh tried to bring up words, but couldn't get them to her tongue. *Where am I?*

Sirens blared in the distance. That brought back the recent past, the terror of being attacked. Her nose and eyes still burned. Tear gas. Her head still throbbed. A name came to mind then, "Mary Beth."

Someone took her wrist. "Are you coming around, Miss Sinclair?" a woman asked her.

"Mary Beth," Leigh managed to whisper, "Get her. She's . . ."

"Mary Beth?" the man's voice came again. "Your friend that we bailed out yesterday?"

Leigh nodded, and the slight motion set off an atom bomb in her head; pain vibrated through her, bringing nausea. She gagged and dry-heaved. "Cop . . . got her."

"I'll see if she's been admitted or arrested."

Leigh recognized it now. She realized it was Dane's voice. She couldn't reply, but her mind brought up, like a newsreel, another memory for her. Mary Beth. Yesterday. Near the Picasso at the Chicago Civic Center Plaza, a crowd of yippies with a large pig—their candidate for president. Police with twisted faces crowded close. Hippies jeered them. After that, she'd met Dane. He'd come to the hotel to help her get Mary Beth out of jail.

Leigh opened her eyes and she tried to get herself to think normally. "Dane," she whispered.

Now, in the lowering light of dusk, a white-coated doctor came in. "Conscious, I see." After his cursory examination, she was headed to X-ray to make sure she didn't have a hairline fracture of the skull. As they rolled her away from Dane, she tried to say, "Don't leave me," but she couldn't form the words. Desperate, she reached for his hand.

He squeezed her shoulder and said, "I'll be here. I won't leave you."

And she sighed with relief.

*   *   *

She woke up in a bed and again smelled the distinctive odor of "American hospital." In the dim room, light seeped over a tall white curtain that cut off her view of the other half of the room. A man with dark hair and broad shoulders sat in a chair by her bed—Dane, true to his word. "Hi," she whispered, glad to see his face.

Dane moved forward, and the light flowed over his hawklike features. Beams of light from above moved over him, and away; they must have been headlights, not moonlight. She gazed at his harsh but handsome face, trying to remember . . . something.

"Leigh, you have a concussion," he informed her. "But otherwise you're okay."

"Obviously . . . ," she joked weakly, "my headache . . . didn't show up on the X-ray. It's colossal."

"Sorry." He touched her shoulder. "Want a pain pill?"

She closed and then opened her eyes, drawing strength from his calm presence. "Yes. It's awful."

Not letting go of Leigh's shoulder, he buzzed for the nurse. She appeared and gave Leigh a pill and a glass of water, and then left without a superfluous word.

Dane watched Leigh as if expecting some unwise action from her and ready to stop her.

"Don't worry." She tried to be wry. "I'm not going anywhere."

"Well, that's not quite true. You'll be going home this afternoon with me."

"Home? With you?" That didn't make sense.

Headlights came again, casting shadows on his face, his high cheekbones. "No, I'm taking you home to your parents."

"But my reservation is for Saturday," she objected with as

much heat as she could muster. "I wanted to do some sight-seeing after the convention. The Art Institute—"

"Sorry." He gave her a wry grin. "When you get yourself on TV being clubbed by a cop, you lose your sightseeing rights."

His ironic comment couldn't be true. "TV? Me?"

He nodded soberly. "Your parents saw you."

"Oh, no." Distress welled up inside her—a geyser. Her mother, who hadn't wanted her to come, would be fit to be tied.

"Your parents were going to fly here, but I persuaded them that the best idea is my getting you out of this crazy city."

"Thanks," she said in warm relief. She didn't want to think how embarrassing it would have been having her parents fly in to take her by the hand and lead her home. "They still think I'm a baby."

Dane shrugged. "Well, how old are you?"

"I'm twenty-one," Leigh defended herself.

"Then you are a baby."

She made a face at him and her head twinged with pain. "I missed the nomination tonight," she said, going through her mind, trying to bring everything back into focus.

"Hubert Horatio Humphrey got the nomination after all—even without your being there," he said dryly.

She grimaced, but with only half her face. She closed her eyes. She wasn't up to repartee. And besides, everything that had happened here was awful.

"What? Didn't Humphrey have your support?"

"Stop teasing. What does my opinion matter? I was just a hanger-on with the Maryland delegation. Tonight has been a total disaster."

"Oh, I don't know about that. At least we got to tour another historic Chicago police station, another *venerable dump*."

She ignored this, worrying her lower lip. "Where's Mary Beth?" She opened her eyes, peering at him through her veil of pain.

His face drew down. "So far we haven't found her. I've got the local police and FBI on the lookout for her."

She relived seeing that cop dragging her friend by the hair. *No. She's okay. She has to be.* "Then I'm not going home. I can't leave without Mary Beth."

Chapter Seven

"What makes you think she wants to be found?" Dane asked with blatant sarcasm in his voice. "The last time we saw her, she was doing a good job of straying from the straight and narrow. She's probably off somewhere stoned out of her mind."

His sarcasm stung. Leigh wanted to say that wasn't true. But unfortunately, it might be. This fact made her quiver inside, feel a bit sick or sicker than she already felt. "She's my friend." Leigh emphasized the word *friend*. "One of my best friends." *And someone has to care about her*.

"Then you should choose your friends with better care. I don't think she's looking for you."

Leigh flushed warmly since, again, she couldn't disagree. "A friend is a friend. I don't abandon my friends just because they make bad choices. Despite what you think, Mary Beth wouldn't leave me behind, and I can't leave until she's found."

"Are you sure about that?" But he gave her no time to answer. "You won't be doing anything until you are released from this hospital today. So you're stuck here until I get back.

And I've got to check in with the local Bureau here." He nailed her with both eyes. "Be here when I come back."

Leigh wanted to argue, but her residual weakness left her mute. She nodded. How had everything gone so awry?

Dane chuckled without mirth and walked out of her room. She watched his back recede from her sight, feeling an inexplicable sense of loss. He was sarcastic, but when he was with her, he made her feel safe.

Viet Nam, August 29, 1968

*F*rank sat hunched over on his cot, a pen in his hand and a pad of paper on his knee. *I have to write her. I can't just let her hear it from someone else.* But why did he feel this way? Why did Leigh rate a *separate* letter, a *separate* announcement? After those few brief letters five years ago, he hadn't written her—at least not *only* her, but her and her two friends. Why did Leigh linger in his mind—always a temptation?

He recalled Leigh's innocent beauty as she'd sat beside the reflecting pool in Washington, D.C., while Dr. King preached. Then he recalled her as she'd marched up the aisle at her graduation, her lovely, long blonde hair flowing from under her black mortarboard. Tightening his lips and his grip on his pen, he knew he had to explain this to her. He owed her that. He owed himself that.

> *Dear Leigh,*
>   *Where have the years gone? Doesn't that make us feel old? You were sixteen and I was twenty-two when we met that evening at Ivy Manor. I still re-member how lovely you looked in the twilight hold-ing a willow whip in your hands.*

He ripped the page off the pad and crumpled it. *I can't tell her that, not with what I need to say to her.* He'd made his decision, and it was a good one. These were just sweet memories of the past . . .

Still wearing her cloying, blood-stained, dirt-smeared outfit, Leigh hobbled defiantly on her broken shoe through the line of police and into the lobby of the Conrad Hilton. In silence, she and Dane rode the elevator to her floor. Again, his presence filled her, driving out the residual fear. Dane stood by as she unlocked the door of her room. The hotel hallways held the sickly odor of tear gas from the night before. Still light-headed, she led Dane inside. The room was empty of her roommates, whom she'd barely known; it looked as if they'd already checked out.

Even hours after last night's events, she felt flat, tired and weak from her slight concussion. Somehow she had to recover enough to start looking for Mary Beth. In spite of wanting to peel off her sticky clothes and throw them in the waste basket, Leigh plopped down on her freshly made bed. "This is a nightmare."

Dane made no reply, but crossed to the phone and picked it up, speaking to the hotel operator. "This is Agent Dane Hanley. I need to make a phone call to the FBI headquarters in D.C."

Leigh closed her eyes and lay back on the bed, wondering if he were going to report everything to her stepfather. As soon as she had the strength, she'd take a shower and change into clean clothes. She'd never felt this filthy in her life. It was as if she were wearing garbage.

"Hi, this is Hanley. Is Gaston there?"

Dane's voice, so businesslike, steadied Leigh. She tried to

think where Mary Beth might go. Maybe Leigh would find her somewhere in Old Town.

Dane turned and offered Leigh the receiver. "Your dad."

With a sigh, Leigh put it to her ear. "Dad?"

"Hi, honey. I hear you had an exciting evening. Are you planning on making a career in revolution?"

In spite of her lingering weakness and tender head, Leigh smiled. Only her stepdad would tease her about being in a riot. How she loved this man. "Not really. No fringe benefits." She grinned. "And I'm not much for being hit with billy clubs."

"If I had any way of finding out," he said, suddenly sounding like an angry father, "who clubbed you—"

"Cool it, Dad. I'm fine. Just feeling a little rough." Her head was still tender where the billy club had struck her. She closed her eyes and turned on her side, longing for a tub of hot water and bubble bath. Dane sat down by her feet, making the bed dip and reminding her of his presence.

"Leigh, here's your mother." Her dad's tone begged her to be diplomatic.

But Leigh didn't feel diplomatic right now. Out of respect for her father and Grandma Chloe, she'd always tried to keep her dialogues with her mother polite, but detached. She'd had to maintain her distance because her mother always did. Her mother always seemed to sit on Mt. Olympus raining down her opinions from on high. Today Leigh couldn't handle that. *Right now I just don't need her scolding me with, "I thought something like this would happen," and telling me to come home.*

"I knew something like this would happen," were her mother's petulant first words. "What were you thinking, putting yourself in harm's way?"

Had her mother ever realized how predictable she was?

Leigh tried to hold onto the ragged ends of her temper. "Mom, I was just getting into the limo headed for the Amphitheatre when everything came undone. It's not my fault the police overreacted and started attacking unarmed citizens—"

"I can't believe that the police would attack without provocation," her mother snapped.

Right. Cops never do anything they're not supposed to do. "Believe what you want, Mother. But I was there. I know what happened."

"Why can't you just focus on finishing your degree and leave politics for the future?"

"Because I can't just sit on the sidelines." Leigh sat up, making her head spin. Dane reached out and gripped her upper arm. "I'm going to be out in this world as a journalist. This is what I'll be doing with my life. This is my time. I can't hide from what's happening all around me." *Like you do.*

They'd had this conversation more times than Leigh wanted to remember. And her mother never understood the insatiable restlessness that drove Leigh. How could she? Her mother's generation had fought its war in the Pacific and in Europe. But Leigh's generation was fighting its war in Viet Nam and in the dangerous streets of Watts, Detroit, Harlem, and now Chicago.

Dane held on to her and she found herself leaning toward his strength—too weak to care how it looked.

"No one can hide from life," her mother said, "but do you have to be on the front lines?"

"Yes, I do," Leigh snapped. Pain spiked over her right temple. "I can't just sit back and watch things happen. I want to report it, to witness it. And fortunately, I can."

Stiff silence.

Leigh rested her palm on Dane's knee, needing to

strengthen the bond forming between them. She'd never played the damsel in distress before and she wasn't "playing" it now. It was real, and Dane had come just in the nick of time.

Her stepfather came back on the line. "Honey, we've been very worried," his voice again entreated her for understanding. How could he know her so well and her mother not at all? "You can imagine how we felt when we saw you being clubbed and gassed on national TV."

"I didn't exactly enjoy it." *I love you, Dad.* "And believe me, I don't plan on getting that close to a billy club anytime soon. Does Mom think I did it on purpose? I was just heading for the limo to go to the Amphitheatre and everything exploded around me."

"I've been in similar situations, sweetheart. We're just glad that you're safe and that Dane's there with you. He's a good man, one of the best, and you can trust him. He'll bring you home. We'll meet you at the airport—"

A good man, one of the best. She turned her thoughts back to her dilemma. "Dad, I can't leave Chicago until I find out what happened to Mary Beth. I'm the one who persuaded her to come. Did you see her on TV, too?"

"No."

"I got clubbed while trying to get to her. A policeman had her by the hair and was dragging her while he beat her." The gut-wrenching memory of witnessing physical violence made Leigh quiver sharply and draw a deep breath. She released it slowly. "That was why I got hurt. I was trying to get to her." Leigh pressed her lips together to hold back the tears.

"You're safe now," her stepfather murmured. "Now let me talk to Dane."

Leigh handed over the phone and then lay down on the bed again. She was glad when Dane stayed on the bed with her as he talked to her dad. Being forced to recall the events of last night had stirred the pot again. The concussion, the tear gas, and being the target of physical violence all rolled together and left her shaky and weak.

It was one thing to see actors fighting in a movie, but it was so much different when it took place in person. She'd never before witnessed physical violence or been near a riot. How did her friends do it—those who had quit school and were protesting the war full-time? Last night, the yippies had sounded exhilarated over the violence. Did a person ever really get accustomed to brutality?

"Right, Ted," Dane said into the receiver. "Yeah, I can do that. What if we don't find her today?" He made sounds of assent and then handed Leigh the phone again.

"Hi, Dad," she muttered, trying to let her affection show in her softened tone.

"Honey, Dane and I have talked. He will spend the day trying to find your friend. If you don't find her, then we'll talk about what to do next."

"Thank you, Daddy. I just couldn't leave her. I mean, I needed Dane last night or I might still be in that awful holding cell." *Thank you for sending Dane, Daddy.* "And sometimes I think Mary Beth has lost her mind or something. She . . ." Leigh didn't want to say what she feared—that Mary Beth was doing more drugs instead of less.

"You were in a holding cell?" Dad asked sharply.

"Yes."

Her father swore under his breath. "Okay, honey, you let Dane investigate while you recover. I'll contact Mary Beth's parents and find out if they've heard from her. We'll talk later."

After thanking him, Leigh hung up and looked at Dane with sudden determination that was quite at odds with how she was feeling. "I'm going with you—"

"No, Ted wants you to lie down—"

Pushing down every scrap of despair and pain that threatened to come bubbling up, Leigh stood up and headed for the bathroom door. "I need a shower, to change clothes and have breakfast. Why don't you order room service for us?"

"I'm going to head—"

"If you aren't here when I get out of the shower, I'll start looking for Mary Beth on my own." With the closet open behind her, she turned to face him, daring him.

"You are a spoiled little brat," he said, sounding half mad, but half amused.

"Sticks and stones," Leigh replied and then began gathering fresh clothing from hangers and her open suitcase. She needed him, but she didn't have to admit it.

"I'll have to go down and order breakfast at the hotel restaurant," Dane gave in with some grace. "I only get to use the phone for official Bureau business."

After a nod, Leigh went into the bathroom and locked the door . . .

Frank started a fresh page.

Dear Leigh,

I appreciate that you and Mary Beth have continued to write me even though our stands about this war are in conflict. I think your point about a lack of will on the part of our leaders to win this war is completely valid. I'm sorry that Mary Beth thinks I'm the one moral man in an army of baby-killers. In every army, there are a few baby-killers as well as many heroes who would die rather than harm a civilian. We are handicapped by the nature of this war. We're fighting against guerrillas in the midst of people who are trying to make a living and simply stay alive. We aren't fighting on distant battlefields. We're fighting in their villages, cities, rice paddies. Civilian casualties make me heartsick.

The wild card in all of this is of course Red China, who is backing the Viet Cong. I think this is what holds the brass back. You and I talked of nuclear war years ago. No one wants to make the Chinese declare war. Wouldn't that draw in their allies, the Soviets, and trigger an atomic war?"

Why was he writing all of this? Was this what he had to tell Leigh before she found it out from someone else? *She should hear it from me first.*

He started a new page.

Leigh, there are things that have never been said between us that should have been said. Or at least, that is how I feel about it . . .

After a nourishing breakfast, several cups of coffee, and two aspirin, and freshly showered and dressed in jeans, an NYU T-shirt, and sandals, Leigh walked beside Dane on the way to nearby Grant Park. Feeling wonderfully human again, she glanced around at the placid setting, contrasting it with last night's carnage. The yellow barricades were back in place, and a few blue-uniformed cops lounged near them. She cringed at the sight of them and hated it. Would she ever see a cop again and not feel afraid?

"Don't you have Bureau stuff to do today?" she asked Dane, looking away, willing herself to look nonchalant.

He gave her a sidelong glance. "Your stepfather is important enough to the Bureau that if he wants an agent to help his daughter look for her missing friend, then that becomes my assignment."

From behind her round, blue-tinted wire-rim sunglasses, Leigh considered this. She'd never thought about her stepfather's career at the FBI except as his job. But that he was held in respect didn't surprise her. And she was more than glad to have Dane at her side as they entered the ravaged park. Trash collected around the base of tree trunks and around overturned trash barrels. Transistor radios turned to WLS played loud rock and roll. "Sgt. Pepper's Lonely Heart Club Band," came from a nearby pup tent.

"Do you know where Mary Beth *and her old man*," Dane mimicked, mocking her friend's terminology, "were camping?"

Ignoring the innuendo, Leigh nodded and led him to an area under tall oaks near the band shell. The bright summer day made the night before feel like an imagined nightmare. The sun warmed her back and neck. In the distance, gulls screeched and sunlight gleamed on the blue water of Lake Michigan. Nearer, Leigh averted her eyes from a nearly naked hippie, obviously passed out in front of a rude pup tent.

Dane made a sound of disgust low in his throat. "How long has your friend been on drugs?"

Leigh tingled with fear. If Dane told her stepfather this undeniable fact about Mary Beth, her mother would freak out and make her change roommates, maybe even schools. She almost opened her mouth to deny it. But then she decided Dane already knew too much for evasion. "She started smoking marijuana in our sophomore year. I tried to talk her out of it." She frowned, still wondering what the attraction of marijuana had been to her friend. Was it just the allure of the forbidden?

Or was she trying to shock her parents into noticing more than her grade-point average?

"Does she drop acid?" Dane asked.

I hope not. "I'm not sure."

"Do I need to tell you that stuff's dangerous?"

"*No.* A girl in my psych class last year had a bad trip and her parents had to come and take her away. She kept having flashbacks . . ." Leigh shivered in spite of the summer heat.

"Are you using?"

Leigh nailed him with both eyes. "Are you kidding?"

"Just checking," he said, deadpan. "I didn't think so."

Leigh punched him in the arm.

He grinned. "Your stepfather thinks you have a good head on your shoulders. Told me so more than once."

The compliment warmed her and took the sting out of his insulting question.

"It's too bad your friend doesn't have one, too."

Leigh looked over the array of tents, campers, and sleeping bags. A young female hippie was sitting under a tree near where Mary Beth and Chance's tent should have been. "Let's ask her if she's seen Mary Beth."

Frank looked down at the second page he'd just written. For once, he'd poured out all he'd felt from the moment he'd met Leigh. All of it was true, but he realized that all of it was impossible for him to say to Leigh. Though they'd only been together a short while that August of 1963, he thought he had a pretty good bead on what she was, where she was coming from. Leigh Sinclair was—or was in the process of becoming—a woman of substance, one worthy of praise. A woman like his grandmother Minnie and her grandmother Chloe.

He crumpled the second page, wrote a friendly ending to

the first page, and signed it. Before he changed his mind, he sealed the letter and addressed it. The chips would just have to fall where they may. If this world were different, it might have worked out for them.

But the world is the way it is. Leigh will just have to find out the news from someone else.

Later that afternoon, Dane and Leigh sat outside at one of a few tables in front of a pub in Old Town, on the near north side. Old Town was Chicago's version of Greenwich Village. A mini-skirted waitress delivered Leigh's Coke with a twist of lime and Dane's draft beer. Around them, heat radiated from the concrete, but the lake breeze was clean and refreshing. The waitress lingered a bit too long next to Dane, eyeing him. A lick of irritation went up Leigh's spine. Did the woman have to be that obvious?

"Do you have any more ideas of where your friend might be?" Dane nodded to dismiss the waitress and turned to Leigh.

With her forefinger, Leigh stroked the condensation on the outside of her glass. She needed some caffeine. A grinding fatigue weighed her down. Along with overwhelming guilt. "I think I want to fly out to San Francisco."

"You believe she's gone back to Berkeley with that guy?" Dane caught her reasoning without a missed beat. And it pleased Leigh.

She nodded. "That's what I think."

"Why do *you* have to go to California to find her? Doesn't she have family?"

Leigh made eye contact with Dane, noting that he was giving her his undivided attention. "Her parents won't do anything."

"What do you mean?" His tone hardened.

Leigh felt for the first time that he was turning his sympathy toward Mary Beth. Two girls in tight shorts walked past, paused, and gave Dane the eye. Leigh looked away, feeling the lick of irritation again. "Mary Beth's parents have always been a puzzle to me."

Dane ignored the girls, and they walked away, giggling. "How so?"

Her own mother drove Leigh nuts at times, but at least she acted like a mother who was interested in her daughter. How to explain Mary Beth's parents to this hard man? "I know they love Mary Beth, so I would think that means they wouldn't want anything bad to happen to her. But they—"

"But they—what?" he prompted.

"But it's like they don't have any common sense. The only thing they have ever really been concerned with is whether or not Mary Beth gets top grades. That's why they sent her to the private girl's school where we met—because it was the best in the D.C. area. But they don't seem to comprehend *anything else* that's happening in her life."

"And does she get top grades?" Dane asked, his eyes strayed to a group of hippies crowding around a nearby table that had just burst into raucous laughter.

Leigh wondered if he were looking the hippies over for any particular suspects. "She did. But not this spring."

"Smoking pot can cloud the mind." He sipped his brew.

Leigh couldn't disagree. She twirled the swizzle stick in her Coke. How had everything gone so terribly wrong? "I'd hoped," she murmured, "that the trip here might wake Mary Beth up, get her interested in more than . . ."

"More than drugs and a hippie boyfriend?" Dane finished for her.

Leigh took off her sunglasses and then twirled them with

one hand, trying to look unconcerned. Instead of helping Mary Beth, inviting her to the convention had backfired. *This is all my fault. Why didn't I just leave well enough alone?*

What if Mary Beth had been injured, but she and her boyfriend were too stoned to get proper medical care in time? What if the violence yesterday had pushed Mary Beth into even more outrageous, more revolutionary . . . violent activities? Leigh could understand that. Her outrage over the police brutality still rankled. Her sense of justice had been trampled, and she wanted someone to pay.

"So when Mary Beth's grades dropped," Dane asked, "did her parents start putting on the pressure?"

One of the hippies nearby wolf-whistled at her. She hated those kind of unwanted overtures. It was embarrassing. She frowned and leaned closer to Dane. "Some, but . . . they seemed to be pleased by her becoming a yippie, pleased that she was protesting the war. They said that some things were more important than good grades." Leigh looked up. "Mary Beth's dad was a conscientious objector in World War II, and both of them are members of the American Socialist Party."

Dane nodded. "I get it. I wonder if they were pleased when they watched what was happening in Chicago last night. They probably think the revolution has finally begun."

Leigh shrugged. What they thought was of no importance. "I'm going to Berkeley and see if I can find her through Chance. School starts in a few days and she needs to be there with me to start classes."

"Why don't you leave this to me?"

Leigh opened her mouth to retort.

Dane forestalled her with an upraised palm. "This is what I do for a living. Do you really think you can do it better than I can?"

She worried her lower lip. "Maybe. People who know

Mary Beth or Chance would probably talk to me before they'd talk to—"

"An FBI pig?" he deadpanned.

That forced a smile from her. She took a cool, sweet-sharp draft of Coke.

"You said this is Chance's senior year, too? Let me put out some feelers to see if he returns to Berkeley." He caught her eye. "I'll deny this if you repeat it, but we have people on campus at Berkeley, and I'll put the word out for them to look for Chance."

"I'm not surprised." She swung her head and lifted her long hair off her perspiring nape. "And I won't repeat it, either." She grinned suddenly. "I'd appreciate your help."

The waitress sashayed back to them and asked Dane if he needed a refill. He shook his head. She gave him a flirty smile. He ignored her. "Then leave it to me. For a while," he replied.

Leigh gave the waitress a cool, superior look. "Okay, just for a while." She realized that she might have to miss a few days of school, but she had to find Mary Beth. She had an awful feeling that her friend was heading down a treacherous path to disaster.

Dane rose and offered her a hand up. She took it, and as their hands touched, an unexpected charge raced up her arm. She ignored it. Starting a flirtation with an FBI agent didn't make sense right now. She had more important things on her mind. *I'll give you a week, Dane, then I'm heading west.*

CHAPTER EIGHT

San Francisco, September 10, 1968

"Chloe? Is that you?" Kitty McCaslin answered the phone from where she sat in bed in her townhouse. She leaned over to read the late hour on her bedside clock, feeling both pleasure and surprise ripple through her.

"Don't act like I never call you," Chloe said with evident feeling.

Pleased to hear from her lifelong friend and sister-in-law, Kitty tucked a bookmark in *The Spy Who Came in from the Cold* and set the hardback on the bedside table. "It's just that you never call me this late. It must be after midnight in Maryland."

"You're right. But I just got off the phone with Leigh in New York City."

Kitty brought to mind photographs of a pretty little blonde girl—Bette's daughter by Curt, all grown up now. Another childhood she had missed during her California exile. "You sound worried, Chloe. What's wrong?"

"She's still insistent on going out to San Francisco to find her friend—"

Kitty recalled a recent letter from her sister-in-law. "The flower child? The one who got lost in Chicago?"

"Yes, I tried to talk Leigh into letting her stepfather take care of it, but she feels she must take action herself, that she was the one who encouraged Mary Beth to go to Chicago in the first place."

The stepfather was in the FBI. "She sounds like an admirable young woman. A loyal friend." Kitty ran her fingers through her tousled gray curls and thought about coloring her hair.

"She is. I just wish she would leave this to her stepfather. He's more qualified."

"She feels guilty over this?"

"Yes, and she's planning on withdrawing from her classes tomorrow before it's too late to get back most of her tuition. She has a ticket to San Francisco and will arrive on Saturday afternoon."

Kitty went on with the natural progression, "Do you want me to pick her up?"

"I want you to invite her stay with you while she's in California."

"Of course." Kitty felt a spurt of anticipation over being able to do something for Chloe, to whom she owed so much. "She's family. When is her flight, and what's the flight number?"

Chloe gave her the information. "I appreciate this, Kitty."

"It's not a problem. Tell her I'm happy to do it." *More than happy. Thrilled.* "Now. How's that ugly brother of mine treating you?"

"Oh, it's a trial being married to the old coot," Chloe teased, "but I manage."

Kitty chuckled. "Let me talk to him. Or is he already asleep and snoring?"

"Hey, little sis, I heard that, and I don't snore. Chloe does." Roarke's gruff voice came over the line. "When are you coming home for a visit?"

The same old question. Roarke never stopped asking, even though he knew quite well why she avoided Maryland. She fell back on her standard reply. "Oh, someday. I'm awfully busy."

"That's what you always say. But if we want to see you, *we're* always the ones who have to do the traveling. We lead busy lives, too, even if I've retired from the bank and Thompson's in charge."

The mention of their family's bank and Thompson brought Kitty too close to the subject they both wanted to discuss, but wouldn't. The old, familiar regret clutched her heart tightly. "I'll come sometime soon, Roarke. Promise. But right now it's good I'm here to take care of your granddaughter."

"Wait till you see her," Roarke crowed. "She's another heartbreaker like her grandmother."

Kitty grinned at the pride in her brother's voice. "I'll look forward to it. Give Chloe a hug for me, and let Leigh know I'll be at the airport on Saturday." Kitty hung up. She looked down at the age spots on her hands. How long had it been since she'd been to Maryland? Not since her father's death back in the thirties. Roarke was right. It was foolish of her to stay away.

All the gossips who'd even remembered that Roarke had a wild younger sister were probably dead and gone. And it would be good to see the old homestead and Ivy Manor again. But none of that had anything to do with the real reason she never went home. There was a truth there she'd never truly faced up to, no matter how many years had passed. Suddenly a glimmer of hope rose in her heart. Maybe someday soon she'd be able to face . . . him in Maryland. *I'll keep my promise, dear brother. I'll visit soon.*

She got up, went to the medicine chest, and opened her jar of fading cream. She needed to get rid of her age spots before Saturday and Leigh's arrival. The thought of having family come for a visit zipped through her once more, making her grin.

San Francisco, September 1968

As Leigh—tired and a bit downhearted—walked down the ramp from the jet plane to the gate, she scanned the people in the waiting area. From family photos, she recognized Aunt Kitty and waved, forcing a smile. Aunt Kitty, who was really her great-aunt, Grandpa Roarke's little sister, stood on tiptoe and waved back.

The obviously genuine smile of welcome on Aunt Kitty's face warmed Leigh's battered heart. She reached the petite, gray-haired woman and was enveloped in an energetic hug.

"Welcome to San Francisco, my dear girl." Aunt Kitty, who was dressed in the latest fashion, a pantsuit in deep bronze, kissed her on both cheeks. "I hope you're hungry because I'm going to take you directly to a late lunch at Fisherman's Wharf."

"I'm starved," Leigh admitted with genuine feeling. Her subdued appetite awakened with a jolt at the mention of lunch.

After retrieving her suitcase, Leigh followed Kitty out of the terminal where she had hailed a taxi. "I don't keep a car anymore," Kitty confided in the backseat of the yellow cab.

"It's such an expense, and I can get anywhere I really want to by bus or taxi. Plus all the walking I do keeps me fit. Has anyone ever told you that you are the image of your grandmother?"

Leigh grinned. She liked it when people told her she looked like Chloe. "Yes."

"You nearly took my breath away. It was like being transported back to 1917. All you needed was a corset, a hat, and long kid gloves. And of course, a dress that came to your ankles—not one that—" Kitty paused to look down at the long expanse of Leigh's thigh, showing beneath her lime-green leather miniskirt. "—displays your charms so . . . blatantly."

"Miniskirts are in," Leigh replied in a long-suffering tone that plainly told Aunt Kitty she was tired of the topic.

Kitty chuckled. "Mother giving you trouble about the length of your skirts?"

"Endlessly."

"Well, that's because she understands men. My dear, men are all about what catches their eye. And you give them so much to admire." Kitty grinned. "Is that wise?"

Leigh didn't know quite how to take her Aunt Kitty. She was teasing, but perhaps she did side with her mother on the issue of miniskirts. But so what? Discussing the fashionable length of skirts wasn't what had brought Leigh to California. "Thanks so much for letting me come out for a visit."

"My pleasure, my dear." Kitty squeezed Leigh's hand. "This will give us a chance to get to know each other. Chloe says you're wonderful, and I don't doubt it for a minute."

Leigh smiled again. Her grandmother's love and acceptance never wavered, was never based on whether Leigh obeyed or not. "Thanks anyway," she murmured.

Kitty pressed her hand over Leigh's again. "You are very welcome here for as long as you wish to stay."

*   *   *

Leigh and Aunt Kitty shared a wonderful open-air lunch of creamy clam chowder and crusty sourdough bread at the Wharf, where Leigh fed the raucous seagulls and watched the antics of the sea lions lying on rocks in the sunny harbor. The harbor streets were also filled with tourists, flower children, street musicians, and panhandlers.

After seeing the sights, she and Aunty Kitty waited in line and rode the creaking trolley car up the steep hill from the waterfront. From there they walked a few blocks and arrived at Kitty's white Victorian townhouse, which perched on the top of another steep hill, overlooking the bay. Leigh couldn't help herself, and she gasped with pleasure. "How cool!"

"Maybe even groovy?" Kitty teased her.

"More than groovy." Leigh nodded with decision. "How long have you lived here?"

"Since 1952."

"Wow."

"What's the wow for—my longevity or the fact that I had enough sense to move here in 1952 and buy this place?"

Leigh grinned. It was hard to be miserable around Aunt Kitty's lively sense of humor. "Both," Leigh teased back.

Leigh carried her hot-pink suitcase up the stairs to the bright-red door.

"I do love your luggage," Kitty repeated.

"Well, it makes it hard to lose at airports." Leigh set down her bag inside the front hall and gazed around her. Family photos of McCaslins, some familiar, arrayed the walls in the foyer and up the staircase. A spectacular crystal chandelier hung high overhead, sparkling and casting little rainbow prisms on the wall opposite the door. Sunlight streamed through the leaded glass panels on both sides of the door, also casting rainbows. "I love this hallway. It's psychedelic."

Kitty laughed out loud. "This is just the beginning. Come on. I'll give you the grand tour."

On the first floor were the dining room, parlor, kitchen, and a powder room under the staircase. They were all light, airy rooms filled with antiques. On the second floor were a den packed with books, two bedrooms, and a full bath with a wonderfully old, deep, claw-footed bathtub.

"I chose to decorate with antiques," Kitty said, "because they fit the house and reminded me of growing up in Maryland. Our house was filled with family pieces. I went through a modern stage in the 1920s—"

"Is that when you bought your Modiglianis?"

"Yes, my first apartment in the Village was done all in shades of gray and white and spiced up with all the wonderful Modigliani and Chagall paintings that hang in my den now."

"They must be worth a fortune." Leigh glanced over her shoulder from the hall.

Kitty laughed again. "Yes, just ask my insurance agent. He loves me. I think I'm sending one of his children to private school. When I die, they will all go to the art museum here. Now you call your family and let them know you arrived safely and are unpacking at my place." Kitty waved to the antique, French-style phone on the table beside the bed in the delightful guest bedroom before heading down the stairs.

Leigh entered and gazed around at the lovely room decorated in a delicate rose-pink and off-white. It reminded her of the bedroom she had always shared with Dory at Ivy Manor, only the furnishings here were more Victorian than Colonial—an iron bed frame painted white, a dark-walnut chest of drawers, a gilded white vanity with a triple mirror, and a beautiful rose-sprigged rug with rich oak flooring peeking past its edges. Period photographs from the Victorian era—more McCaslins—were in groupings on the walls, along with a few period paintings of pastoral scenes and a few watercolor portraits. Leigh fell in love with the room immediately.

She closed her eyes to settle her volatile emotions so that she would be able to stand up to her mother, then she dialed her home number. Each time the dial clicked around, number by number, her nerves tightened another notch.

"Hello," her mother answered.

"Mom, this is Leigh. I just wanted you to know I got here safely. I'm at Aunt Kitty's. She has a lovely house, and I can see the Pacific from my window."

"I'm glad you arrived safely," her mother said tersely. "Cherise called and asked me to ask you to call her. Here, Dory wants to speak to you."

"Hi," came her ten-year-old sister's small voice. "Are you okay?"

Leigh's heart melted. "I'm fine, ladybug. How are you?"

"I miss you. When will you come home?"

Leigh wondered if her mother had put Dory up to asking these questions. But she'd give her mother the benefit of the doubt, which was more than her mother usually did for her. "I have to see if I can find my friend Mary Beth. I'll come home as soon as I find her."

"What if you don't find her right away?" Dory sounded lost and alone.

"Don't worry, ladybug. And I wouldn't have been home this fall anyway. I'd have been away at school."

"I know."

The little girl's sadness scored Leigh's heart. "Tell Mom that I'll call again soon. I love you, ladybug."

"I love you, too." Her sister hung up.

Leigh sighed, pressed down the button on the phone, and

dialed Cherise's home number. She'd put off talking to Cherise about Mary Beth. Cherise was a junior at Howard University and commuted to classes from her home.

After talking with Mrs. Langford briefly, Cherise came on the line. "Hi, Leigh, I called, and your mother said you'd gone off to California on a wild-goose chase and that Mary Beth was missing. What's going on?"

Leigh gave Cherise the facts.

"That's awful."

Leigh could hear the sincere sympathy in Cherise's voice. "I'm worried about Mary Beth. She's been doing drugs."

"*No*," Cherise said with audible shock.

"Unfortunately, yes." Leigh stood by the window, staring out at the rooftops and the blue Pacific in the distance. The view soothed something deep inside her. How could anything bad happen here? "I've been covering for her, trying to get her back on track. But obviously I failed. Now I just want to make sure she's safe."

"Keep me posted. What's your address there?"

Leigh gave it.

"I just can't believe Mary Beth . . ." Cherise's soft voice trailed into silence.

"I know. And her parents just think it's great that she's gone counterculture." Leigh's resentment leaked into her words, twisting them. "They haven't heard from her and think that's just fine—that 'she's just growing, exploring,'" Leigh quoted them with the sarcasm she felt.

"Do they know about her drug usage?"

"I didn't tell them." Leigh grimaced at her own cowardice. "Don't you think they should be able to put two and two together?"

"Maybe, but they've always been odd, don't you think?"

Cherise's words bolstered Leigh. "Yes, that's exactly what I think."

"My dad calls them aging Bolsheviks."

Leigh chuckled dryly. "He's probably right."

"Have you heard from Frank?" Cherise asked in an odd voice.

Leigh tried not to feel jealous, but she had guessed that Frank wrote Cherise more often than he wrote her. The correspondence between Frank and the trio had continued but separately. "Yes, you?"

"Yes, I'm worried about him even though no big attacks are on right now. I'm so glad he came through Khe Sanh."

"Yeah." Leigh tried to keep her voice normal though Frank's last letter had left her wondering about him. The letter had possessed an oddly incomplete feeling. Leigh couldn't have put it into words, but it was real.

"Write soon," Cherise urged.

"I will." Leigh hung up and sat staring at the ornate phone. Who would have believed in 1963 that five years later, Frank would be in Viet Nam, that Cherise and he would be courting by mail, that Mary Beth would be on drugs and lost somewhere in San Francisco. Was life always like this? Did the last thing one expected always happen?

She walked downstairs, intent on hiding her low mood. Her great-aunt didn't need a depressed relative. A noise made her turn her head. Through the leaded panels on both sides of the front door, she glimpsed the form of a man. The doorbell rang and Kitty called for her to please answer it. Leigh hurried down the last two steps and opened the door.

"Hi." Dane Hanley looked back at her, his dark-brown eyes studying her. His strong chin already showed the beginning of five o'clock shadow.

His unexpected appearance took her by storm. No words

came. Leigh just stared at him, wave after wave of awareness and pleasure echoing, soaking through her.

Kitty came up behind her. "How delightful! A handsome young man at my door. I knew there'd be more than one advantage to having a beautiful young woman as a guest. Do come in."

Dane nodded at Kitty. "I will, if Leigh will stop blocking the entrance."

Leigh felt her face warm with embarrassment over letting him affect her, and even warmer for letting it show.

Kitty chuckled and touched Leigh's arm. "Let the poor man in. I'm dying to hear what he's come for."

"He's come to spy on me for my mother," Leigh snapped as she gave way. How did this man get to her, make her so conscious of him? She stared at him. "Isn't that right?"

"Not even close." Dane took the hand Kitty offered him. "I'm Dane Hanley, FBI, and a friend of Ted Gaston's."

"Oh," Kitty exclaimed with obvious pleasure. "Come in. I'm just making tea, and I've never had an FBI agent to tea before. And certainly not such a handsome one."

"I'm sorry," Dane apologized, "but could you hold that tea for about an hour? I'm afraid I need to take Leigh on an unpleasant trip downtown."

Leigh eyed him. "Where?"

"The morgue."

The scene was surreal to Leigh. She stood in an overly bright gray room filled with stainless steel and looked down at Chance lying on a cold tray pulled from a wall of drawers. Were they all occupied by white, bloodless corpses?

"Is this Mary Beth's Chance?" Dane asked.

A white-coated coroner's department assistant stood

with them. She hated being here, hated having to do this. Chance's head looked odd somehow, but she recognized him. "Yes, it's him." She turned away abruptly, weak in her knees.

Dane took her arm and helped her to a molded orange-plastic chair against the wall, the only blotch of color in the deadly, gleaming room. The assistant slid the drawer back into the wall and without a word left her with Dane.

"I'm sorry I had to make you do this, Leigh," Dane said close to her ear, "but there is more than one Chance in California. I hadn't met him in Chicago, and I needed to be sure that he was the one Mary Beth came out here with."

Leigh stared at the highly polished speckled-green linoleum floor, trying to blot out the formaldehyde odor of the room. "How did he die?"

"It looks like he took a fall from a fire escape or a roof. They'd cleaned him up already. You didn't see the back of his head. It was pretty much a cracked eggshell. Who knows how long he'd lain there before he was found."

Leigh shuddered. "Do you know where he was found?"

"Yeah, a driver for a waste company found him when he came to empty a Dumpster behind an apartment house."

"Do you think Chance was living in the apartment building?"

Dane took out a paper from his suit pocket. "Let's go talk to the detective on this case. Up to it?"

Shutting out the images that Dane's explanation had brought to mind, Leigh nodded and stood up.

A short walk down the street brought them to a police station. Walking beside Dane gave her a quiet source of strength. Dane showed his badge and asked for the detective in charge of the case, and an officer led them back to an office. After her experience in Chicago, Leigh found herself prickling with anxiety. Dane's solid presence reassured her, but she hated that she craved his support.

Dane whispered in her ear, "Let me do the talking." And then the two men were shaking hands. Dane introduced her to Detective Shay, and they all sat down facing each other in the crowded, cluttered office. "So you ID-ed our latest dead hippie." Shay looked her up and down.

Leigh suddenly wished she'd worn a longer skirt. She didn't like how the man's eyes slid over her.

"Miss Sinclair," Dane replied for her and gave the detective a hard look, "has identified him as the companion of her friend, who is a missing person."

"Right." Shay leaned back, his chair creaking, and pulled out a file folder. "Miss Mary Beth Hunninger, twenty-one, missing for over a week. Last seen in Chicago. What's the FBI's interest in Miss Hunninger? Is she SDS or involved in the Weathermen, or something like that?"

If it hadn't been all so macabre, Leigh would have laughed at the man trying to connect "puppy dog" Mary Beth with the Students for Democratic Society and the Weathermen, a group of violent protesters. Chance dead. Mary Beth a missing person. The events of Chicago played in Leigh's mind like a newsreel. *Mary Beth, where are you? What have you gotten yourself into? Why didn't I leave well enough alone?*

"So far we don't have anything on her," Dane replied, "But Miss Sinclair's father is FBI, and he's personally interested in finding his daughter's girlfriend before something like what happened to Chance happens to Miss Hunninger."

This thought sent another shiver of dread through Leigh.

Shay nodded. "We're on it. But we have so many hippies around Haight-Ashbury. All over the city, really. And if someone doesn't want to be found, it's hard. Their living situations are so fluid. Guys and girls shack up together, and friends of theirs float in and out of apartments. Some even become squatters, camping in old houses or canneries until the wrecking ball sends them all to the next deserted house or factory." He shrugged and then looked at Leigh. "I'd be careful about looking for your girlfriend yourself. As the daughter of an FBI agent, you'd be prime bait for kidnapping by one of these violent protest groups."

Leigh frowned. Kidnapping?

Dane stood and pulled her up by the hand. "Well, we'd really appreciate it if you'd keep us posted on your progress, and if there's anything we can do, just ask." Dane handed the man his card.

Shay pushed to his feet and shot out his hand to Dane. The men shook hands. Leigh murmured her thanks. And within minutes, she and Dane were back outside in the cool sunshine. Leigh lifted her face skyward, feeling the sun's rays cleanse her, as Dane led her to his car. He helped her into the passenger seat and drove them off without a word.

Leigh felt folded up inside, her emotions a tight little bundle she didn't want to open and examine. "Thanks," she murmured.

"For what? For taking you to the morgue?" Dane's tone was sarcastic.

"No," she replied, looking down at her hands. "For coming, for helping." *For caring*. But that was only a mirage. Dane was just doing this because he was a friend of her stepfather's.

Suddenly she felt adrift on a strange, murky sea without a compass. She turned her head away as if looking out her window. Propping her elbow, she pressed the back of her hand to her mouth, pressing her lips shut so no sound of her tears would be heard.

Dane's hand took her other one and squeezed it. His palm was warm and strong, and his touch had power. "I won't say,

'Don't worry. Everything will be all right,' because I have no control over Mary Beth or what may happen to her. She's left the straight and narrow and is walking the wild side—an innocent—so everything is up for grabs."

Leigh turned toward him with sudden gratitude. He did understand. "I know. She's like her parents and doesn't seem to think there is evil in the world—except in Viet Nam or the federal government. And the way she's using drugs. It scares me to death for her."

He squeezed her hand and nodded solemnly. She left her hand in his, drawing comfort and strength from him for the rest of the drive home, where they parked down the street from the townhouse. He tucked her hand into his arm as they walked up the steep sidewalk. No words were needed. She felt her heart opening like a blossom to sunshine. And she had no way to stop it.

Leigh led him up to Kitty's door and rang the bell. With her usual gaiety, Kitty welcomed them in to tea in the white-and-ivory parlor. Leigh sat silently while Kitty and Dane carried on polite conversation. The sweet and creamy tea warmed Leigh and helped her think. *What do I do now?* In a lull, she addressed Dane, "How long are you going to be in San Francisco?"

He shrugged. "When your stepfather received notification from the San Francisco police about finding Chance's body, he sent me to be with you so you could make a positive ID. I'm also going to be pursuing a few other cases that have shifted from the East to the West."

"So you're going to be here?" She tried not to be glad about this mixed blessing. Dane was all too tempting, and she was much too vulnerable right now. *He's all wrong for me.*

"Why do you ask?"

She resisted the enticement of leaning on this man. "Because I want to go looking for Mary Beth myself, and I don't want you trailing around after me." *Distracting me. Tempting me.*

He looked amused at her bluntness. "All right, then. I'll go with you."

"No, you didn't get what I'm saying." She shook her head vehemently. "I can get people to talk to me who wouldn't talk to you." *And I'm beginning to notice things about you, like the part in your thick, dark hair and the way your eyelashes beckon me to stroke them.*

"I can wear blue jeans, too, you know," Dane said in that way of his—somehow deadpan, somehow taunting.

"Look at your haircut. Everything about you screams establishment. The kind of people who would know about Mary Beth's whereabouts would keep mum around you."

"You're probably right. I'll need a wig and some tie-dyed T-shirts."

Leigh shook her head at him; this time in amusement. "No, I don't think so."

He lifted one eyebrow. "Were you paying any attention to Shay's advice about your not looking for Mary Beth alone? Some of these groups would be thrilled to take an FBI agent's daughter hostage. Some of them have been able to get classified documents. They know stuff they shouldn't know. Your stepfather is very visible in the inner circle at the Bureau. And with your mother at the CIA, you'd be a plum bargaining chip all right."

She ignored this. "I'm going to look for Mary Beth."

"And I'm going with you."

Leigh let her irritation flow over her face and put her cup down with a snap. "No—"

Kitty interrupted with a laugh. "I love the battle of the

sexes, don't you?" She lifted the vintage teapot, her bright brown eyes crinkling up in amusement. "More?"

Over a week later

*L*eigh, with Dane at her side, strolled down Haight Street, trying to look unobtrusive. She had become accustomed to Dane's hippie disguise—a dark, long-haired, untidy wig and mustache, and ragged blue jeans and stained T-shirt. He looked raffish, and it somehow heightened her growing unease around him. Relations between them had subtly changed, progressed over the past week. She knew what it was, but refused to examine it.

They stopped to listen to a long-haired street guitarist who was singing Peter, Paul, and Mary's, "Where Have All the Flowers Gone?" Dane slouched against the pole of a streetlamp and pulled her against him. She didn't want him this close, because she, of course, *did* want him close. But she knew that to him it was only part of their disguise. Dane wouldn't want her. He thought she was too young, too impulsive, too naive. So she let herself lean against Dane's hard body, feeling the latent strength there, aware that it could be unleashed in an instant. Dane possessed a dangerous quality beneath his cool exterior. It fascinated her. And that troubled her.

The song ended, and Dane muttered, "Hey, man. Groovy." Then he pulled her along as they sauntered down the street. Leigh noticed a shop that sold incense, handmade soap, and long strings of beads to hang as doors in hippie apartments. There was a Help Wanted sign in the window. Leigh led Dane inside, making the bell above the door jingle, and then walked up to a red-haired woman, dressed in a gauzy multicolored caftan, perched behind the counter. "Hi, you need someone?" Leigh pointed back toward the window.

Dane gave her a private "What's this about?" glance, but then began examining love beads hanging on a nearby rack.

"Yes, do you know how to run a cash register?" the proprietress asked, eyeing Leigh in her jeans and Columbia T-shirt. Of the two of them, Dane looked the more counterculture.

"No," Leigh admitted, "but I'm sure I could learn."

"Okay," the woman said, handing Leigh an application and a pen. "Fill this out. Do you have a phone where you are?"

Leigh nodded and then quickly filled out the application. "I came to town to visit a friend of mine, but she'd moved and didn't leave a forwarding address. Maybe you've seen her. She's a little shorter than I am, long, dark hair, and her old man was named Chance."

The proprietress accepted the snapshot of Mary Beth from Leigh. And then she eyed Leigh and the photo with vague suspicion. "No, haven't seen her. We get a lot of coming and going around here."

Leigh nodded and put the snapshot back into her crocheted shoulder bag. "Thanks. Will you call me, or should I just come back tomorrow?"

"I'll call you."

After giving the woman the obligatory peace sign, Leigh led Dane out of the store. He murmured, "I've got to see you home now. I have another appointment about a different case."

After disappointing days with no leads, Leigh didn't have the energy to object. After a few changes of buses, she left him and walked to her Aunty Kitty's townhouse. She collected the mail from the box by the door, unlocked the door, and entered the quiet house. Her great-aunt, though over seventy, still worked a few days a week doing *pro bono* legal work for the needy. She'd come home each day around five, and then the two of them would cook dinner together and eat it by the windows overlooking the bay.

Leigh loved San Francisco and Aunt Kitty. If only this were just a pleasure visit.

She sifted the mail and found another letter addressed to her from Cherise. It was good to have another friend who was as concerned about Mary Beth as she was. Leigh dropped the other mail on the table in the foyer, which was, as usual, alive with shimmering light and rainbow prisms. She slit open the letter. She read the first page and then the second and froze. Gripping the carved finial on the bottom post of the banister, she slid down and slumped on the bottom step. *No. No.*

CHAPTER NINE

*L*eigh couldn't believe she was able to dial the phone. Her fingers actually felt stiff. But this was like witnessing a train wreck—she couldn't look away. She must learn every detail. "Hello, Mrs. Langford, this is Leigh calling from San Francisco. Is Cherise home?" Her cool voice didn't even quaver.

Enduring the agony of Mrs. Langford's friendly greeting and inquiries, Leigh waited on the line for Cherise to pick up.

"Leigh, have you found Mary Beth?"

Of course, dear Cherise would ask about their mutual friend first. That was so like her. Leigh didn't like the cold, hard feeling growing inside her. Cherise was a good friend, a good person, and Leigh knew she truly was concerned about Mary Beth. "No, sorry. So far we haven't found anything except that her boyfriend has turned up dead."

"That's *awful*," Cherise said with undeniable sincerity.

Why do I always think Cherise has an ulterior motive? Is it just because I knew Frank was attracted to her, writing her, too? "It was rough. I had to identify his body at the morgue."

"Oh, Leigh, I'm so sorry." Cherise aggravated Leigh further by sounding deeply sympathetic.

"I just got your letter." Leigh couldn't make herself say any more.

"I feel awful," Cherise said with audible regret, "with Mary Beth missing and all. It's like, why do I have a right to happiness when Mary Beth may be . . ."

Leigh was glad Cherise stopped there. Leigh couldn't allow herself to think that Mary Beth might be dead, too. *I thought I was helping her.* Leigh had tried to pull Mary Beth along, interest her in politics, get her back on track. *And maybe I got her killed, too. Or at least, I helped her to be drawn deeper into the drug-saturated counterculture movement.* "I feel so guilty," Leigh muttered in spite of herself.

"What's happened to Mary Beth is not your fault," Cherise defended her fiercely. "Her parents and—from what she told me herself—her professors encouraged her to fall off the edge of the earth. Don't blame yourself. Mary Beth has always been persuadable. Or at least, as long as I've known her."

Leigh didn't want to agree with Cherise, but part of her did. She felt grateful to Cherise, but resented that, too. Leigh had always thought that Cherise had exercised a great deal of self-serving charm in high school. But she'd never blamed Cherise for this, because as the first black student in an all-white school, Cherise had faced stresses that Leigh hadn't. And that ambiguity had set the stage for how she felt now. How could she like and dislike Cherise, trust and distrust her, all at the same time? Perhaps this was all tied up with her feelings about Frank.

"So . . . ," Cherise said, sounding apologetic, "what did you think of my news?"

The moment had come. Leigh steeled herself to say what

she must, what she had to in order to salvage even a scrap of her self-respect. "I was surprised, but of course, I'm so very happy for you, Cherise, for both you and Frank." Her heart constricted so tightly it felt like it might fracture into slivers. "Have you set the date?"

"We're going to wait until he comes home from Nam. I worry so. So many GIs are dying there every week, and with sabotage so rampant, Frank doesn't even have to be part of a mission to be in danger."

"I know. I worry, too." *I do.* Two of the people she cared about the most were in danger.

"I know it might be difficult for you. But I'm hoping that you will be my maid of honor," Cherise said softly.

Raw pain whispered through Leigh's every nerve, enveloping her in a haze of red-tinged agony, like going up in flames. She pictured herself standing beside a white-gowned Cherise as she exchanged vows with Frank in his uniform, lethally handsome. Why had Cherise said, "I know it might be hard for you?" Was that because of Mary Beth's disappearance or because Cherise knew that Leigh still had feelings for Frank? Could Cherise be knowingly cruel?

No answers came to her and, of course, there was only one possible reply for her to make. "I'd be honored," she pushed the rasping words through her dry lips.

"That will mean a lot to me and Frank, especially since I wouldn't have even met him if it hadn't been for you."

With these innocent words, Cherise slid the knife neatly into Leigh's back and twisted the blade. Leigh nearly gasped aloud. "My pleasure," she murmured, reeling. "I have to hang up now." Leigh fell back on the pat, polite phrases her mother had taught her. "I just wanted to tender my best wishes."

"Thanks, Leigh. And please keep me posted about Mary Beth. You know I'm terribly worried about her."

"Of course. Bye." Leigh hung up. She crumpled Cherise's letter and dropped it onto the hall table.

The doorbell rang.

Leigh groaned. *What now?* Still, she forced herself to the door and opened it. It was Dane.

He stepped inside and stared at her. "What's wrong? Did you get news about Mary Beth? Did she turn up at the morgue?"

Too much had happened that day. In that moment, Leigh ceased fighting her attraction to Dane. She walked up to him, flush against his chest, resting her hands on his shoulders. "Hold me." *Keep me together before I shatter.*

Dane looked as if he wanted to say more. He gazed at the crumpled letter on the hall table. But after another glance at her, he wrapped his arms around her and pressed her even closer to him. "Let it out." His deep voice drifted over her, sifting through her like soft, soothing powder. "Let it all out."

She burst into tears, not gentle ones. Hurricane-force emotions swept through her.

Dane didn't waste words. He held her and stroked her back, ran his fingers through her long hair, and murmured to her, words she barely heard, didn't even try to comprehend. The presence, the essence of Dane enfolded her, seeped into her—lush, comforting, commanding.

Finally, she straightened, shaky, but oddly not embarrassed. She felt as though she'd just survived an earthquake of the heart. Nothing would ever be the same. She would never be the same. She wiped her wet cheeks with her fingertips.

"Sorry I broke down like that," she mumbled. Maybe Dane didn't feel the same attraction to her. Certainly, he hadn't experienced the same catharsis she just had. So she pulled away and looked down. *But I can't help or hide what just happened.*

Dane halted her retreat. He slid a hand into the hair just above her nape. "Someone write you a Dear John letter?"

She looked up at him, wondering how he'd guessed so accurately. Her body overwhelmed her thought, calling, shouting for her to go back into his arms.

He leaned close to her face. "I've tried to hold back, but do you know—" His breath fanned her mouth. "—how much I've wanted to kiss you?"

She stared at him, too shocked to speak. The thought of kissing Dane reverberated inside of her.

"But I won't. You're just a kid—"

"I am not a kid," she snapped, leaning forward. *Not after today.* She let her lips hover over his, daring him.

Then his mouth took possession of hers. His skilled, delicious assault swept away her resistance, and she clung to his shoulders. "I shouldn't be kissing you. Something in that letter has upset you," he whispered as he nuzzled her ear. "And you're vulnerable. That's why you're kissing me."

She turned her face and initiated their second kiss, forcing him into silence. He didn't refuse her, but deepened their kiss, drawing it out, lingering.

When his lips finally released hers, Leigh found it hard to draw breath. She stayed within his arms, feeling the full effect of his kisses, his embrace undulating through her, melting her.

"I shouldn't take advantage of you." He fingered a lock of her golden hair. "What's upset you?"

She shook her head and wouldn't answer him. Thinking about Frank and Cherise together was like stepping out of an airplane. Free falling. *Then why am I kissing Dane? Does anything make sense anymore?*

He nudged her chin upward and gazed into her eyes. "This isn't about Mary Beth. These aren't that kind of tears.

Bad news about her wouldn't force you into my arms. Who's hurt you enough to make you seek consolation?"

She refused to answer. She pulled away, even though stepping out of his arms chilled her. Turning to the oval hall table, she tugged a pale-pink tissue from the box there. "Why are you here?"

"I have to fly back to D.C. in a few hours." His voice went back to normal. "I came to say good-bye and to warn you not to get yourself into anything dangerous while I'm gone."

She glanced over her shoulder at him, a grim look. "Why do you think I'd—"

"I know. I know." He moved to grip her arms with both hands. "You're Joan of Arc and you're on a mission for God that doesn't permit concern for your own safety." He pressed a soft kiss below her right ear.

"Don't make fun of me." Her back to him, she dried her cheeks with the soft tissue.

"I'm not. You can't help it if you're Joan of Arc." He kissed her in the same spot behind the left ear. "She didn't choose to be God's instrument—God chose her."

She turned and faced him, feeling defiant. "Call me what you like. I can't leave San Francisco until I feel like I've done everything I can to find Mary Beth."

"Well, that's progress. Before it was, 'I won't leave until I've found Mary Beth.'" He lifted her chin with his forefinger. "Whoever he is—he's not worth this reaction. No man is. Let him go. I won't offer you love, but I'll take better care of you than he evidently did."

His words didn't faze her. His touch did. Tingling wherever his skin grazed hers, she expected him to kiss her again, and she teetered on the edge of decision. Did she want him to or not?

A kiss on her forehead, and without a word he left her there, shocked out of her pain, shocked at her deep response to him. Sunlight and rainbows danced on the foyer walls. And McCaslin ancestors in their frames had watched and listened. Was she already falling in love again? Could she be that stupid?

"No, Mother," Leigh replied over the phone two days later, "I won't be coming home soon. Aunt Kitty said I can stay with her as long as I want, and I'm going to accept her invitation."

"I don't understand what you're doing. I'm sorry that Mary Beth is still missing. I'm sorry her boyfriend was found dead, but I fail to see why you must interrupt your senior year—"

"Mother," Leigh cut in, "it's too late for me to take classes anywhere this semester. Next semester I may enroll out here. I don't know."

"Are you going to throw away the chance to have a college degree? I don't understand you."

At last, she admits it. "Mother, I have plenty of time to finish. I'm just taking a semester off. It isn't the end of the world. Just let it go, all right?"

"I don't think you should be a burden to Aunt Kitty. And I don't think your stepfather and I should support you unless you're a full-time student."

Whatever. "I can get a job out here, then."

Her mother made a sound of irritation, kind of like a tea kettle releasing steam. "Your little sister wants to talk to you."

Dory's soft voice came on the line. "Leigh, I miss you. If you aren't in school, why can't you come home?"

Denying her little sister was harder, and her mother knew that. "Ladybug, I'll come home for Christmas just like I would have anyway. I miss you, too. How is your friend Lucy?"

"She's okay. But she's not you."

That made Leigh grin. "I love you, ladybug. Bye."

"Love you, too. Bye."

Leigh hung up and walked into the parlor where Kitty, wearing half-glasses, was reading. "Mom isn't happy about my staying. But I just can't go home."

Kitty looked up. "I understand, dear. Your mother reminds me a little of your great-grandmother Lily Leigh Kimball. She thought Chloe, your grandmother, was a china doll. Miss Lily wanted to be able to set Chloe down where and when she wanted her and she expected her daughter to stay put. No one ought to try to do that to another person. And you're going through one of those awful times when life comes in like the ocean and sweeps you away."

Leigh sat down on the arm of her aunt's chair and gave her a half smile. "Thanks for letting me stay." *For understanding.*

"Have you thought about what you'd like to do while you continue to look for Mary Beth?"

Leigh sighed. "It's a little late for classes anywhere. I think I should get a job and pay you room and board."

"You may get a job, but I don't need any room and board from you. For heaven's sake, you're family."

A few days later

Leigh stood behind the cash register near the end of her first day of work. She'd gotten the job at the little shop where she'd applied that day with "hippie" Dane at her side. She still had hopes that Mary Beth might walk by. At least this job gave her a reason to hang out in the Haight-Ashbury area. Learning to run the cash register had been no stretch, and she just had to dust and learn where everything was in the store. The proprietress would work the same hours as she did for the first week, and then she'd be on her own. Leigh hoped that there would be lots of customers to distract her from the troubles of her life.

Her mind was much too busy chewing painfully over and over on where Mary Beth could be, the upcoming nuptials of Frank and Cherise, why she'd kissed Dane and let him kiss her—and why it had affected her so. She couldn't think about it without reliving the sensations he'd triggered in her. No other man had ever affected her this way—except Frank. And Frank was marrying Cherise.

The bell over the door jingled. Leigh looked up and froze.

"Hi, Leigh," Mary Beth muttered.

Leigh scanned her friend and didn't like what she saw, but simple, bone-deep relief sluiced through her anyway. "*Mary Beth*, I've been so worried!"

Mary Beth—much thinner, dirty, bedraggled—shrugged. "What are you doing here?"

"I was worried." Leigh held onto the edge of the counter to keep herself from rushing over to her friend. She wanted to hug Mary Beth, but her appearance, her stance warned Leigh away. "I came to California looking for you."

Mary Beth nodded. "I saw you once with that guy. Who is he? Are you dating him?"

"He's just a friend." *Of my stepfather*. Then her lips tingled with the memory of Dane's kisses. Those weren't *friendly* in any sense of the word.

"Well, I just wanted to say hi." Flashing the peace sign, Mary Beth turned to go.

"No, Mary Beth, wait." Leigh stepped around the

counter and hurried forward. "Why don't you come home with me for dinner? I'm staying with my Aunt Kitty. She'd love to meet you." *Don't leave me. Let me help you.*

Mary Beth stood, looking at her. She looked drugged, hungry, subdued. "Okay, why not?"

That evening in Kitty's parlor, Leigh sat on a tapestry sofa across from Mary Beth. Her friend had tucked her bare feet under the light-blue kimono Aunt Kitty had loaned her after Mary Beth had taken a long hot soak in the claw-foot tub upstairs. Mary Beth's clothes were spinning in the dryer off the kitchen. Leigh tried not to stare, but this Mary Beth had none of the spark that her friend had always possessed in abundance. Her eyes were sunken, and dark circles rimmed them. Where had Mary Beth, the eager puppy dog, gone? Leigh felt like crying. But at least she'd found Mary Beth—or Mary Beth had found her.

Anyway, now Leigh could help her friend. Everything would work out all right. But first, did Mary Beth know about Chance? And should she tell Mary Beth? Might that derail her friend again?

On the loveseat, Mary Beth and Aunt Kitty were having a discussion on early blues singers. A conversation that ignored all the issues Leigh wanted to discuss with her friend. What did she care about Bessie Smith? What did that have to do with 1968? There were things she needed to discuss with Mary Beth. What about going back East? What about school?

"Mary Beth, do you know that Chance is dead?" Leigh asked abruptly, unable to hold back any longer.

Absolute silence in the parlor was the only reply. There was only the sound of the dryer spinning in the distance.

"Yeah, he had a bad trip." Mary Beth looked away.

Leigh waited for some further comment, some expression of sorrow. Something that would sound like Mary Beth.

"That happens," Mary Beth finished and turned to Kitty. "I really like your pad." She gazed around at the room, where a fine collection of early-twentieth-century art glass was on display.

"Thanks." Kitty smiled. "I like it. I'm glad you came. Leigh has been worried about you."

"What are your plans?" Leigh asked her friend.

"Plans?" Mary Beth looked at her as if she'd spoken in a foreign language.

"Yes, we both should have been finishing college this year. I came to find you."

"Why?"

"Why?" Leigh echoed. "Because you're my friend. Because I was worried about you. I was afraid you'd gotten hurt in Chicago."

"Chicago," Mary Beth repeated, as if finally catching something of what Leigh was saying. "That was a heavy scene. Heavy."

Leigh felt like slapping Mary Beth. She was acting like a caricature of a hippie, not Mary Beth.

Kitty intervened. "Well, I think we've discussed old times long enough. Why don't you two turn in for the night? We can discuss the future tomorrow after a good night's rest and a hearty breakfast. What do you think?"

"Cool," Mary Beth assented.

Leigh took the hint from a pointed look Kitty sent her. There was always tomorrow. "Fine. I am tired."

This strange Mary Beth with the hollow cheeks and emaciated body followed her up the stairs and perched on the rose-pink bedspread. She watched Leigh prepare for bed and then joined her at the sink, where they both brushed their teeth like they had so many times during childhood sleep-overs and in the dorm. Mary Beth got into bed first. Leigh turned off the light and climbed in on her side of the bed.

"Have you talked to my parents?" Mary Beth asked in the darkened room, her first *real* question of the evening.

"Yes." Leigh didn't know what to add.

"What did they say?" Mary Beth pressed, for the first time showing any interest in what Leigh had to say.

"They ... they said that you were an adult," Leigh repeated what she remembered from her conversations with them. "That you didn't need them telling you what to do and that maybe our generation would finally bring about revolution. That capitalistic America was long overdue for one."

"Oh." Her friend sounded ... what? Leigh couldn't identify the emotion. Mary Beth had been "blunted" some-how, and Leigh didn't know what more to say. How had Mary Beth gotten along with her parents?

Leigh recalled Frank's description of his mother's bland acceptance of everything he did, good or bad. And she thought of her mother, who had a firm and usually negative opinion about everything Leigh did and didn't mind giving it. Why couldn't parents be more like Grandma Chloe, who loved, tried to speak the truth, but never tried to control or dominate?

"Thanks for worrying about me," Mary Beth whispered in the dark. " 'Night."

" 'Night." Leigh lay on her side watching city light flow into the room from the tall window beside the bed. She didn't know what she'd expected upon finding Mary Beth. But whatever it had been, this wasn't it.

*   *   *

In the early hours of morning, Leigh suddenly opened her eyes. In the moonlight she saw what looked like the light-blue kimono Mary Beth had been wearing lying on the floor. She rolled over and patted the other side of the bed. She was alone. She sat up and threw back the covers. She ran lightly to the bathroom first. It was empty. She checked the den. Also vacant. Then she hurried silently down the stairs and walked through the rooms, heading for the kitchen. Had her friend gotten up for an early-morning snack? The kitchen was dark and quiet except for the hum of the refrigerator.

Leigh switched on the light. A note written on Aunt Kitty's shopping list pad sat on the table. "I needed a fix. Don't look for me anymore. M.B."

Leigh slid down onto a kitchen chair at the small table for two. She re-read the note, rejecting what it said, all it implied. Her heart pounded in her ears, tears pooled in her eyes.

She didn't know how long she sat there, holding the note. Aunt Kitty came into the kitchen, tying the sash of her beige robe. "What's wrong?"

"Mary Beth left." The words plummeted through her like an avalanche. She handed her great-aunt the note.

Aunt Kitty sat down in the chair opposite. "I'm so sorry."

"None of this makes any sense. Marijuana isn't addictive."

"But some people are prone to addiction. At least, that's what I think. And if a person prone to addiction gets a taste for being high . . ." Kitty shook her head and sighed.

Leigh burst into tears. *No, not Mary Beth*. Had it been all for nothing? Had she come all this way in vain?

Kitty rose and came to her. She patted Leigh's shoulder, murmuring comforting words.

Leigh stood up and rested her head on her great-aunt's slender shoulder. "I wanted to save her."

"A person has to want to be saved. Obviously, Mary Beth isn't there yet."

"Why? Mary Beth would have been the last person I would have expected to . . ."

"Leigh, from what your mother told your grandmother, Mary Beth was extremely impressionable and her parents were odd themselves. Maybe they didn't give her a solid foundation or maybe they tried and failed. Parents aren't always to blame. Mary Beth is just one of thousands of young people seduced by the nationwide vibrations from the 'Summer of Love' here in 1967. 'Flower power.' 'Make love, not war.' 'All we need is love,'" Kitty recited the pat phrases.

Leigh folded her arms in front of her stomach. She felt as if a gaping space had opened in her midsection. "What do I do now?"

"What she says." Aunt Kitty nodded toward the note on the table. "Don't look for her. She doesn't want to be found—"

Leigh couldn't accept this. "But—"

"Where's your purse?"

Leigh looked at Kitty. "Why do you ask that?"

"Where's your purse?" Kitty repeated.

"Hanging on the hall tree in the foyer."

"Go get it."

Returning, Leigh was astounded and unable to hide it. She held out her open purse. "My money's all gone."

Kitty nodded, not looking surprised. "I took my purse to bed with me. I should have taken yours, too. But . . . Let's see if she lifted anything else."

Dumbfounded, Leigh trailed after her aunt as she walked from room to room, tallying what Mary Beth had stolen. Two small pieces of art glass, a pair of eighteenth-century spectacles that had sat on top Kitty's secretary in her den, and some cash Kitty had had in her desk. "I'd better call the police," Kitty said matter-of-factly. "The art glass is insured, so I have to put in a theft report to make a claim."

Stunned into silence, Leigh sat down on the carved Victorian loveseat in the den while Kitty dialed the police. Soon, an officer came to take down a description of the art glass and spectacles. Leigh watched, but said nothing.

"They'll probably turn up in antique stores in town," he said, looking at his notes. "We'll send out a description of them to the reputable dealers," the officer said. He turned to Leigh. "I wouldn't bring any more hippies home. Some of them are harmless, but some of them get into drugs way over their heads. She's probably on heroin now, or coke. Or maybe she just has a taste for acid. In any event, she isn't to be trusted anymore."

Leigh wanted to rail against him, tell him he didn't know Mary Beth—how sweet she was, how smart. But the words melted on her tongue, sour and bitter. She merely nodded.

Kitty walked him to the door and then called to Leigh to follow her to the kitchen. "I think we need a hot cup of tea. Or maybe we should just have coffee. I won't sleep anymore."

Leigh made no answer, just wandered into the kitchen and sat down.

"This isn't your fault, Leigh. Mary Beth has chosen her path to destruction, and there's no way you can save her or stop her." Kitty filled the yellow-enamel kettle at the sink. "You came and found her. She could have decided to stay here with us and get back to her life. But she didn't."

"I don't understand." Leigh ran fingers through her long hair, feeling for sleep tangles. "I just don't get it."

"Of course, you don't. But this isn't the first generation that's waded out into deep waters and foundered."

"What do you mean?" Leigh glanced up.

"Ever hear of the Roaring Twenties?"

Leigh nodded.

"Well, that was my generation. Speakeasies, bathtub gin, and the Charleston." Kitty set the kettle on the stove and lit the gas burner. "I spent the whole decade in an alcoholic haze. And then I nearly died on some colored wood alcohol I got at a club."

Leigh gawked at Kitty.

"Don't look so shocked. Your generation isn't the first to turn its back on conventional mores. We flappers talked a lot about Freud and inhibitions and wanted to rid ourselves of ours." Leaning against the counter, still in her robe, Kitty smiled sadly and shook her head. "I thought I was 'the thing,' all right. No one could tell me how to live my life. Not even my parents, who loved me so much, or my brother, who'd suffered so much in the war. Or even my beautiful best friend, your grandmother. Kitty McCaslin had all the answers, but unfortunately, she hadn't even figured out the questions."

As Leigh listened to her great-aunt, a deepening feeling of loss and despair wrapped itself around her heart. Though she'd never really "had" him, she'd lost Frank to Cherise, and somehow that meant she'd lost Cherise, too. And tonight she'd lost Mary Beth. They wouldn't be graduating together in the spring as they'd planned or going to Europe together in the summer. Was this the way life was going to be? Didn't anything ever work out the way you planned?

Chapter Ten

San Francisco, January 1972

From the chill night, Leigh led Dane inside Kitty's warm quiet, dimly lit townhouse. He folded her into his arms. She came to him without demur, molding herself to him, letting her arms creep up to circle his neck. She loved kissing Dane, letting Dane kiss her. When their lips parted, she sighed, prolonging the seductive thrum through all her nerves. "You do know how to kiss."

But I want more, need more than kisses. These three years together have been wonderful, but maddening. I need to know whether you love me or not. And if you love me enough to make a commitment.

He chuckled. "Offer me something warm to drink before you send me out into the dank night again." He was already taking off his black leather gloves and helping her out of her fur-collared coat to hang on the hall tree. As if nothing crucial were about to happen, she smiled and waved him to follow her. Earlier tonight she'd decided that this was it. After a few years of an on-again-off-again, long-distance relationship, she had to ask what Dane's intentions for them were.

In the kitchen, she put the kettle on the stove and lit the gas burner. As she pulled mugs and hot cocoa mix from the shelf, she searched for the right words—without success. Dane came in and sat down at the tiny table. "Hey, Ted gave me that article you did on the chances for the Democratic Party in this year's election. Well done."

She smiled in reply but had her own agenda tonight. "How long are you here for this time?" she asked him as she pulled out the half-and-half. She set it on the counter next to their mugs. Dane liked his hot cocoa rich and creamy. And she liked performing this homey task for him. He would accept so little from her. And she longed to do so much more.

"Just this long weekend. I'm here to give a deposition in a case."

"Sure I can't persuade you to stay a bit longer?" She turned to him and lifted one eyebrow, trying to ease into her overriding question. She never knew quite what to expect from this man.

With one swift move, he took her back into his arms. Within seconds, he had backed her against the wall and she was drowning in his embrace. "You tempt me," he murmured.

Dane, tell me that you love me. I need to hear the words.

Then he was back in his seat and she was breathing deeply and reaching for the kettle, which was just beginning to whistle. The words, "I've fallen in love with you," hovered just behind her lips, clamoring to be voiced. Instead she asked once more, "Why do you do this—drop in and out of my life?"

For the first time, he didn't try to evade her question. "I can't help myself. I keep telling myself to stay away, but I can't resist what you offer me."

Feeling her way, she poured the hot water into the mugs. His words puzzled her. "And what is it that I offer you?"

"I come to warm my hands by your bright fire. In this cold world, there is so little warmth." He accepted the mug from her hand, letting his fingers brush hers.

She stood over him. He always made it sound as if she was from Mercury, the molten planet nearest the sun, and he was from the dark, frozen side of the moon. Of course, he was nearly a decade older than she, and they lived very different lives. But it was time to put her feelings and his to the test.

"It's been three years since Chicago. I was an innocent then, but I'm not naïve anymore."

"You will always be naïve." He blew on his hot cocoa. "You were born to be an innocent in this wicked world."

"I don't see that." She propped a hand on her hip. "I'm not the girl I was in Chicago. I'm a woman out in the world every day, writing about it, trying to get others to see the injustices I see."

"That's what I mean." He gazed up at her. "You're still Joan of Arc, still the crusader who wants to save the world. The world doesn't want to be saved. It wants to go to hell. Let it."

She sat down across from him and shook her head. "I have to speak out."

He nodded and took a tentative sip. "That's your unquenchable fire, your bright passion. That's what I can't get out of my mind. That's what always lures me back to you."

His words were criticism and praise all in one. She wouldn't let him dismiss her this way. She'd refused other men and waited for Dane's intermittent calls or for the next time he'd just appear at Aunt Kitty's door once again. She drew up her nerve. "Why not stay?" she asked, boldly reaching over and placing her hand on his. "Why not get transferred to San Francisco? Why not buy me a ring?"

His fingers closed around hers, weaving together the two hands. "I've thought of that. But I wouldn't do that to you."

Would he never open up and tell her what really kept them apart? "What are you protecting me from?"

"I'm in a dangerous line of work—"

"Don't give me that," she snapped. "My stepfather's FBI, remember?"

Dane shook his head with an apologetic but closed expression. "I'm not the man for you. I'll try not to come back here again."

He tried, but she wouldn't let him pull his fingers from hers. "What holds you back? And don't give me that Joan of Arc story." *I can't go on just waiting by the phone.* Even Aunt Kitty had suggested she pin Dane down, with the caution, *"Dane's wonderful, but, Leigh, you only have so many years in your youth."*

He wouldn't look at her. "Do you know how I met your dad?" His deep voice was low, almost inaudible.

Hope sprang up even as she tried to force it to remain under control. "Tell me." *Please.*

"Ted was working on a kidnapping case." Dane looked away out the window as if it weren't black night outside. "I was the kid who'd been kidnapped. I was fifteen."

Leigh stared at him. "Why did that . . . why—"

He stood up and walked to the window, keeping his back to her. "My father engineered the whole thing. He was in debt, gambling debt, and needed money from his father-in-law." He stared out the window as if he could see the rooftops below. "My father paid someone to kidnap me—someone very unstable, and I nearly got killed. Your stepfather figured it all out in time and saved my life."

Leigh held her warm mug within two hands and took her time reacting. She'd ask for the truth, and he'd given it to her. Now what should she do with it? "So you had an idiot for a father." She rose. "That's all in the past. Why does that mean we can't be together?"

"You're fearless." He shoved his hands into his pockets. "You don't have a clue to what life can throw at you. I do. I don't want you hurt because of who I was, who I am, who my family is."

None of what he said gave her the answer she needed. "Why won't you tell me what's really keeping us apart?"

"I know you don't understand, but that's the way it's going to be. I'd better be leaving." He walked out into the hall.

Frustration and the fear of losing him pushed her. She followed him. She pleaded, "Stay for a while. We'll make a fire and sit in the living room." *Don't leave like this. I need to know the truth.*

He halted and without words preceded her into the living room, where he began to lay a fire in the vintage fireplace. Leigh stood beside him and then led him to the sofa and pulled him down next to her. She knew how to snare him. She knew he'd respond to her.

He wrapped his arms around her and nuzzled her neck.

Leigh wanted to persuade him to tell her more, but every time she opened her mouth, his lips smothered her words with kisses. Frustration fumed inside her, but she'd already said too much, and for once he'd given her something to think about. She sighed and rested her head on his shoulder. Maybe this couldn't be done in one night. She would have to be content with what he'd told her that night and bide her time for the rest.

*   *   *

In the darkness of early morning, the phone rang. Leigh woke up and realized that she'd dozed off in Dane's arms. Dane's cheek had been resting on her head. Now he sat up straighter and looked around.

"I'll get it," Leigh said, reaching for the phone, a sudden fear zinging through her. *Who would be calling at this hour?*

"Hello?"

"Leigh," her mother's strained voice came over the line. "I'm so sorry to call so late, but . . . your grandfather's had a heart attack."

Leigh gripped the receiver. "Are you with Grandma Chloe?"

"Yes, your stepfather and I are here at Ivy Manor, or really, at the hospital. Leigh, you need to tell your Aunt Kitty, and you both need to get here as soon as you can. Your grandfather wants to see his sister before . . . before . . ."

Before he dies. Leigh squeezed her eyes shut and then opened them. "I'll call you to tell you when to expect us at the airport."

"Hurry. Hurry."

Leigh couldn't ever remember her mother's voice sounding this way, shaky and uncertain. "I will, Mother. Bye." Leigh put the receiver back into place. She relayed her news to Dane and rose to go upstairs. She halted.

Aunt Kitty in her robe already stood in the doorway to the foyer. "I heard you on the phone. Is it Roarke?"

"Yes. He's had a heart attack." Leigh went to her aunt and took her hands in hers. "Are you all right?"

"No, I'm not." Aunt Kitty's voice trembled. "But, I don't have time to take this all in now. We have to pack." But her great-aunt just stood there.

"You two go up and dress and pack," Dane said, taking charge. "My rental car's parked outside. I'll drive you both to the airport. No travel agency is open now, but the airport is open around the clock. I'll take care of everything. Just go get dressed for the trip and pack."

Still hearing her mother's shaky voice in her mind, Leigh looked back at him, the low glimmer from the fire backlighting him. His outline looked so strong and capable. "Thank you."

She led Kitty back upstairs to her room. When Kitty still seemed bewildered, Leigh selected an outfit for her and told her to dress. Leigh then quickly selected a few more outfits and laid them on Kitty's rumpled bed. "After you dress, pack these in your suitcase."

Leigh went to her own room and slumped down on her bed. She felt like she'd been hit over the head and was still vibrating from the assault. *Dear God, don't let him die before we get to see him one more time.*

Dane had taken charge, and now, late on Sunday afternoon, he drove them in his car the last few miles toward Ivy Manor. Aunt Kitty rode in the backseat, unnaturally silent. Leigh sat close beside Dane. She hadn't tried to persuade him that she didn't need him. She did need him. She was having trouble concentrating on anything; her thoughts drifted away, bringing up memories of her grandfather. *He loved me.*

Then Leigh realized that she'd used the past tense, and a tear slipped from her eye.

Before long, Leigh directed Dane to the side street that took them to the small hospital. After parking the car, he walked them inside to the information desk, where he asked for Roarke's room number. He then escorted them up to the second floor and down the long hall filled with Sunday visitors to the private room on the end. At the door, he stepped back, letting her and Kitty enter first. The room was filled with family. Leigh immediately walked into her stepfather's embrace.

Grandpa Roarke lay in bed, looking very pale and old—much older than Leigh remembered from her last visit at Thanksgiving, just a few months ago.

Grandma Chloe sat in a straight chair beside the bed, holding one of Roarke's hands. When she spied Kitty, she rose and opened her arms. Kitty came and hugged her. Then Kitty moved to stand beside her brother on the other side of the bed. He moved his hand and she took it.

"You came, Kitty," Roarke said in a thready voice that almost didn't sound like him.

"I'm sorry I waited so long," Kitty said in a shaky voice. Still holding Roarke's hand, she sought the chair beside him as if her legs wouldn't support her.

Leigh watched the scene unfold. Her mother came and stood on Ted's other side and Dane kept his place beside Leigh. Her little sister, who was now a teenager, came over and kissed her, casting a glance at Dane. Leigh hugged her. Leigh's uncles, Rory and Thompson, and their wives hovered in the background, greeting her with soft hellos, smiles, and nods.

Leigh felt the warm blanket of family wrap itself around her. She drew strength from it as she watched Aunt Kitty weep silently and her grandmother's lips move in soundless prayer.

Later that night as Chloe watched her husband's labored breathing, she recalled a hospital scene from long ago. That night, over forty years ago, when she and Roarke had kept vigil over Kitty, whose life had hung in the balance. Tears swelled in Chloe's throat, but she kept them down. If she started crying, she wouldn't be able to stop. And how long did she have left with Roarke? She wouldn't let her final hours with him be marred by tears.

"I'm so sorry I didn't come sooner," Kitty from the other side of the bed repeated once more.

"I wish you had, too, but you're here now," Chloe said.

Sleeping, Roarke was draped in an oxygen tent. It reminded Chloe of the passing away of his mother, Estelle, in 1930. The last few days she'd been under an oxygen mask on and off. Was it always like this at deathbeds? Did one always remember all the passings that had come before?

Chloe clung to Roarke's hand, already cool within her grasp. *I love you, my dearest. Always.*

As if he'd heard her thought, Roarke opened his eyes and smiled at her. He couldn't speak because of the oxygen tent, but she saw his love for her in his tender glance.

Kitty began weeping softly against the background shush of the oxygen.

Chloe's favorite hymn hummed in her mind, "Oh, Lamb of God, I come. I come."

Grandpa Roarke's funeral took place six days after Leigh had arrived with Aunt Kitty. After the funeral at St. John's, everyone gathered at Ivy Manor to draw comfort from each other. At first, longtime neighbors and friends filled the downstairs of the house along with the hum of low respectful voices, the scent of fried chicken, and the fragrance of lilies, the type of flower Roarke had requested for his funeral.

Grandma Chloe and Aunt Kitty sat side by side in the parlor on the loveseat. With Dane at her side, Leigh glanced around the crowded room. In addition to her uncles and their families, many others had traveled a long way to pay their respects. Her uncle Jamie had flown in from Hawaii. He stood nearest Chloe and Kitty. Minnie and her husband, Frank, had come from New York along with Drake Lovelady and his wife, Ilsa. Even Aunt Gretel had flown from Israel in time for the service. Leigh had been awed by this woman, who'd been her mother's best friend and who had fought in 1948 to create the new state of Israel in Palestine.

But most of all, Leigh was so grateful to Dane, for his solid presence that made everything easier for her. He'd come and gone from work until her grandfather had died, then he'd taken a few days off. Leigh squeezed his hand, letting him know how much his presence meant to her.

Then suddenly Frank and Cherise walked into the parlor, shocking and wounding Leigh. A very pregnant Cherise came over to her immediately and hugged her. "We're so sorry, Leigh. We got here as soon as we could."

Leigh was thunderstruck. She hadn't expected Frank and Cherise to come. She couldn't find a single word to say.

Frank came up behind his wife. "My grandmother called us. I didn't know if I could get away from the base in South Carolina, but my commanding officer said, 'Of course.' " He shook Leigh's hand and smiled down at her.

Leigh was still dumbstruck.

Dane offered Frank his hand. "I don't know if you—"

"You were Leigh's guest at our wedding," Cherise said and smiled at Dane. "It's so nice to see you again. Dane, isn't it?"

Stark images from Frank and Cherise's wedding flashed through Leigh's mind, stung her heart. She'd worn a blue dress and stood mutely beside Cherise as she became Mrs. Frank Dawson III. "Thanks for coming," she finally managed to say to them.

Then Minnie was at Cherise's elbow. "How's my favorite granddaughter-in-law?" She hugged Cherise while Frank leaned down and kissed Minnie's cheek. "Come over," Minnie said, "and pay your respects to Chloe. And you haven't met Roarke's sister, Kitty, have you?"

Leigh watched Frank as he followed Minnie's suggestion. Dane leaned down and murmured into Leigh's ear, "Why don't we take a walk outside? I could use some fresh air."

Leigh nodded, suddenly eager to put distance between herself and the quiet somber gathering . . . and Frank. Dane snagged her coat off the hall tree and draped it around her.

Outside, the light breeze lifted Leigh's mood. It was one of those balmy February days that whispers, "Spring." She let Dane lead her down the dirt lane toward the creek behind the little cottage. The scene reminded Leigh of Aunt Jerusha, who'd died a year ago in her nineties.

"You weren't happy to see Cherise and her husband?" Dane asked quietly.

Leigh recalled the night she'd met Frank in this very place almost a decade ago and their conversation here beside these willow trees. On that night, she would never have imagined everything *or anything* that had happened in their lives over the following years. Although she was only twenty-five, this made her feel old somehow. "I was surprised. That's all."

"You cared for him once. Ted mentioned that your mother was bent out of shape about it."

"I did have feelings for Frank, but . . ." She shrugged. "That was a long time ago. I was just a kid."

Without warning, Dane pulled her flush against him. "Will you marry me?"

Leigh stared at him, struck mute again.

"I know I've surprised you," he said with a wry grin.

Shock made her feel a little lightheaded, and she clutched

Dane's arm. "Surprise doesn't even come close to describing how I feel," she said at last. "I thought you just turned me down last week."

"A lot can happen in a week."

"You mean my grandfather?"

"Your step-grandfather. As I understand it, your real grandfather died before your mother was born. And your own father died when you were just a baby."

"Who told you all of this?"

"Ted told me this week while you and your mother were gone making funeral arrangements."

"What's all this leading up to? What has that got to do with us?"

"I finally decided that you are the only woman I've ever loved, the only woman I've ever wanted to marry and have children with. And I've decided that I shouldn't throw you away just because I have an awful family and work a job that can be dangerous at times."

Leigh stepped closer and rested her head against his worsted coat. "Oh, Dane, I do love you. And all that stuff doesn't matter."

"Well, it may matter, but it doesn't today. Set the date."

Leigh stared at the stream running fast and dark with spring run off. "Let's marry in March. It will give me time to plan something small and elegant, and it will give my grand-mother and Aunt Kitty time to recover a bit from today."

"March is a good month, and I don't want to wait any longer to claim you as my own." He increased his pressure on her arms and pulled her up to him for a kiss that left her gasp-ing. Her spirits rose. "Thank you, God," she whispered thankfully.

Now, she could bear Cherise giving Frank a child because she wouldn't be alone anymore. The only thing that still hurt was that just as Mary Beth hadn't been present at Cherise's wedding, neither would she be at Leigh's. The sixties had ended, and Leigh had never seen her friend again. Sometimes before she fell asleep at night, she still wondered where Mary Beth was and what she was doing. Would she ever see her again?

Dane kissed Leigh and all thoughts apart from him vanished from her mind.

Washington, D.C., March 1972

Leigh looked into the three-way mirror at her bridal gown, which had just come in. With the high waistline and pearl-encrusted bodice, she looked like a medieval princess in it.

"I love it," Dory said.

Leigh turned and smiled at her. "And I think you look lovely yourself." Dory was trying on her bridesmaid's dress, an empire gown in pale blue that went beautifully with her eyes. Dane had asked Ted to be his best man, as well as the father of the bride, and Leigh's sister would be her only attendant. Dory grinned and twirled around in her dress.

"I have been blessed with two lovely daughters." From a chair beside the mirror, their mother beamed at them.

Leigh felt an overwhelming love for her mother and sister. All the old conflicts had died. She was going to marry Dane, and they'd have a family of their own. Her mother would be a doting grandmother, and Dory a proud aunt. Everything was going to be all right from now on.

* * *

Later that day, Leigh, her mother, and sister walked into the backdoor of their home in Arlington, carrying the large gold-and-white boxes that held their wedding finery. Leigh had been living back at home for the past month in order to carry out the wedding preparations. She and Dane would marry at St. John's in Croftown, where her grandparents and parents had been married, and a small reception would be held at Ivy Manor.

As soon as they entered the house, Leigh realized it wasn't empty. They put down the boxes and entered the living room. A large man with heavy jowls was talking to another man in the living room. Leigh's mother froze in her steps. "Mr. Hoover?"

Then Leigh recognized him. He was J. Edgar Hoover, the head of the FBI.

"Yes, Bette, I'm so sorry, but I thought it best we wait here for you."

Dory looked back and forth between her mother and the tall man with wavy gray hair.

"What's happened?" Bette said, going to Mr. Hoover, both her hands held out in front of her. The older man paused a moment, clearly unhappy to speak. He looked sorrowfully at Bette.

"I'm very sorry, Bette, but we lost Ted this afternoon."

Dory moaned. Leigh took hold of her arm.

"Lost him?" Bette echoed.

"He was working the Delaware investigation of that radical group, and it literally blew up in our faces. He was killed instantly, an explosion."

Bette went white. Wordlessly she sagged against Mr. Hoover, who helped her onto the nearby sofa.

"I can't tell you how sorry I am," he said. "Ted Gaston

was one of my best men and a good friend. I'm so sorry, Bette."

Dory hurried to their mother and sat down beside her. Leigh stood in the doorway between the dining and living rooms, unable to move or speak.

The other man, a stranger, cleared his throat and nodded toward her. Mr. Hoover turned to her and looked even more forbidding. "And you're Leigh, aren't you?"

She nodded, mute.

"I'm afraid that Dane Hanley was working the same case."

"What happened?" Leigh whispered, though she was already tightening up inside, already realizing what the man might say.

"Dane was killed, also. I'm so very sorry. I know you were his fiancée. We're all so very sorry."

Leigh's head swam in a rush of disorienting emotion. She put a hand out to catch herself, but she couldn't find the wall. Strong hands pulled her forward and urged her down into an armchair.

"My wedding dress just came in from New York," Leigh said, as if these words would work some magic, change what had happened. "We just picked up our dresses." She leaned back, unable to halt the chill washing through her. The bright sunny day was suddenly cast into alternating shadow and a bleak light.

It isn't true. There's been a mistake. We're going to be married next Saturday. I have my dress, and everything is planned.

"They always say deaths come in threes," Grandma Chloe said. "I just never believed that kind of thing."

Leigh, Bette, Aunt Kitty, and Grandma Chloe huddled

together in the parlor at Ivy Manor. The house was empty of guests now that the double funeral was over. Dory had been given a sedative and was asleep upstairs in the little bedroom on the trundle bed. Leigh would join her as soon as she had the strength and will to walk up the steps.

"This is worse than losing Roarke," Aunt Kitty murmured.

No one bothered to agree, but Leigh felt this, too. Grandpa Roarke had been over seventy and in ill health.

"Leigh, Dory will need you during this time," Bette said, "please come back home."

Leigh glanced at her mother, whose face had aged a decade over the past few days. Leigh read between the lines. Bette was the one who really needed her. Leigh had expected some plea like this from her mother, but Leigh didn't want to leave Kitty, either. Who needed Leigh more—her little sister, her mother, or her aunt? And who or what did Leigh herself need? With the loss of her stepfather and Dane, a gaping rent had been opened up inside her heart. She felt empty, broken, bereft of hope. Who would comfort *her*?

Leigh gazed at her grandmother and mother. Years before, both of them had lost their first loves—her real grandfather and father. She wished she could ask them how they'd survived such a loss. But how could she ask them that when now they'd lost their second loves?

Leigh felt cheated. *I didn't even get to marry Dane. If it had only been Dane who'd been killed, I would be the only one receiving comfort.* And then she felt guilty for being so self-centered. As it was, since she had only lost her fiancé, she felt as though she should be the one comforting them. But she had no comfort in her to give.

"No one from Dane's family came," Aunt Kitty went on,

sounding like a radio turned on low. "I can't believe he didn't have any family."

"Dane broke with his family years ago," Bette explained.

Leigh closed her eyes, trying to block out the one conversation she and Dane had shared that had touched on his family. He hadn't wanted to invite any of them to his wedding, and none had come to his funeral. Or maybe they had attended. There had been a few strangers at the funeral, but maybe they'd just been FBI colleagues whom Leigh had never met.

Dane's and her wedding day was only five days away now. *But I'm not getting married. Dane isn't coming back.* Leigh felt as if she'd slipped out of her skin. She was raw and defenseless. Her love for Dane pulsed inside her like an aching of her very soul. Would anything ever be right again? She'd lost so many people—Mary Beth to drugs, Frank to Cherise, her grandfather, now her stepfather and her own love. How did a person who had lost almost everyone she loved find a reason to go on?

CHAPTER ELEVEN

Ivy Manor, May 1972

Leigh followed Grandma Chloe as she walked down the lane behind Ivy Manor. Leigh carried a basket, as did Chloe. A local family had just had a new baby, so Chloe had packed a cold meal and gifts for the family. In the weeks since the double funeral, Leigh and Kitty had lingered at Ivy Manor, unable to find the strength to return to San Francisco. And though Bette had taken Dory home so that she wouldn't miss high school, they both returned to Ivy Manor every weekend. Leigh still felt ripped open inside, and her grandmother seemed unusually quiet. The phrase "walking wounded" was a perfect description of how Leigh felt.

Every morning when Leigh awoke, she tried to come up with a destination, a goal that would give her a purpose, a reason to move forward. But every morning she came up with no answer. She knew there had to be one. She couldn't just stop living because Dane was gone. Now, as she walked beside Chloe, she wondered if she could use this private time with her grandmother to make some sense of what her future could, should be. If anyone had answers, it would be her wise and loving grandmother.

Unable to get up the energy to begin this kind of discussion, Leigh let herself drink in the warmth of the sunny day, the lavish greens that surrounded them, and the sweet, clean scent of mown grass that permeated the air.

"It's hard to believe that dreadful George Wallace is speaking in Maryland today," her grandmother commented in a faraway voice.

Leigh made a sound of acknowledgment. Chloe didn't like Wallace, and it was far too beautiful a day for a racist rally. Cocooned from the world, Leigh was vaguely aware that another presidential race was in full swing, with Hubert Humphrey and George McGovern fighting over which of them would face off against Nixon, the incumbent. As a third-party candidate, George Wallace was campaigning on state's rights and white supremacy all over the South. Peace talks over Viet Nam had also begun in Paris. But all of that strife and striving was a world away from the soft breezes laden with the fragrance of late lilacs, lacy boughs of bridal wreath, and periodic bouts of tears. Losing Dane filled Leigh with an emptiness, a weepiness she'd never imagined, never known before in her life.

Beside her, Chloe began humming "Amazing Grace." Leigh frowned. "I didn't like them singing that at Grandpa's funeral," she murmured, the basket weighing heavy on her arm. "He wasn't a wretch who needed saving."

Chloe smiled at her, cocking her head toward Leigh. "Your grandfather requested that hymn especially to be sung. He loved the story of its author, a slave owner who'd seen the light and turned from his sin of selling other humans. Dearest, you only knew my Roarke as 'a lion in winter.'" Chloe used the title of a recent award-winning movie. "You've never been told how he struggled after the war."

"You mean because of his arm?" Leigh stepped over a shallow puddle in a rut in the road.

"That and other things." Chloe looked away.

"You mean *other things* I'll never be told," Leigh said with a snap in her voice, "because I'm too young to understand?"

Chloe ran a hand lightly over Leigh's cheek. "No, I just can't talk about it now, dearest. I will someday. Just realize that no one comes through this life unscathed. Your grandfather had his battles, too."

Leigh understood not being able to speak about certain subjects, so she nodded, thinking of her own battles. *And I'm only twenty-five.* That wasn't a pleasant thought. What else might she be expected to endure? She looked up as if to God, gazing at the blue sky through the chartreuse leaves on the trees. Everything around her was in fresh blossom, and yet she felt frozen in the dead of winter.

The ache inside her was relentless, an all-consuming vacuum. "Will I ever feel normal again?" The words flowed out from deep inside Leigh before she'd realized she was ready to speak.

Grandma Chloe kept walking, but glanced at Leigh. "I ask myself the same thing every morning. I grieve over losing Roarke. I grieve over Bette losing Ted and your losing Dane. All our griefs are multiplied."

"Sometimes I find it hard to breathe," Leigh admitted.

Chloe nodded. "When your grandfather was under the oxygen tent, I kept having trouble breathing along with him."

Leigh wanted to say, "It's not fair. You had forty years together." But, of course, she couldn't. What did it matter? Would she have loved Dane more if they'd had more years?

That didn't seem possible. "How could we lose them all at once? I keep thinking of how many fathers, husbands, and sweethearts are dying over in Viet Nam, and yet we lost all three of them here in peace. What sense does that make?"

Chloe reached over and patted Leigh's arm. "I don't know how, but we will heal. No one can avoid mourning, but somehow it does end at last. It's best just to accept that the sorrow will work its way through us like a horrible virus that must run its course."

"What do we do until then?" Leigh lowered the basket from her arm, swinging it near her knees. What would take away this raw sorrow?

"We go on living—keep busy and comfort one another. That is what losing my first love and my parents and the Depression taught me. That's the only way. And God is here to comfort us."

Leigh glanced at her grandmother. "I don't have your faith. I believe in God, but . . ."

"Just remember, He believes in you." Chloe gave Leigh a gentle smile. "He loves us just as we are, with all our frailties and failings. He's always just waiting for us to turn to Him, to lay down our pride that insists we can *do* this life without His forgiveness. When we let Him, He takes us just as we are, and we must do the same for each other and even ourselves. Don't forget that, dearest Leigh. If you never remember anything else I've ever said to you, don't forget that."

Leigh absorbed the words deeply and felt a solemnity in that moment that seemed at odds with their mundane errand, a walk down a country road, listening to robins and cardinals calling their mates. "I won't forget, Grandma," she murmured. She didn't understand what this really meant, but her grandmother's earnestness touched her.

Chloe turned and gave her another of her sweet, loving

smiles that warmed Leigh from her head to her toes. "I love you, dearest."

"I love you, too, Grandma." *I do. I always will. You are the dearest of all to me.* "I wish . . ."

"What do you wish?"

"I wish I could be closer to my mother." Leigh sighed. "I wish she and I could talk like this."

"Why can't you?"

Leigh stared down at her sandals. "She won't let me. She always keeps busy telling me what to do, not listening to me, not seeing me and what's going on in the world. Why is she like that?"

Chloe walked along, gazing down. Finally, she glanced at Leigh. "Your mother is a strong woman, and she suffered greatly with your father. She doesn't want you to make the same mistakes she made."

"What mistakes? All I know is that my father died after the war. Is there more—more I've never been told?"

"There is always more, dear." Chloe smiled sadly.

"What, then?" Why wouldn't Grandma tell her the truth?

Chloe shook her head. "I try not to let myself get in between you two. I love both of you, and this is up to both of you to deal with, not me."

Leigh heated with frustration. "Tell *that* to my mother. Whenever I try to talk to her, all I get is a lecture. She never listens."

"Do you listen to her?"

"Yes, but she never *gets* it. This isn't 1942. It's 1972. The world's different, but it's like she can't see that at all."

Chloe nodded with a wry grin. "You always remind me of Theran Black, your mother's real father and your real grandfather, the husband I lost in 1917. He was just like you."

Chloe suddenly gave Leigh a dazzling smile. "He was so dashing— he intended to go to France and bring the Kaiser to his knees single-handedly." Chloe shook her head. "That's you, dear. You're going to grab the world and teach it how to behave. I love that about you, but it scares your mother to death. She knows it will put you on the front lines, just as it did in Chicago."

Leigh pondered her grandmother's words, and in her mind, she heard Dane again: *"You're Joan of Arc. The crusader who wants to change the world."* Tears slipped down her cheeks. She tried to hide them, not wishing to trigger more weeping in her grandmother. *Dane, I didn't want to save the world. I just wanted us to have a life together. Where do I go from here? When will this awful emptiness be filled?*

Later, when they returned to Ivy Manor, Aunt Kitty met them at the backdoor. From the look on her face, Leigh felt a tingle of dread. "What's happened?"

"It just came on the news."

"Not another assassination?" Chloe asked, dropping the empty baskets in the back hall.

Kitty shook her head. "Well, it would have been if the man had succeeded. George Wallace has been shot during a rally at Laurel, Maryland. They think he's paralyzed."

"Well," Chloe said, wiping her muddy shoes on the rough mat. "I hated his politics, but that doesn't mean I wanted someone to shoot him. When will this end?"

Leigh felt the same shock. In the years from 1963 through 1972, JFK, his brother Robert, Dr. King—all had been cut down by lesser men. How many politicians had to be killed before this terrible scourge stopped?

"Leigh, you got a phone call while you were out." Kitty handed her a slip of paper.

"From whom?" Leigh looked down at the phone number and name.

"From someone in the Maryland Democratic Party. She asked you to please call her back. It's important, she said."

Washington, D.C., June 1972

*L*eigh sat in a row of maroon, banquet-style chairs in the back of a meeting in the McGovern for President headquarters in a Democratic pre-1972-convention meeting. People milled around in the aisles. She'd been asked to take the place of the original woman delegate, who'd died suddenly in an auto accident. They'd needed a woman to fill Maryland's quota of women delegates, and she had been remembered from 1968. Grief made it hard to sit in her chair and not get up and pace. But she was afraid that if she got up, she'd leave. And it had been hard enough to make herself come.

When she looked toward the front of the room, she realized that the man who was chairing the meeting appeared to be gazing at her steadily. Avoiding his eyes, she scanned the large room. In the weeks at Ivy Manor after Dane's death, she'd been asking the universe for something strong enough to make her want to get up in the morning and change out of her nightgown. And then the day George Wallace had been wounded, she'd been asked to serve as a Maryland Democratic Party delegate and go to Miami in August. She'd also been invited to visit both the Humphrey and McGovern campaign centers. Perhaps this was her answer.

This wasn't anything like the closed and secretive sessions

she'd heard of in previous election years. She glanced at the front once more and found the man still looking in her direction, although he was speaking to a large, gray-haired matron on his right. Who was he?

Then the chairman stopped his conversation and faced the microphone, asking for volunteers for a subcommittee on the pro-peace plan.

Leigh lacked the energy to raise her hand. Wasn't it enough that she was here? She felt like an imposter. She expected someone to walk up to her at any moment and demand, "Who let you in?"

A young woman sat next to her, a brunette with long, straight hair who wore bell-bottom jeans and a jersey-knit blouse in a wild yellow-and-green print. She leaned forward to read Leigh's identifying badge. "You're from Maryland?"

"Yes," Leigh replied uneasily.

"I'm Nancy Hollister." The woman offered Leigh her hand. "I'm a delegate from New York."

Leigh returned the handshake, glad to have someone cheerful to talk to.

"It's unbelievable being here, isn't it?" Nancy asked.

"Yes." At last someone else who felt a little like Leigh did. This was an exciting opportunity, but still grieving, she just couldn't generate any strong emotion. "I had forgotten that in Chicago the way delegates are chosen has been changed, that they had voted to set up quotas for all the different groups—youth, women, minorities."

Nancy snorted. "With everything that happened in '68, who noticed? But when they called me and asked me to put my name in to be a delegate, I didn't hesitate. I was a precinct worker in '68. That was my first election."

"Mine, too."

Nancy chuckled. "And here we are four years later, delegates to the national convention. Power to the people in action."

Leigh smiled, but the radical phrase still brought back unhappy memories of the violence she'd been caught up in outside the Conrad Hilton, the very day she'd met Dane.

"Some men still don't like women having access to power. They call our influence the 'Nylon Revolution.'" Nancy snorted again. "Personally, I'm not going to wear pantyhose to any party meeting or function. I think pantyhose—or worse, girdles and garter belts—should be relegated to the past along with corsets."

Leigh, who was wearing pantyhose under her lemon-yellow miniskirt, was in the minority. She'd already noticed most everyone, male and female, was wearing jeans or polyester slacks. Pantsuits for women had revolutionized fashion. She looked down at her legs. "I'll keep that in mind."

"Hey," Nancy conceded as if she'd just noticed Leigh's pantyhose, "if you like skirts, do your own thing. If I had legs like yours, maybe I'd wear skirts, too."

This made Leigh almost grin, just as the chairman asked one last time for volunteers for the pro-peace committee.

Then Nancy surprised her. She raised her own hand and at the same time lifted Leigh's. "Hey, we might as well jump in with both feet!" she exclaimed.

Leigh lacked the will even to object.

Their hands were acknowledged, and Leigh let Nancy draw her to the back of the room to meet the other delegates on the committee. The man who'd been watching her from the front of the room left the platform and walked toward them, his eyes on Leigh.

* * *

Later, after buying lunch at the campaign headquarters, Leigh, along with the other delegates and volunteers, walked outside the McGovern headquarters in Washington, D.C., and paused at the corner of 19th and K. The campaign workers were all picnicking on a grassy slope nearby.

"So what do you think of McGovern's idea of giving everyone in America a thousand dollars?" Trent Kinnard, the man who'd been staring at her earlier, asked Leigh. Trent was older than she and did not wear denim or polyester bell-bottoms but a crisp, summer-weight suit in light tan. His wide tie was salmon pink, and his black hair had just a touch of gray at the temples and was just long enough to give him a raffish air. Altogether he was a polished, expensive package.

Holding a white-plastic plate of quiche in one hand and a green bottle of Coke in the other, Leigh concentrated on finding a place to sit. She'd purposefully not replied to anything Trent had said to her or in her direction so far. She wasn't in the mood to be charmed.

"Still not talking?" He grinned at her. "You know, you're the most beautiful Democrat at the meetings—does that mean you can't be bothered talking to the *hoi polloi*?"

She gave him a sharp glance. "I'm always wary of men who are as suave as you are."

"I'm crushed. My hopes dashed," he teased.

She grimaced, knowing she was being borderline rude. Still, she couldn't drop into easy conversation. Silently she walked to a place on the grass and sat down modestly in her miniskirt.

"I don't remember seeing you," he proceeded undaunted, "at any of the Democratic fundraisers or McGovern rallies."

"I've been busy with family business this year."

"Then how did you become a delegate?" he asked, sounding sincere for the first time.

"I'm a replacement." She closed her eyes for a moment, wishing him away. She didn't want to feel attractive, desirable.

"I see. Have you heard about the break-in a few days ago?"

"What break-in?" she asked automatically.

"It happened on the eighteenth. Five people broke into the Watergate Hotel—into the Democratic National Committee suite."

"Some radical group?" Memories of what had happened to her stepfather and Dane when they'd investigated one of these groups stole what appetite she had.

"Three Cubans, a Miami businessman, and a former CIA security specialist."

"What a strange group." She put her fork down and sipped her cold Coke.

"They've all been charged with breaking and entering. Some people think they were acting for the Republican Party."

"I have a hard time believing that."

Trent shrugged. "All's fair in love, war, and politics. What are you doing tonight?"

His casual, unexpected question ripped her wide open. Hurting, she looked away and acted as if she hadn't heard him.

"What's wrong?"

"Nothing." She scrambled, trying to come up with something to distract him. "Do you think any of this will do any good?" She waved her hand at the other delegates all eating *al fresco* on the grassy slope.

"What do you mean?"

"Meetings. Platform committees. Politics. After the last convention . . . ," her voice trailed off.

"We do this sort of thing every four years as the Constitution says we must."

His glib reply grated on her nerves. All she wanted to do was get away from this easy-talking man, away from this sunny slope overlooking Lafayette Park. So she did just that. With a mumbled excuse to the others around her, she escaped Trent and fled back to the Willard where she was staying. When she picked up her key, the desk clerk gave her a letter that had been forwarded to her. It was from Cherise.

She entered the elevator and opened it as she began to rise. After reading the first paragraph, she found herself leaning against the back wall of the compartment, tears again streaming down her face.

CHAPTER TWELVE

Maryland, July 1972

After doing her part on the Democratic Platform meetings, Leigh had been asked to campaign for McGovern in a series of town hall meetings as an example of the new woman Democrat. On this night, Leigh had come to participate in one in an auditorium in a suburb of Baltimore. She'd never appeared in a public panel before and now she knew why. She didn't have butterflies in her stomach, she had elephants. And they were all doing the cha-cha. She sat at a long institutional table and resisted the urge to fidget.

At first, she'd put off deciding about whether to participate or not. She'd made no bones about her lack of enthusiasm for all three presidential candidates—Humphrey versus McGovern, and both of them versus Nixon. But the party still wanted her to take part in these meetings. So she'd given in and agreed. It was something to do, something that might, at least, help others decide who to vote for. And maybe, somehow, by taking part she'd begin to feel alive again.

Everyone stood as the national anthem was played by a

young bugler. Then, at one of the platform microphones, Trent Kinnard—well-dressed and groomed as usual—welcomed everyone to the meeting. She wondered if Trent followed the progress of the Democratic campaign as doggedly as he pursued her. It made her nervous. Now, after his few opening comments, he invited people to stand and move to speak into the microphone in the middle aisle.

Immediately, a burly retirement-aged man rose and shouldered his way to the mike. "I want to know what in the heck McGovern thinks he's going to do with our military. As far as I'm concerned, when I hear what he said about Viet Nam, I think he's nuts and abetting the enemy while Nixon's trying to get peace in Paris."

Leigh frowned. After receiving Cherise's letter in June, she had come to dread the whole topic of Viet Nam. Why had Frank requested another tour of duty there? Wasn't putting himself in harm's way twice enough?

"Is that a question?" Trent asked smoothly. "It sounds more like a speech."

The man wasn't put off. "What would McGovern do to end the war with honor?" he shot back, jabbing a forefinger in the air. "And how would he defend the U.S. with the military cuts he's said he'd make? I don't ever want America to be as unprepared for war as we were in 1941."

Leigh leaned into her microphone, suddenly unable to remain silent. The topic of Viet Nam stirred her. "We're all concerned about the war. One of my dearest friends is a career military man, and he's in Nam for his third tour of duty. Stateside, his wife is expecting their second child." Leigh suppressed a tremor that went through her. "I would say that Mr. McGovern is merely saying what he thinks, and I don't find that treasonous."

"Are you one of those woman-libbers?" the man blustered, looking at her with narrowed eyes.

"What has that got to do with anything?" Trent took over. "I think Miss Sinclair has given you an honest opinion. No one likes the war in Viet Nam. Why did we get into this war in the first place? Is the American taxpayer supposed to bear the burden of policing the world against Communism? McGovern says no."

Others stood up to add to this discussion. Leigh tried to look interested, but she was too shaken to take part. She kept thinking about her friends. Cherise and Frank already had a little boy, named James. Frank had said three Franks were enough. Cherise tried to sound brave in her letters, but it was obvious that she feared Frank might never live to see their second child. Leigh couldn't rid herself of the feeling that Cherise might be right.

Finally, the meeting with all the stupid questions from the local John Does ended. Delaying his departure, Trent finally managed to escort Leigh out to her Nova in the new fire-engine chartreuse. So far he'd not scored one point with the most gorgeous Democrat in the U.S. What was going on behind those beautiful but sad eyes? They told him that she was on the rebound, which could work to his favor if he could get on her good side. Easy. He was good at that. He'd just have to play this a little more subtly than he had been.

"Go to a late supper with me?" he offered, trying not to sound as if this meant anything like a date. Women on the rebound didn't want to date.

"I'm driving to my grandmother's house—"

Oh, ho, little Red Riding Hood. "But surely you have to eat," he said, trying to sound sympathetic. Heck, at forty, he was a little young for the role, but he'd even attempt fatherly if that would do the trick.

Leigh looked at him. Sudden tears moistened her big cornflower-blue eyes. She blinked, trying to hide them from him.

"Why are you sad all the time?" Trent asked in the softest and most caring voice he could manage. "Don't you think it might help to talk about it?"

In the empty parking lot, Leigh burst into tears. Trent gathered her into his arms, making sure that he kept the embrace comforting, not sensual. "Let it out. Let it all out. I can take it." Dear Abby would be proud of him.

"I just lost my fiancé," she said, her tears subsiding. "I'm sorry. It's just—"

"It's hard, I know." What jerk would leave this luscious armful behind? Well, one man's stupidity could be this man's luck. Over the past few weeks, this young woman had lingered in his mind, not just because of her beauty, but because she had *something*. She made him want to be near her for a long time, a very long time. Meeting her had made him finally realize that he needed someone who'd commit to a longer-term relationship. He was tired of one-night stands and casual affairs. And of women who were on the prowl just like him. What he wanted was right here in his arms—a beautiful woman who projected a delicious tempting innocence.

They'd shared a relaxing supper at a homey little café. That had been just the right setting for Leigh to begin to open up to him. He'd felt a flicker of sympathy when she'd revealed that she wasn't suffering from a broken heart but from her fiancé's death. That was heavy, but it also would work for him. She didn't know it, but she was looking to replace what she'd lost—a wedding night. And he was more than willing to supply—if not the wedding—the night, and much more. He wouldn't be stingy with his time or his money. Leigh was luxury class all the way, and that's how he'd treat her. But first he had to help her fall from grace and into his waiting arms.

Aware of her naïve idealism, he'd spent the evening convincing her that he was deeply concerned about America and very sympathetic to her grief. She wasn't the kind who was impressed by influence, agreeable to his pragmatic enthusiasm for power and money. He'd keep that to himself. Feeling as if he'd made good progress, Trent walked her to her Nova once more.

"I'm sorry to be such poor company," she murmured.

Trent put his arm around her in a comforting gesture, again calculatingly devoid of sensuality. "You? Poor company? Never. You've been through hell."

She sighed with obvious fatigue.

"I don't like you driving home alone at night," he said. "Why don't you stay at a hotel?" He stopped himself from adding—"with me?" *Patience. Patience.*

"Ivy Manor's not far—just around twenty-five miles." She unlocked the door of her Nova and then turned back to him. "Thanks. I enjoyed your company."

"I'm glad." *Someday soon you'll enjoy something much more exciting than just my company.* He lifted her chin with his hand. "You'll survive this, you know. You're a strong woman."

She blushed. "Thanks."

He gave her a light, fatherly kiss on her cheek. And wondered how soon he'd be able to kiss her deeply with all the passion she ignited in him. "I'll see you in three days then."

She nodded and got in.

"Fasten that seat belt," he ordered in a mock-severe tone. "And I'll see you at the next town-hall meeting."

She smiled and buckled up before starting the car and driving away. He waved until she was out of sight.

An image of her lying in his arms, her golden hair flowing over his skin, floated through his mind, and his breath caught in his throat. He would be the envy of every man when she was his. And it wouldn't take long. He just had to lull her into trusting him, and then he'd overcome the strong scruples he sensed she still possessed—even though the sexual revolution had changed the social landscape. It was kind of cute that she still hadn't had much experience with passion. And maybe that would bind her to him for that "long, long time." He breathed in deeply. So much to look forward to. She would be his. He'd just chipped out the first chink in her armor.

November 7, 1972

Leigh didn't know why she'd agreed to attend the McGovern election-night festivities in Baltimore. Victory did not seem to loom on the Democratic horizon. But she'd come because she'd gotten caught up in the campaign, the town-hall meetings, the knocking on doors to get the vote out, the writing letters to the editors of various newspapers, challenging the government to do better.

Her mood had lifted as she'd thrown herself into the campaign. After all, there were important things to fight for. LBJ's War on Poverty had not been won. Viet Nam dragged on, killing men day by day, and radical groups were still planting bombs and robbing banks. The debates, the campaigning, the being a part of something that mattered had lifted Leigh out of her grief for brief periods.

But tonight had lived up to the depressing election predictions. The hope for a happy outcome for the Democratic candidate had been in doubt from the start of the evening and had worsened minute by minute. All around her, McGovern supporters had been—for many exhausting hours—putting up a good front for the local TV station cameras. In fact, as state after state swung to Nixon, the gaiety took on a frantic quality of desperation.

It made her nervous. It brought back too many memories of the days just after her stepfather and Dane had died, when life had become darker and more impossible each day. Her nerves tight, Leigh found herself drifting toward the door. Then a familiar arm around her shoulders stopped her.

"Let's abandon this sinking ship. I need a drink," Trent murmured into her ear. "I hate wakes, especially when the corpse is still breathing."

Leigh glanced up. Trent's look of grim disappointment snared her sympathy. He'd tried so hard to make this election a success. And he probably hadn't realized he was helping her—day by day—to recover from losing Dane. Now he looked like he needed a friend, and she owed him.

She took the hand he offered. "Yes," she said, feeling suddenly overwhelmed and repelled by the disaster all around, "get me out of here."

With her hand in his, he led her out of the banquet room and into the nearby hotel lounge. She slid into the comfortable leather of the corner booth. Masked by the low light, she relaxed, breathing easier. Beside her, Trent motioned toward the cocktail waitress. "Are you going to have your usual Coke with a twist of lime?" he asked Leigh.

The way he said it was somehow a dare. It was almost as

if he'd said, "Have you grown up yet, or are you still a little girl?" And she didn't feel like a little girl tonight. She felt ancient. She gave him a wry look. Maybe he was right. The slaughter of McGovern called for something stronger than soda. And she didn't want to look so young to him. She hesitated.

"Let's make it rum and Coke just for tonight," he said smoothly, taking the decision from her. He turned to the waitress, ordering for them.

Her pulse sped up, but she didn't stop him. After Mary Beth got lost in drugs, Leigh had shied away from every intoxicant. But tonight was different. Tonight, everything that Leigh had fought for had gone down to bloody defeat. Would life ever make sense again?

The waitress left for the bar, and Trent faced her. "You and I need a little medication tonight. How could McGovern . . ." He shook his head and fell silent.

Trent looked so defeated, and she knew how he was feeling. *I backed the losing side again.* Just like she had when she'd quit college and went looking for Mary Beth. *And what is the use of all this campaigning, caring anyway?* Dane had called her Joan of Arc. Well, where did a discouraged crusader—make that two discouraged crusaders—go to resign?

This election had kept her going for months. Now it was over. McGovern had lost. No, not just merely lost, but gone down in flames to Nixon, who'd won one of the largest landslide victories in history. What would keep her going now?

The cocktail waitress returned with their drinks, and Leigh sipped her rum-laced Coke and tortured herself by picturing Dane—alive and strong—walking through the door of the lounge. Why had he died so young, so senselessly? She closed her eyes, sipping the cold, sweet Coke, willing away her sorrow, willing away the desolation that awaited her when she woke tomorrow morning with nothing to look forward to.

"We backed the losing side," Trent said, sounding like a different man. He sounded crushed, completely beaten as if the defeat were his fault.

Sympathetically, Leigh touched his shoulder. "You were a great campaigner."

He shook his head and took a sip of his drink. "I knew this would be a hard election to win. But . . ."

That even upbeat Trent was in danger of being depressed worried Leigh. Trent had kept her busy, kept her involved. She'd never seen Trent discouraged. "We did the best we could." She squeezed his arm and tried to smile. "There always has to be a winner and a loser."

Trent snorted and drained his martini. He waved to the waitress, and she appeared with refills for both of them. Leigh then realized that she'd already drained her first glass. She'd forgotten it contained rum, not just Coke. Trent put the fresh cold glass in her hand. Again, she didn't want to make a scene. *I'll just have to drink this one slow and make it the last.*

"I don't know what's going to happen to our country. Nixon has his strengths, but I've never trusted the man. The voters completely ignored the issue of the break-in at the Watergate Hotel. But I think Nixon was behind it, and has been busy breaking laws to cover it up." Trent looked downward, speaking in a disgusted tone she'd never heard him use before. "Should a man capable of such low, underhanded behavior be elected president of a world superpower?"

Leigh moved a little closer to him on the seat. Trent had always been so strong. Now to hear his disillusionment and despair troubled her. She sipped her drink and tried to think of something comforting to say. He'd been so good to her.

Before she could say anything, a wave of people sporting

McGovern buttons flowed into the lounge, filling every stool at the bar and every booth. Three other campaigners Leigh recognized by sight crowded up to their booth. "Do you have room for three more losers?" one of them asked with an attempt at dark humor.

"Take the booth." Trent rose and drew Leigh with him, abandoning it. He led her out of the lounge. She wondered where Trent was taking her, but before she could form words, he gave her the answer.

"Let's go where we can talk privately." He drew her hand to his lips and kissed her fingertips.

She felt as if she were floating just above the carpet. She realized then that she had downed her second drink as fast as the first. Unaccustomed to alcohol, she was a little light-headed and more than a little shocked at herself. But she didn't stop herself as Trent led her into the elevator, where she dreamily watched the buttons for the floors light up one by one. Then she was in the hall, waiting for Trent to unlock the door to his hotel suite. "I should be going," she murmured. She felt funny about going to his room. Her mother would have a fit if she knew. *Well, Mom, this is 1972, not 1942.*

"Don't go yet." Trent squeezed her hand. "Just stay a bit longer with me. You're the only one I want to be with right now."

As he said the words, Leigh realized that she felt the same way. Somehow even tonight, in this dark mood, he gave her hope. "All right." Inside the room, she sank down onto an amber sofa, feeling a bit unsteady on her feet.

Within minutes, Trent sat down beside her, handing her another Coke that he'd poured at the small wet bar.

"No, no," she muttered.

"You don't have to drink it. But rum and Coke isn't that strong. It's not like drinking martinis, you know."

Leigh didn't want to make a big deal about it, so she just held the drink. Again, this wasn't the dark ages of the forties, but she still felt odd about being alone with a man in his hotel suite. "I should be going," she said again.

Trent sat forward, his elbows on his knees. "You loved him very much, didn't you?"

The question came out of nowhere, freezing her in place. She'd never really discussed Dane with Trent. She drank some of her Coke, trying to act nonchalant. And then she realized she could feel the rum loosening the rough cords of anguish that had bound her for months. Everything was relaxing in and around her. Less pain—it felt good. Was that so bad?

"You don't have to talk about it if you don't want to," Trent said as if he expected her to rebuff him.

She ached with loneliness and gratitude for his tact.

Trent folded her hand into his. "He was a fortunate man. You are a woman of quality, a woman worthy of notice. I hope he realized that."

Leigh looked away, feeling loneliness and despair creeping close again. She took another sip of her drink and then hazarded a look at him.

Trent drew her hand to his mouth and kissed her fingertips again. "You've suffered."

Leigh felt hot, embarrassing tears dropping down her cheeks. "I'm sorry to break down like this."

He pressed the back of her hand against his cheek. "I just wish I could do something to make you feel better."

His sympathy made the tears come faster. "I . . . feel like I'll never . . . love again."

He drew her into a comforting embrace. "That's not true."

Her mind was moving much slower than usual, but his

words finally spread over and through her. She tingled with their effect. "Have you ever been in love like that?"

Trent met her gaze. "No." Then he gave her a sad look. "I'd like to be. To be honest, I don't know if I have what it takes."

She felt the familiar pain of loss, but something new had been added. She wished she could help Trent know what it was like to be loved.

"Love has never been part of my life, Leigh. Until I met you, I didn't care. But you're so special, so wonderful. You've tempted me to hope." He stopped, then went on in a different voice, "I wish I could soothe away your sorrow at least a little."

As he said these words, Leigh found herself floating in a lovely cocoon. The anguish that had racked her for months had released its hold on her, and Trent's touch warmed her, excited her. She suddenly realized that the man beside her wanted to help her, wanted to know her . . . The longing to let go, to let Trent comfort her, to move *toward* someone instead of just drifting in painful limbo swept over her. "And I wish you could know what it is to love and be loved."

"So do I." He folded her into his arms and kissed her.

Somewhere in the back of Leigh's mind, a tardy warning rang and rang. But she was deliciously detached from it. She closed her eyes and hummed softly, blocking it out. Trent was holding her, kissing her. As his lips dipped lower down her throat, she sighed and leaned back, encouraging him. One last breath of caution whispered through her. Trent's kisses became more insistent. How could she just get up and go? How could she do that to him? He needed her. She needed him. She knew she couldn't face tomorrow alone. And for the first time in months, she felt good, alive. She wasn't alone in the darkness anymore.

*   *   *

The next morning, a phone rang, and Leigh opened her eyes. Her mouth was dry, and a slight ache pounded over one temple. An unusual languor made it hard for her to move. But she rolled over. And then she realized where she was.

She'd spent the night in Trent's suite.

With Trent.

Flashes of the night played in her mind. Then she felt as if Grandma Chloe were standing right beside her, looking hurt and very disappointed. Leigh buried her face in her hands. *How did I let this happen? Why? I don't approve of this when others do it.* Then she recalled the three rum and Cokes she'd drank. *Why did I do that? I don't drink.*

But she'd let herself get into a questionable situation and then she'd let down her guard—and the only explanation she could come up with was that she'd been weak and weighed down with her grief. Was that an adequate excuse? In her mind, she heard Sister Mary Margaret at St. Agnes saying, "There's always a reason for why people do the sinful things they do. But that doesn't mean that there is ever an excuse."

Leigh massaged her temples. She didn't really want to remember Sister Mary Margaret right now. It was bad enough, hoping that her grandmother would never find out about last night. She didn't even try to deceive her conscience with the popular sop that these were the seventies, after all, and things were different between the sexes now. She would never again let herself fall into the sin she had last night. She wouldn't rationalize her way out of this. And she'd have to make that clear to Trent. Or maybe he was feeling the same guilt as she this morning.

A phone conversation in the other room came to her in bits and pieces. Trent raised his voice as if winding up a conversation, "Yes, I won't forget. The game's at 6:30. I'll be there." She heard the phone receiver being put down.

Fearing that Trent would come back in the room, she sat up and pulled the sheet to her chin.

He appeared in the doorway, still wearing only pajama bottoms. She realized she was wearing his pajama top under the sheet and blushed furiously. In the cold light of morning, her situation was too humiliating.

Trent chuckled. "I was wondering if I should wake you up. I called room service a while ago. I hope I ordered what you like for breakfast."

Fierce embarrassment made it impossible for her to reply.

Trent came and sat down beside her on the bed. "You look beautiful when you blush like that." He ran a finger down her cheek.

Her face flushed hotter, and she moved a bit away from him. "Trent, please, I—"

He interrupted her with a kiss. Then he murmured, "You're so beautiful. I can't wait to show you off."

His words did not reassure her. She pulled away and grabbed at something to stop him from going any further. "Who were you talking to?"

Trent shrugged. "Family." He ran a finger around one ear and down her neck to the top of the sheet she held against herself. His touch still had the power to move her, but she refused to give in to it. When she held tight, he chuckled again. "Why don't you shower before breakfast? I can wait and shower afterward." He stood up.

She felt distinct relief that he was leaving her to get herself together. And yes, she wanted and needed fresh clothing to face breakfast with him and the conversation they had to have. She must let him know that she wouldn't fall from grace again. Once was already more than she could handle. The only thing that made this bearable was that she was sure Trent was a good person who had fallen in love with her and that he'd understand why it had to be that way. They'd just have to go back and begin dating, getting to know one another a bit better. She had no doubt that she felt love for this man. Otherwise, she wouldn't have allowed him to make love to her.

So she gave him the key from her purse, and he told her he'd call the bellman to go out and bring up her overnight bag from her car in the hotel lot. That even an unknown bellhop would realize that she'd spent the night with Trent made her cringe. Then he left her, and she scrambled into the bathroom.

Later, fully dressed but with her long hair still wet from the shower, Leigh sipped her first cup of hot coffee. It did wonders for her slight headache. She looked over the rim of her cup at Trent and wondered how to begin to tell him of her regret over her lapse of judgment last night. She wasn't the kind of woman who did this type of thing.

"I have to go back to Annapolis today, Leigh. I have a case coming up soon, and I have to meet with my staff."

Leigh took in a deep breath. "We need to discuss—"

"Believe me," he cut in, "I wouldn't go if I had any choice. And I have to attend my son's football game at 6:30 today."

The word "son" startled her. "Son? You didn't tell me you'd been married."

He gave her an odd look. "Everyone knows I'm married."

It was like a clawhammer to her head. She gaped at him.

"Didn't you recognize me?" He lifted one brow quizzically. "My wife's father is the governor of Maryland. How could you not know that?"

His words cut her in two. She could barely draw breath. She gaped at him. Finally, she managed to say, "But you said you'd never known love." Was Trent teasing her or playing an awful joke?

He snorted. "There's no love between my wife and me. It is purely a marriage of convenience, an open marriage for both of us. She wanted a husband who was able to impress her father, and I wanted his political connections. I'm building a reputation for myself, and when her father eventually retires, I'll run for his office."

Leigh was too stunned to speak. Her mouth opened and closed soundlessly. She realized then that she'd taken Trent at face value, never asking other women about him. She'd kept her distance from others at the town meetings and had never gone back to the McGovern headquarters in Washington or Maryland. Her grief had cut her off from the regular flow of getting to know people. She'd only talked to that girl Nancy and the man across from her.

He reached over and took her hand. "We can play this any way you want. I plan that our affair will last as long as you can put up with me. In fact, forever if you wish. You're beautiful, intelligent, and I've never felt anything for a woman like what I feel for you. I didn't think I was capable of falling in love. But I think this is the real thing this time."

Leigh felt as if he were speaking a foreign language. This Trent was nothing like the Trent she'd known over the past few months. Which one was real—the caring, more mature man who'd been so understanding, or this cold stranger who spoke of a wife, a son, and political ambition?

He paused to sip his coffee. "Why don't you come to Annapolis with me today and look for an apartment? I think you'll find me very generous. Or—" He gave her a roguish grin. "—are you one of those liberated women who doesn't want a man to provide for her?"

That Trent would even say the words to her appalled her. Her nerves felt as if someone had set fire to them. She wanted to lie down on the floor and writhe with the agony, the shame. *This can't be happening. I can't have really done this. Oh, dear God, no.* "I didn't know you were married," she said at last, her throat as dry as sand.

"Leigh, I really care for you, more than I've ever cared for anyone. And I've wanted you and waited longer for you than any other woman. But I am married. I can't divorce her. I've put too many years into the marriage, and it's part and parcel with my political ambitions. We have a son, too. This isn't going to be a problem, is it?"

Yes, this is going to be a problem. She stared at him, feeling as if he had just yanked out her insides. *Dear God, I've been such a fool.*

CHAPTER THIRTEEN

*T*oo shocked to react. Too horrified at her own foolish-
ness. Too crushed by his assumption that she would
knowingly, *willingly* enter into an affair with a married man.
How Leigh had survived the rest of the minutes till Trent left
her, she didn't know. Finally, after a fast kiss on her forehead
and a reminder for her to call him at his private office number
so they could make plans for their future, he departed.

Alone at last, she stood in the center of the luxurious suite
and stared around. "What do I do now?" she asked the empty,
mocking room. "How could I have been so stupid?"

*"Everyone knows I'm married. You must have recog-
nized me. My wife's the governor's daughter."*

But she'd lived in San Francisco and before that in New
York City attending college. And before that, she'd lived near
Arlington, Virginia. She hadn't known who the governor of
Maryland was or who was married to his daughter. And she
hadn't become chummy with any of the other McGovern
campaigners except Nancy Hollister, who was from New
York and wouldn't have known, either. Leigh had kept to her-

self, and only Trent had pursued her. And now she knew why—he'd needed a new mistress.

Her knees suddenly weakened, and she staggered to the amber sofa. Staring at the smudged glasses left on the coffee table from last night, she moaned, feeling almost physically ill. How had she sunk this low? Was it only that she never drank and the rum had weakened her resistance? Her conscience refused to allow this excuse. She'd drunk the alcohol of her own free will. She'd consented to come to Trent's room alone. She'd let him make love to her, knowing no vows had been spoken between them.

"I have no one to blame but myself."

What kind of man married for political connections and then had affairs? It was hard to reconcile this kind of cold-blooded behavior with the warm and caring man whom she'd spent hours with over the past few months. *I must be a very poor judge of character*. Or had he been busy seducing her and she hadn't even realized it? Was she that naïve? Evidently she was.

Trent's charming words played in her mind: *"I've never felt anything for a woman like what I feel for you. I didn't think I was capable of falling in love."* Was that what men said to their mistresses? Did they try to dress up the relationship as a "love" affair so that the woman didn't feel the full weight of the guilt of committing adultery?

That's what I did. I committed adultery. She recalled memorizing the Ten Commandments as a little girl in Sunday school. She remembered wondering why she'd had to be-cause—*of course*—she'd never break any of those command-ments. Without meaning to, she moaned again. She couldn't ever remember moaning aloud in her life, not even when she'd lost Dane. But each one felt wrenched from deep inside her.

What do I do now? How can I ever live this down? Oh, God, forgive me. Forgive me.

Minutes passed, and finally Leigh pulled herself together and left the hotel room. Downstairs, still wobbly, she saw a bank of public telephones off to one side of the lobby. It suddenly dawned on her that she hadn't driven home to Ivy Manor last night or even called. Her grandmother might be worried. She got change for a couple of dollars from the desk clerk and went to the end phone, trying for some privacy. She dialed the long-distance number, deposited the requested number of coins, and heard the call go through. When her grandmother's sweet voice came over the line, Leigh nearly burst into tears.

"Grandma," she said, controlling her shaky voice, "I'm sorry I didn't call last night. I was up quite late and then stayed with . . . a friend here at the hotel." Pain twisted through her nerves again. *A friend, right.* Now she was lying to her grandmother.

"That's what we decided had happened, dear. After all, you had taken an overnight bag with you," Chloe replied as if this were just an ordinary day, not the day Leigh would regret for the rest of her life. "After McGovern's defeat, it must have been a rough night for everyone there."

Who cares about McGovern? "Yes." *This morning was the worst. Oh, Grandma, I didn't mean this to happen.*

"Are you coming home today?"

"I don't know," she lied. *No, I can't come home. If I did, I'd break down and tell you what I've done. I can't face you or anyone else in the family. No one must ever know what I've done. Oh, Grandma, I hate myself.*

But if she did not go back to Ivy Manor or her mother's house, what was she going to do? She had no place of her own to limp off to and hide from everyone. But suddenly, grasping for straws, she remembered her conversation with her friend Nancy. Nancy's parting words came to mind: *"If you're ever in New York City, give me a call. I've got a sleeper sofa."*

"Grandma, I think that I'm going to go up to New York City." What possible reason could she give for this? Her frantic mind searched for a reason and came up with, "I might see about starting graduate classes in January. I've been at loose ends. Maybe I should go back to school."

Her grandmother responded with the usual encouragement and request that Leigh call her when she reached New York City safe and sound. "Do you want me to call the Loveladys? I know they'd love to have you stay with them. Or you could stay with Minnie."

"No." Leigh's denial came swift and strong. She couldn't face anyone she knew well. "I—" She softened her voice. "I'm going to stay with a friend I met in D.C. in June. She lives in the Village."

Within seconds, Leigh was able to end the phone call. With almost desperate determination, she dug out Nancy Hollister's card, buried in her billfold. She dropped more coins into the slot and dialed her friend's number. No answer. Leigh hung up and retrieved the change from the coin drop. She stood there. Should she go to New York? Did she have a choice?

In times of trouble, she'd always run to Ivy Manor and her grandmother's open arms. Never before had she run *away* from Ivy Manor. But she'd never before broken the seventh commandment.

The drive to New York helped Leigh get hold of her stormy emotions. She couldn't land on Nancy's doorstep, burst into tears, and confess all. She suspected Trent would never tell anyone about their night together, and certainly she wouldn't. And Trent would just have to figure out by himself why she didn't call him. She had no desire to speak to him again, and there was no way, she decided with dark, bitter humor, she could leave a message with his secretary like, "Please tell Mr. Kinnard that I've decided not to become his mistress." No, her absence would have to speak for her.

A heavy feeling weighed her down. She finally identified it as pure guilt, overwhelming regret.

It had been a long time since she'd prayed, but evidently, this event required confession, an act of contrition. She felt foolish somehow, but at the sight of a church spire, she pulled off the highway and drove up the street. She parked beside the white-frame church and turned off the motor. She couldn't go in—if she met someone, what would she possibly say? *I came to confess to committing adultery.*

A large sign announced that the church was an historic one, dating from colonial times and with a cemetery beside it. Leigh got out of the car, pulling up the collar of her coat against the sharp November wind, and wandered around the cemetery, reading the weathered headstones. If anyone saw her, they'd think she was one of those people who visited old cemeteries to jot down dates and names of people long gone.

She looked over the gravestones, some leaning with age, some nearly illegible after years of torrents and winds had worn away their etched messages. One of the most common epitaphs was merely, "Beloved Wife." None of them read, "Beloved Mistress."

I was supposed to be Dane's beloved wife. When I lost him, I allowed my grief to stop me from living. And I ended up easy prey for a calculating man. But that's no excuse. I knew better.

She put a hand on a newer marble headstone and bowed

her head. She recalled the biblical tale of David and Bathsheba's adultery. Now she knew how David must have felt when he'd finally faced his sin—shattered and ashamed. *God, You know I'm not very religious, but I feel terrible about what happened last night. I have no good excuse except human stupidity. Please forgive me. I'll do my best never to be that brainless again. I guess that's all. Amen.*

She wished a dove would fly down from heaven and let her know God had forgiven her. Of course, she knew that was not going to happen. But her words were the best she could do in the way of a confession. The hymn "Amazing Grace" from Grandpa Roarke's funeral came back to mind. She hadn't believed that he was a wretch in need of salvation, but that was exactly how she felt right now. How did one stop the overwhelming wave after wave of guilt?

"Hello," a little woman in white orthopedic shoes hailed her from the churchyard. "Can I help you?"

Leigh pulled herself together and walked toward the woman.

"Have you come to do some genealogical research?" the little gray bird of a woman asked.

"No, just needed to get out of the car for a few moments."

"Our church dates from 1736. And keeping it and the cemetery in good repair is costly. Would you like a tour of the church? There is a box for donations next to the guest register."

Ah, a walk in the graveyard didn't come free. Leigh put her hand in her pocket and drew out the change she had left from her morning phone calls. "Why don't you put this in for me? I must be getting on."

"Oh, thank you," the woman called after her. "Have a nice day!"

Leigh wondered how many weeks, months, years would pass before she would "have a nice day" again.

After parking her car in a long-term lot across the river in New Jersey, she found a pay phone and called Nancy's number again. On the very last ring, just as Leigh was about to hang up and look for a nearby hotel, Nancy's breathless voice came on. "Hi! I heard the phone just as I was unlocking my door."

"Hi, Nancy, this is Leigh Sinclair," Leigh started, feeling more uncertain with each syllable. What if this woman didn't even remember her? "We met in June—"

"Oh, the beautiful blonde. Hi. What's going on?"

"I just got in, and I wondered if the offer to use your sleeper sofa was still—"

"Great! Can't wait to see you." Nancy gave Leigh the address and said to come over right away.

Leigh hailed a taxi, and in spite of the traffic, she soon stepped out of the cab in front of Nancy's vintage apartment building in the Village. Just as she reached for the door to the vestibule, it burst open. "Hey! Great to see you!" Nancy crowed, looking as if Leigh were Stanley and she were Livingston. Leigh couldn't help it. Tears filled her eyes. She blinked them away as she followed Nancy up the narrow staircase to the second story and into her apartment, which had obviously been decorated from thrift stores and sported rock band and travel posters on every wall.

"I only have one bedroom," Nancy, with her long dark hair and denim bell-bottoms, filled her in. "And just a postage stamp of a kitchen and bath, but it works. How long will you be staying?"

The question yanked Leigh out of her misery and back

into real life. "I'm going to look for a job. Can I stay during the job hunt? As soon as I have something, I'll get my own place."

"Sure," Nancy agreed with easy humor, "I'll love having you. With that long blonde hair, you'll attract men like bees to honey and maybe I can commiserate with those you turn down."

Leigh turned away, the horrifying events of this morning replaying in her mind, fiery remorse blistering her raw conscience. She couldn't tell Nancy that. But how to explain her easy tears? "Maybe I should tell you that my fiancé was . . . He died this spring."

"Oh!" Nancy put an arm around her. "I'm so sorry. I didn't mean to hurt—"

"It's okay." Leigh made herself smile. "I'm . . . just not in the market for romance right now." *Or an affair with a married man.* Suddenly she wished she'd screamed at Trent this morning, slapped his face, raged at him. But, of course, she'd been too numb to react at the time. *Stupid little fool,* she scolded herself. *Stupid, naïve, little blonde fool.*

"Sure." Nancy snagged her denim shoulder bag from a faded chintz chair that didn't match the crushed-velvet avocado-green sofa. "Let's go get something to eat. I'm an awful cook."

Leigh followed Nancy out the door, silently sighing with relief. She'd found a haven.

Two days later, Manhattan

Since Leigh had finished her degree in English and journalism in California, she didn't go to an employment agency, but instead to a career counselor—otherwise known as a "headhunter." The day before, she'd filled out a long application that the agency would turn into a résumé. Today she was keeping her appointment with the *head* "headhunter." A tall, very business-major-looking man, he rose as she entered his compact office with its one small window. "Miss Sinclair."

"Mr. Johnson." Leigh shook his hand and took the seat in front of his desk.

"You have quite an impressive list of credits for your writing. You're interested in finding a job with a newspaper or magazine, I see."

"Yes, since I finished school," Leigh recited the phrases she'd rehearsed mentally, "I've lived with an elderly aunt in San Francisco and have done—"

"Quite a bit of freelance writing there." He looked up from the paper and stared at her.

She waited for him to go on, but he continued to stare at her. Finally, it began to make her uncomfortable. If he made a pass at her, she'd throw something at him. She prompted, "Mr. Johnson?"

He grinned. "I was just thinking that now that I've seen you, I would suggest that you make a career change. You could make much more as a model. My wife runs a modeling agency. Perhaps you would like to go there and—"

"No." Leigh held up her hand. "I'm not interested in anything like that. I'm a writer, not a fashion model."

"Well, you can make a living by writing, but you could make a fortune in modeling. Are you—"

Leigh slid forward on her seat. "Let me be very clear, Mr. Johnson. I came here for help with getting my résumé in order," she made her voice sharp and determined, "and to get a few interviews with papers and magazines. I am not interested in posing for a camera." Grandma Chloe had been a model on Fifth Avenue in 1917, but that was when very few professions were open to women. Did this man actually expect her to turn her back on her education and model instead?

Mr. Johnson tapped her application on his desktop. "I see. In that case, I think our secretary has a rough draft of your résumé done for you to approve, and I have three positions for which you can interview in the next few days. Is that satisfactory?"

"Yes, just what I expected." She gave him a measured smile. After Trent Kinnard, she had no patience with meaningless flattery or men who used it. She wanted to write, and who cared what a writer looked like?

He pressed a button on his intercom, and within minutes his secretary brought in the typed pages of her résumé. Leigh looked them over and gave her approval.

"Now," Johnson proceeded, "one of the journals you'll be interviewing with is pretty stodgy, so don't wear a miniskirt to the interview."

Leigh gave the man a long look. "Don't worry. I know how to handle an interview." *But the first man who makes a pass at me will be in serious danger....*

Three days later, Leigh sat on a chair in an editor's office. She'd worn a new gray pantsuit and had pulled her hair back into a low ponytail.

The woman editor glanced over her résumé one more time and then looked up. "Your credentials are quite good. I see that you've been active in politics. What do you think of the Equal Rights Amendment?"

Leigh hadn't really made a decision on the topic. It sounded good, but was it really? "I think American women have been held back for generations," she said diplomatically. "And that isn't right."

The editor nodded. "You realize that we've only been in business a little over a year. I can't promise you that we'll stay in business." She gave Leigh a tight smile. "Publishing magazines is a touchy, uncertain way to make money. We aren't *The Saturday Evening Post*."

"I know."

"Okay, then. The job's yours—if you want it."

Sudden fear snaked through Leigh. She'd never worked a real job. She'd only done freelance assignments over the past few years. Was she smart enough to do this? After that awful morning in Baltimore, she'd begun doubting herself. But this job would mean that she'd have a reason for getting up every morning. "Yes, I want it." *And I'll do a good job if it kills me.*

New York City, December 21, 1972

Leigh sat across from Shirley Chisholm, the first female African-American congresswoman—the first also to receive delegate votes for president in this year's presidential race—at her Brooklyn office. Leigh had just finished jotting down Ms. Chisholm's reply to her last question. Leigh looked up. "I want to thank you again, Ms. Chisholm, for giving me this interview. The readers of *Women Today* are definitely interested in helping more women get into politics and into Congress."

Ms. Chisholm stood up and offered her hand. "When you first walked in and I saw you, I wondered if this was going to be a fluff piece. But you really did your homework on what I've been trying to do down in Washington. I apologize for assuming that such a pretty girl couldn't do a good job. I'm afraid all of us are guilty of judging by appearances at times."

Leigh smiled, accustomed to this kind of conversation. Thanking her again, Leigh shook Ms. Chisholm's hand and then left. She didn't tell the woman that in many ways, she'd reminded Leigh of Aunt Jerusha. What could Aunt Jerusha have accomplished if she'd been born a century later than she was?

At that, the germ of another article sprang to Leigh's mind. Maybe she could interview Minnie Dawson and put that very question to her. Perhaps she could contrast Minnie's life with her mother, Jerusha's.

In the outer office, she sat down and took time to jot down this idea and then she stood up quickly. For a moment, everything wavered around her and she sat back down.

"Are you all right?" the secretary asked.

She couldn't say, "I think I'm coming down with the flu"—not after just meeting with the congresswoman. "No. Just all the holiday activities. I haven't been getting enough sleep and haven't eaten lunch today. Merry Christmas!"

The secretary wished her the same, and Leigh took the elevator down to the street, where she spotted a sign: "Women's Clinic. Walk-Ins Welcome."

Without any further thought, she entered the door. After a twenty-minute wait, she was ushered into a cubicle, and within another few minutes, she was joined by a woman doctor, the first she'd ever seen. "I hear you think you are coming down with the flu and don't want to take it home with you for Christmas."

"Yes, if I'm really going to be ill, I'll just stay here. My grandmother and great-aunt are in their seventies. I don't want to infect them with anything."

"Very thoughtful of you." The doctor shook down a

thermometer and slipped it into Leigh's mouth, and then while waiting, took her pulse and blood pressure. "The flu has already hit here, or my nurse would be doing this. It's slowed me down today." She slipped the thermometer out and read it. "Your temperature isn't elevated. What are your symptoms?"

"I'm lightheaded sometimes when I stand up too fast. I felt a bit queasy in the mornings over the past week and also sometimes when I pass a restaurant or sandwich shop and smell the food aromas."

"When was the first day of your last period?"

Leigh gave the doctor a look. *What has that got to do with the flu?* But it was just easier to give her the information. She thought it over. "My last period was in late October." Her own words surprised her a bit.

"Is it usual for you to miss a month?"

"No, I'm as regular as clockwork." Apprehension buzzed inside Leigh.

"Your symptoms sound like pregnancy. Do you think you could be pregnant?"

Now shock burned through Leigh. *Oh, no. I never gave that a thought. Am I insane or just totally brain-dead stupid?* "Yes, I could be." Each word she spoke swung back and hit her like a hammer stroke.

"Why don't you give me a urine sample," the doctor went on matter-of-factly, "and we can know by tomorrow if you are."

Leigh nodded and somehow made it through the rest of the appointment. She promised to call back after 1:00 p.m. the following day.

Outside again, she stood looking around as if she didn't know where she was or what she had planned. Finally, it came to her. She needed to go back to her office and begin writing up the article while the interview was still fresh in her mind. But would she be able to put a word down?

Pregnant, no, please, no.

The next day, she stayed home from the office. She'd just rented the apartment above Nancy's, but she couldn't move in until the first of January. She sat on Nancy's green sofa beside the phone. On the TV, *Concentration* was on. She watched the players but couldn't compete along with them today. It was as if her mind had taken a vacation. Brain failure must have started yesterday after visiting the clinic. This morning, she'd reread what she'd written yesterday afternoon and had ended by tearing it up.

Finally, the clock ticked over to 1:01 p.m. She dialed the clinic and asked about her test.

The receptionist transferred the call to the doctor from yesterday. "Miss Sinclair?"

"Yes?" Leigh's voice sounded like a croak. She cleared her throat. "Have you gotten back the test results yet?"

"Yes, you are pregnant."

Yes, you are pregnant. With those four words, Leigh's world tilted on its axis.

"Miss Sinclair?"

Leigh suppressed the urge to retch. "Yes?"

"You will be due early in August. You should see an obstetrician and begin prenatal visits so you have a healthy pregnancy and a healthy baby."

A healthy baby. "Yes."

"Would you like to come and see me about your options?"

I'm pregnant, and Trent's married. "My options?" She tried to focus on the conversation.

"Well, I want to caution you about the risks of backstreet abortions. If this child is coming at a bad time for you, or if you and the father aren't planning on marriage . . ."

Her mind repeated, ". . . *a bad time for you, or if you and the father aren't planning on marriage* . . ." Marriage. Oh, no.

"There is always the option of adoption," the doctor went on as if discussing the weather. "There are many, many couples looking to adopt—"

"Thank you." Unable to bear speaking about it one more second, Leigh hung up. She slumped as if boneless onto the sofa and lay there looking up at the ceiling. *This can't be real. I can't be pregnant. I was only with him one time.*

Her conscience taunted her in a smug tone, "It only takes one time."

She'd just begun to move on with her career, with her life, to put the one-night affair behind her . . .

Her conscience sprang up to accuse her, "Make that *your* one-night stand."

In pain and utter humiliation, Leigh closed her eyes. She'd been so naïve she hadn't even thought about birth control and Trent must have assumed she was on the pill—like all his other women. The thought was a stinging lash to her heart. *Pregnant. I thought no one would ever have to know. What do I do now?*

CHAPTER FOURTEEN

December 23, 1972

$\mathcal{L}$eigh drove up the road to Ivy Manor, still feeling as if she'd been flattened by a truck and then dragged for a mile or two. The generations-old house looked like a Christmas card: a dusting of snow on its roof and over the hardy green ivy around the entrance, a large evergreen wreath with a bright crimson bow on the front door, and a lovely Christmas tree glowing in the front window. Woozy from too little sleep, Leigh tightened her self-control to the maximum. She wouldn't ruin her grandmother's holiday celebration with bad news. No one here needed to know she was pregnant.

Leigh parked her car in the large garage that had been the stables for the manor long ago. She was weak from crying, and carrying her luggage had never been more wearing. She passed the empty little cottage and the summer house on her way to the backdoor. Then the door swung open, and her grandmother was there with her arms open wide. "My darling! My sweet girl!"

The physical warmth from the house wafted into Leigh's

face, and the warmth of the welcome blew into her heart. She hurried forward. Dropping her luggage, she fell into her grandmother's arms. She'd practiced what to say, to keep her sadness from her grandmother. She opened her mouth to recite her greeting and blurted out instead, "Grandma, I'm pregnant." Then she burst into tears, sobbing against her grandmother's soft shoulder.

Kitty was standing behind Chloe and heard Leigh's wail and weeping. She closed her eyes. What had the poor child gotten herself into? "Bring her inside, Chloe," Kitty instructed, knowing someone had to be strong at this moment. "She needs something hot to drink, and she needs to sit by the fire. Thank heaven Bette isn't arriving until tomorrow."

Chloe obeyed Kitty and drew Leigh into the house. Kitty dragged the luggage inside and shut the back door. Chloe's housekeeper, Rose, was standing in the toasty kitchen at the stove, watching the timer. She was baking sugar cookies. From her expression, Kitty knew she'd overheard Leigh, also.

"Don't worry, Miss Kitty," Rose said with a grim expression. "What's said in this house stays in this house."

Kitty nodded. "Thank you. Would you put the kettle on for tea?" Rose assented, and Kitty went into the parlor. Chloe had Leigh sitting beside her on the loveseat near the hearth. To give Leigh time to compose herself, Kitty stopped to stir the coals and put kindling and a few more logs on the cozy fire. Flames danced up. She turned. "How far along are you?" she said in as businesslike a tone as she could manage.

Leigh looked up. "Almost two months."

"Who's the father?" Kitty sat down across from Chloe in the wingback chair. This scene brought back her own sad memories.

Leigh winced as if Kitty had slapped her. "It doesn't matter. We can't marry. He's got a wife." This admission brought on another gale of weeping.

Kitty absorbed this blow, knowing that this was worse, much worse, than what she'd thought. She'd hoped they'd just be planning a hurried wedding. But that was impossible unless . . . "Is it a happy marriage?"

"I don't have a clue, and I don't care." Leigh's voice rose, the beginning of hysteria.

Kitty fell silent while Chloe stroked Leigh's long blonde hair, murmuring love phrases and kissing Leigh's temple. Kitty let Chloe do her work. She was good at understanding and comforting. Much better than Kitty.

Finally, Kitty asked, "Do you want to tell us about it? I don't see you having an affair with a married man. Didn't you know?"

"No! I didn't." Leigh looked crestfallen. "He said . . . he said that everyone knew he was married. But I didn't." As if exhausted, Leigh rested her head on Chloe's shoulder, almost panting from the exertion of weeping. "He didn't wear a wedding band, and I didn't think . . ."

Kitty nodded grimly. "We know, honey. You're not the first one to find out too late . . ."

Chloe looked across the room at Kitty, obviously pleading with her for help. Chloe couldn't address falling in love with a married man, but she knew that Kitty could.

Kitty looked inside herself at the old scars and wealth of regret. She possessed the awful experience that might help her very dear great-niece through this disastrous valley. She could only hope it would be enough. "Leigh, what do you intend to do? You aren't thinking of an abortion, are you?"

Leigh sat up and looked at her. "The doctor wanted to warn me of the dangers of backstreet abortions . . . I can't imagine doing that. It terrifies me. Then she said something about adoption. I don't know if I could do that, either." Leigh looked at Chloe. "But Uncle Jamie was adopted, and you adopted my uncle Thompson, didn't you?"

"Yes." Chloe squeezed Leigh's hand. "And he's been such a blessing to us—to me. Especially now since Roarke's gone and Rory's living in Philadelphia."

"But I don't know if I can face going through a pregnancy alone," Leigh said, weeping quietly, one hand over her eyes. "I feel so stupid. So alone."

"You're not alone, dear." Chloe patted Leigh's shoulder.

"That's right, my dear," Kitty said, drawing up her strength to reveal here and now what she hadn't spoken of since 1931. "Your grandmother and I will help you. Just as Chloe and Roarke helped me when I got pregnant out of wedlock."

Leigh stopped crying abruptly and stared at Kitty.

"Thank you, Kitty," Chloe murmured.

"You had a baby?" Leigh said. "But . . ."

"I gave birth in California in 1931," Kitty said in a grim voice, "and then brought my baby to Washington, D.C., to the same orphanage that Jamie had been adopted from. Your grandmother and my brother met me there and adopted my son as theirs."

Leigh's eyes widened. "Uncle Thompson is your son?"

At that moment, Rose stepped into the parlor with the tea tray in hand. For a few seconds, all four women froze in place. Then Rose reiterated in her calm way, "What's said in this house stays in this house. Though I think most of Jerusha's generation—black and white—figured it out for themselves. If the good Lord had wanted Thompson to look any more like a *born* McCaslin, He'd have had to stamp the name 'Mc-Caslin' on the boy's forehead."

Kitty chuckled at this—in spite of the bottomless guilt and regret that still tugged at her, tortured her from time to time. If only times had been different, if only she had been different, wiser. But the past was dead and gone. The present was all she could affect. "Why don't you take tea with us, Rose? Leigh needs all of our support now."

"I brought four cups." Rose grinned and then set the tray on the coffee table. She took the chair beside Kitty's and began pouring and handing around the hot tea. "I can hear the oven buzzer from here. Don't want to burn the cookies. Dory asked for them special."

"Now start at the beginning, Leigh," Kitty urged. "Tell us how this happened."

The three of them listened to Leigh's tearful recital of the facts of her one-night affair. "It doesn't seem fair," Kitty sighed.

"Who . . . who was Thompson's father?" Leigh asked.

Kitty had been expecting this question. "Do you remember that photograph I keep on my desk at home in San Francisco?"

"Him? I always wondered who he was. What happened to him . . . to you?" Leigh looked as if Kitty had grown another head.

"You mean why did we part, and why do I keep his photo around?"

"Both." Leigh studied Kitty, her face twisted in concentration.

"I keep his photograph on my desk to remind me that even the most intelligent woman can make horrible mistakes, commit the most foolish sins. You see, I thought I was desperately in love with him. But in truth, I was just desperate. I was thirty, and he was charming and tragically married but separated from a wife who wouldn't give him a divorce. I thought ours was a grand love story. But I was just a fool, living in sin with an unfaithful alcoholic. When I finally figured that out, I left him and moved to San Francisco."

"And you gave your son to Grandmother to raise?" Leigh sipped her tea at last. "I don't know if I can do that. Give my child away."

"Well, as I told my own three daughters," Rose cut in, "some men come and go in a woman's life, but babies are forever. Miss Kitty was right to have her baby, and Thompson didn't suffer none from being raised here by his own blood. But times are changin'. Miss Leigh, you can keep your baby and raise it yourself." Rose aimed her cup at Leigh. "You keep your own blood. You'll never regret it."

"We'll help you, sweetheart," Grandma Chloe said, squeezing her shoulder. "I want my first great-grandchild very much."

"Mother won't want me to keep my baby," Leigh said, looking resentful, hunted.

"That doesn't really matter, does it?" Kitty lifted her chin. "This will be your decision."

"Does Uncle Thompson know?" Leigh asked. "I mean . . ."

"Yes," Chloe replied, "I asked him when he turned twenty-one if he still wanted to meet his mother. When I couldn't persuade Kitty to come to him, he flew to San Francisco at her invitation."

Leigh looked to Kitty. "How did that go?"

"He was kind enough to understand why I'd given him to Chloe and my brother. He told me he hadn't suffered because Chloe had been such a wonderful mother. And she'd told him as a child that he was McCaslin by blood and not to worry about who his real parents were, that she would tell him when he became a man."

Kitty paused before she could go on. Speaking of Thompson like this was costing her more emotionally than she'd feared. But she went on resolutely, "Both he and I are sorry that we missed so many years together. But I write him regularly. And he calls and writes me. He's visited me and brought his bride to meet me on their honeymoon."

Leigh nodded slowly as if pondering all this.

"It's your life," Kitty said, switching back to the main topic: Leigh and her baby. "You've made a mistake—you trusted someone who was untrustworthy. You aren't the first woman to make that mistake."

Rose snorted over her tea. "Ain't that the truth," she muttered and continued, "We women got a way of hearin' things men don't remember saying."

Kitty almost smiled. "But we all have to go on. And no one can say that this hasn't been a rough year for you."

"Yes," Chloe took over, "I don't think you would have done this if you hadn't suffered such overwhelming loss this year. If Dane hadn't died, you might have been pregnant by him now. But he's gone, and *no matter what*, we'll all love this baby."

Kitty leaned forward. "We will."

Chloe put her arm around Leigh's shoulder and hugged her. And Rose raised her cup and said, "That's a fact."

The next evening in front of another warming fire, Leigh sat in the same spot beside Chloe. Kitty was in the same chair as the day before, but Dory had taken Rose's place. Bette stood nearby. A cold December wind was buffeting the old windows and rattling the panes. Leigh leaned closer to the fire. The Christmas decorations that gave the room a festive air didn't fit the occasion. Just a few minutes before, Leigh had told her mother about her pregnancy.

She'd wondered what her mother's reaction would be. She hadn't had to wait long to find out. Her mother had immediately tried to send Dory from the room as if she would be contaminated by the discussion. But now a teen, Dory had refused, and Grandma Chloe had backed her up, saying this was a family matter and Dory was part of it. Visibly fuming, Bette had paced up and down a few minutes and then turned to face Leigh.

"Of course, you must give the baby up for adoption." Her mother was pink in the face. "We'll find you a good unwed-mothers home out of state, and you'll just go away and no one will ever have to know."

"No," Leigh objected, revolted by the idea of being *sent away* like a leper, "I don't—"

"How could you have let this happen?" her mother interrupted her, "when Dane is barely cold in his—"

"That's enough," Chloe snapped and then she tempered her voice. "Don't say things you'll regret, Bette. Leigh made a bad decision, and we all know why this happened. You lost Ted. But Leigh lost both the man who'd been her loving father *and* the man she was going to marry this year. She wasn't thinking like herself. And someone took advantage of that."

"I feel like an idiot," Leigh admitted. "I'd do anything to change this, but I can't."

"I don't know why you just can't do what I suggest," Bette said, her voice becoming pleading, "Honey, this could ruin your life."

Leigh shook her head. The love from her grandmother, Kitty, and Rose had given her strength and brought her first night of deep sleep after many sleepless ones. Both had settled her nerves. "I talked to Grandma and Aunt Kitty, and I think they're right. I don't want to give up my baby. I want to raise him or her—"

Bette huffed her displeasure; her face twisted with it. "Who is going to marry you with an . . . an illegitimate child?"

"I don't think I'm ever going to marry," Leigh said, gazing into the dancing flames.

"Of course, you are," Bette snapped.

"I never did," Kitty put in. "Staying single isn't the end of the world."

"A woman needs a man like a fish needs a bicycle," Dory recited the popular women's lib slogan.

Bette glared at her.

Chloe shook her head. "I don't ever remember seeing a fish and a bicycle mate."

Dory began, "I never thought—"

"Let's stick to the subject," Bette cut in. "Leigh, if you won't do what I suggest, you can't come back and live with me. What will the neighbors say?"

"Well, if they're good neighbors, they will come over and ask if they can help," Chloe replied. "If they're bad neighbors, what does it matter what they say?"

Leigh stood and stirred the wood with the black iron poker. She stared into the flickering red coals. She didn't want to look at her mother, see rejection in her eyes.

"This doesn't make any sense." Bette finally sat down in the chair opposite the fire. "Why is it always *something* with you, Leigh? Dory never gives me an ounce of trouble. Isn't it enough that I lost your stepfather this year—"

"Don't worry, Mother," Leigh flared up, holding the poker like a pointer. "I won't soil *your* reputation with my *love child*. You'll never have to see—"

"No, I want to see the baby," Dory pleaded, holding out her hands. "Mama, please."

"Bette, I asked you not to give into the emotion of the moment," Chloe said, "and say things that you will regret." Chloe turned to Leigh. "And that goes for you, too."

Leigh turned and put the poker back in its stand on the hearth. She folded her arms around herself.

Bette burst into tears. And Leigh looked away into the fire, her jaw set.

On January 2, 1973, in the kitchen at Ivy Manor, Leigh dialed the number of *Women Today* and then the extension for her editor. Leigh didn't want to do what she was going to do, but she didn't have a choice.

"Hello, Dorcas, this is Leigh." Her mouth was so dry she could barely speak. How many times must she make this confession?

"Hi, are you calling for an extension of the Christmas hiatus? If you need another day or—"

"No." Might as well take the plunge. Leigh sucked in air. "I'm pregnant."

"Pregnant," Dorcas repeated sharply. "How pregnant?"

"About two months." Leigh felt like crying again. She loved this job.

"Do you need time off for a honeymoon?" Dorcas asked, sounding uncertain.

"I'm not getting married." Leigh knew the conversation would end now. She wanted to plead with her editor, but that wasn't professional, possible.

"I see."

It was 1973, but most professional women—still primarily teachers and nurses—customarily quit working as soon as they found out they were pregnant. And certainly no magazine would want an unmarried pregnant writer. "My grandmother here in Maryland has asked me to stay with her."

"Can't you have your baby here?" Dorcas's tone was incisive and slightly combative. "We have doctors in New York, too, you know."

At this unexpected salvo, Leigh gathered her wits. "I didn't know what your policy was about pregnant . . . unmarried employees—"

"We don't have one—yet—but I know this," Dorcas said. "We aren't going to fire you or appliqué a red A on your blouse. If you want to work, I want you here working. You can take time off when you have the baby. But I'll want you back as soon as you can. You're my best interviewer. I can send you anywhere and you always get exactly what I want."

Leigh began crying, but tried hard not to let it be heard over the line. "Thanks, Dorcas. I'll talk it over with my grandmother and aunt."

She hung up. The idea of continuing her work gave her a spurt of pure joy. But could she, should she go on working?

She turned toward the three women around the kitchen table, who'd been listening to the one-sided phone call, and gave them the news.

"Told you," Aunt Kitty crowed.

"But do you want to go on working?" Chloe asked. "You know you don't need to. Roarke left me more than comfortable."

Leigh sat down. "I want to keep writing. It's what I do. I just didn't think they'd want me working there—"

"Yes, the scarlet-letter syndrome," Kitty snapped.

Leigh gazed at her great-aunt. She'd probably suffered from gossip all those years ago. Having an illegitimate baby in 1931 was worlds away from having one in 1973.

"Well, it's always better to have a father around when you're raisin' a child," Rose commented from the stove where she'd moved to stir the fragrant navy-bean soup made from a leftover ham bone. "But lots of women have had to do it all alone. And why shouldn't you go on doing what you want? Black women don't usually get to stay home and take care of their children. The grannies do that. The women work."

"But Leigh's granny is going to be here in Ivy Manor," Chloe complained, almost pouting.

"Perhaps a great-aunt will do in a pinch," Kitty said. "I used to live in the Village. You said you've taken a two-bedroom apartment. Why don't I come and stay with you?"

Leigh stared at her aunt, stunned but pleased.

"She's *my* granddaughter," Chloe said with a glint in her eye.

Leigh laughed through her tears. "Hey, you two don't need to fight over me. You can share this baby, okay?"

"Maybe Bette will want to come and help out, too," Rose suggested, pausing with the wooden spoon in hand. "When a woman has her first baby, it's a good time for a mother and daughter. Bette was left with you, a baby to raise alone, until Mr. Ted persuaded her to marry him. And it's good for Dory to learn about babies."

Leigh bit her lower lip before replying, "Rose, you're dreaming. Mother left right after Christmas, and you know they had intended to stay until today. Poor Dory was crying as they drove away. Mother doesn't want her to get the idea that what I've done was right. Well, I know it's wrong. What I don't get is why she'd think I'd encourage my sister to get pregnant out of wedlock?" Anger flared. "I'd have to hate my sister to do that. And I certainly don't hate Dory."

Leigh hadn't been able to bring herself to tell her mother that the baby's father was married to someone else. As it was, just the out-of-wedlock pregnancy had been enough to turn Bette away from her.

Chloe reached over and put her hand on Leigh's. "Your mother is suffering, mourning, too. She's lost Ted, remember. And your mother sometimes acts angry when she is really more worried and upset than anything. She wanted everything to be perfect for you, and life isn't cooperating."

Leigh didn't want to disagree with her grandmother, but it seemed to her that Bette had never been happy with her. Why did Leigh have to lose her stepfather along with Dane? She could have used Ted's help in bridging this gap between her mother and her. But he was gone and her mother had made it clear—without saying a word—that if Leigh wouldn't give up her child, Bette would give up Leigh.

Two days later, Kitty returned to New York City with Leigh. After looking over Leigh's apartment, she made arrangements to have some of her furniture moved from the San Francisco townhouse. The rest was put into storage, and the townhouse was given to a rental agent to manage. Until the furniture arrived, Kitty was sleeping on Leigh's new bed, and Leigh was back at Nancy's apartment, which was just below hers, on the sofa. And back to work.

The next day, Leigh returned home from interviewing women trying to get apprenticed to unions in New York City about the discrimination they were fighting. Through the dark, early winter night, she headed home, bundled up with her fur hat and lined gloves. It was her night to cook, so she stopped on the way home and picked up Chinese at their favorite restaurant in the neighborhood.

Over the past few weeks, she'd found that she did tire more easily, though she'd decided not to mention it to anyone. She was going to be a single mother. She might as well get used to the fact that her life had changed.

She entered Nancy's apartment. Kitty was already there, beaming at her like Christmas had come again. "I just got off the phone. I've already signed us up for Lamaze classes!"

"Lamaze?" Leigh echoed, not prepared for this.

"Yes, modern, natural childbirth," Kitty enthused. "They say it's all the rage."

Nancy stepped out of the bathroom. "Yeah, you don't want to have your kid the old-fashioned way, do you?"

I guess I don't have a choice. "Right. I got Chinese." Anyway, Aunt Kitty's enthusiasm was contagious, and Chloe had confided to Leigh that maybe Kitty needed to do this to put some demons of her own to rest. After all, Chloe felt that Kitty still struggled with guilt over giving up Thompson. Leigh tried to visualize what Aunt Kitty had gone through in the 1930s as an unwed mother and felt a rush of love and compassion for her grandfather's little sister.

July 29, 1973

Aunt Kitty sat on the green mat on the floor at the Lamaze class next to Leigh. "You're doing great, honey. Breathe in, now out."

Lying on her back and gazing at her focus point, Leigh didn't know if she agreed with Kitty. When would this pregnancy ever end?

The instructor, a young woman with long, straw-colored hair who wore jeans and a white T-shirt, looked at the clock. "Now remember at the end of your labor, you will get the urge to push. But don't push until you're fully dilated to ten or you could tear the perineum. At that stage, when you get the urge to push, blow. You can't push at both ends at once."

The class, which consisted primarily of couples, chuckled. Leigh had been grateful to find that two other women classmates had brought female relatives like Leigh had. She wondered if any of the other women were as nervous as she secretly was.

"Well, that's our last lesson," the instructor said. "I'll expect each of you to contact me after you deliver. I always love to come and see 'my' babies."

Kitty helped Leigh up and then rolled up the avocado-green exercise mat. Leigh looked down and couldn't see her slightly swollen feet. She had about ten days to go until her due date. She rubbed the ache in her lower back and was glad it was summer and she could wear sandals. She couldn't imagine trying to wear real shoes right now.

As she and Aunty waited their turn to say farewell to their instructor, the baby started kicking with both feet on the right side of Leigh's abdomen. When the baby had dropped and engaged a month before, it had evidently landed on one side and now didn't have room to turn over. At times like this, Leigh felt like the baby was complaining about the cramped conditions. Leigh pressed against the painful rhythm.

Finally, they bid the instructor farewell and then, calling good luck to the others, they headed for the subway and the short ride home. Well, ready or not, Leigh didn't have much longer to wait. *And then I'll be a mother.* As usual, she tried not to think too much about what the birth process was really going to be like.

It was still light out when they walked into their apartment and found Grandma Chloe waiting for them. Worried that Leigh might need her earlier than expected, she'd called and said she'd decided to come early and stay with the Loveladys until Leigh delivered. Leigh hurried over and threw her arms around her grandmother's neck. "Oh, I'm so glad you came. So glad!"

Kitty hugged Chloe, and then Nancy unlocked the door with her key and came in. "I could hear you squealing through my ceiling. It sounded like all of you were having fun without me. No fair!"

"I'll pour us some iced tea," Leigh said as she moved into the small alcove that was her kitchen. She opened the refrigerator—and then stood stock still in shock. The three women behind her chattered away while she stood there contrasting how she'd thought the delivery would start—and how it actually had.

"Where's that iced tea?" Nancy asked.

Leigh turned. Fluid was trickling down her legs. She had to clear her throat to reply. "I've . . . I'm . . . I think my water just broke. I'll get the mop." But she didn't move.

"Mop!" Chloe moved to her. "We'll get you cleaned up. Are you sure I can't persuade you to go to the hospital? I just don't feel right about this midwife thing."

"Now don't upset her," Kitty said, shaking her finger. "The midwife will have a doctor on call in case of emergency, and the hospital's only ten minutes away." She came and took Leigh's arm. "Nancy, you call the midwife. Chloe, you mop up that puddle. I'll get Leigh changed into a clean summer nightie."

Leigh was relieved to be told what to do and so happy that her grandmother had come early. *My baby is coming*. The thought filled her with awe, fear, and relief. Her pregnancy was ending.

* * *

Within an hour, the midwife, a plump thirtyish mother of three, arrived. Eight and a half hours later, she told Leigh she could stop blowing and start pushing.

Chloe watched as her granddaughter gave birth to her great-granddaughter. The years rolled back for Chloe as she remembered giving birth to Bette and Bette giving birth to Linda Leigh. Now another generation had been born. *How can I be seventy-two years old and a great-grandmother?* And then tears moistened her eyes as she wished Roarke could have been here. And Ted and Dane. *This should have been Dane's baby, Lord.*

But this little one wasn't. And the wayward father didn't even know about the sweet little girl. The midwife handed Chloe the naked, squalling baby. And Chloe took her to the nearby plastic basin in the kitchen sink and gave her great-granddaughter her first bath, just as Jerusha had bathed Bette and she and Jerusha had bathed Leigh. Kitty hung over Chloe's shoulder, watching, cooing. Then the two of them carried the baby, clean and dressed in a pale-yellow newborn gown, over and laid the child in Leigh's arms. "She's beautiful," Chloe said.

"She's outstanding," Kitty said.

"She's here." Nancy yawned.

Leigh couldn't believe that the ordeal was over. The Lamaze classes had prepared her, but going through childbirth had not been what she expected. Now she fully understood why they called labor, "labor." She felt as if she'd been dragging stones large enough for a pyramid.

All that fell away, though, when she looked down. Tears hovered close as she gazed at her precious little daughter. *I'll never make you feel unloved, my darling.*

The women around her, the ones she loved, cooed and patted the baby. The midwife said in a crisp voice that a nurse would be coming in the morning to check on Leigh and the newborn, to call the hospital if anything came up. Then she left, waving good-bye.

"What have you decided to name her?" Chloe asked.

This was something Leigh had given a great deal of thought. "I'm going to name her Carlyle Leigh Sinclair."

"Carlyle? My mother's family name?" Chloe asked.

Leigh saw that her grandmother didn't want to say she didn't like the name.

"Yes," Leigh explained, "because even if my mother wants to deny she exists, she's the next generation."

Chloe squeezed her granddaughter's shoulder. "Don't be bitter, honey. Bitterness is poison."

"I'm not bitter. I've put it into perspective," Leigh said, though her mother's cool treatment of her over the pregnancy still pained her. "Our family carries on in spite of all the changes, all the wars, all the political stuff like Watergate. Ivy Manor still stands, and I'll stand, too."

"Of course, you will." Kitty sat down on the edge of the bed. "And so will we."

As Leigh struggled against the sudden weariness that overtook her, a knock came at the door. "Who could that be at nearly 6:00 a.m.?" Kitty commented as she went to the door and opened it. "Dory!"

Chloe and Leigh turned to see Leigh's younger sister enter. She was wearing jeans and a yellow T-shirt and carrying a duffle bag.

"Oh, the baby!" Dory squealed, rushing forward. "You had the baby!"

"Dory!" Leigh felt her heart lift, buoyant and refreshed.

"Dory, what are you doing here at this time of the morning?" Chloe scolded. "Where's your mother?"

A policeman stepped inside. All together, the older

women gasped. Leigh, disbelieving, tried to cover herself and her daughter. Dory ignored them all and bent to look at her niece.

The officer stopped short, obviously embarrassed at having walked into such an intimate scene. Backing up a pace, he stood by the door and cleared his throat. "Dory, is this your sister?" He gestured at Leigh, who was still shocked to see a stranger standing in front of her birthing bed.

Dory nodded, cooing over the baby.

Leigh finally found her voice. "She's my sister," she replied faintly.

"She's my granddaughter," Chloe said.

"She's my great-niece," Kitty crowed. "And this, Dory, is your little niece, Carly."

"Cool," Dory crowed. "She's so cool."

Leigh continued to stare at the policeman—the handsome, auburn-haired policeman. Her hand absently smoothed her hair and pulled the bed sheets closer to her chest. "What's going on?" she asked. "Dory?"

The policeman nodded, looking as if he were drawing up his professionalism for this occasion. Leigh could see, though, how his eyes softened as he looked at her and the new infant in her arms. "We picked up your sister at the train station. We routinely pick up a lot of runaways there."

Carly suddenly whimpered, and the policeman, along with everyone else in the room, smiled. Leigh felt his kind eyes move over her and her child, and suddenly she didn't mind his attention. He looked like he liked babies.

"I told them I wasn't running away," Dory declared suddenly, raising up and giving her grandmother a wary eye. "I was just coming to see my sister. But they wouldn't believe me so they drove me here."

Leigh knew her mother would never have let Dory travel

alone to New York City, especially not to see her sister and her sister's illegitimate child. So she was sure that Dory had, in a sense, run away. Well, that was their mother's fault, one she'd never learned to stop. But this policeman didn't need to know all the details.

"Thank you, officer. We didn't realize Dory was coming this early, or one of us would have met her at the station. But as you can see, even coming early, she missed the grand entrance of our newest family member."

"Bummer," Dory said.

The policeman looked at each of the women in turn, obviously uneasy, but unwilling to pursue it further. Finally, he smiled. "Well, I'll be going then. Congratulations." He nodded to Leigh and walked out the door.

As the rest of the women descended upon Dory demanding explanations, Leigh stared at the closed door and thought about the man who'd suddenly been thrust into her life, however briefly. She thought of his eyes, the softness that had come over them as he looked at her and Carly. She couldn't help herself from the unexpected, wistful thought, *Why couldn't I have fallen for someone nice like that?*

Six weeks later, in early autumn, Leigh headed down the street toward the subway station. Back into her pre-pregnancy skirt size, she was almost feeling normal again, and she was starting to go in for half days this week. She hoped to be full-time again at the magazine by the time Carly was two months old.

"Leigh." Without warning, a familiar, but upsetting voice summoned her from behind. She turned and there he was. Trent Kinnard. The shock was overwhelming, especially her physical reaction. Images from their one night together flooded her consciousness. She nearly reached for him, but then she turned to run.

Before she could take a step, he caught her wrist. "We need to talk. Let's go somewhere for coffee."

"I don't want to talk to you." She pulled from his loose grasp as if his hands were unclean. "We don't have anything to discuss."

"Yes, we do." He looked angry with her. "Do you think I don't know that you just had my baby? I can count to nine, you know."

She stared at him, her heart pounding so hard it made her nauseated. "How did you find me?"

"When you dropped out of my life last fall, I hired a PI to find you. It wasn't hard, and he's sent me reports about you every week. When our baby—"

"*My* baby—just *mine*. I don't want or need to have anything to do with you." She swept him away with her hand.

"Why? Leigh, I thought we had the start of something good—"

"Good?" *You have gall, all right.* "I didn't know you were married. I don't *do* affairs with married men. You can't imagine how I felt . . ." Her throat started to close up on her. "I've never been so insulted, so humiliated."

She paused to calm herself so she could breathe. All the things she'd wanted to scream at him over the lonely months since last November clamored to be unleashed. She suppressed them. She didn't want him, couldn't let him know how much he'd hurt her. "I don't want anything to do with you." She looked down at the broken sidewalk.

Trent moved closer. "Would it make any difference," he said, urgent and low, "if I told you that now I know I'm in love with you? I've been miserable every day since you walked away. Doesn't that count for anything?"

"No, it doesn't." She wanted to hit him. How dare he try that line on her? Didn't the man know when to give up? "You should have realized that I wasn't what you thought I was. You knew . . ." She refused to continue.

"I knew that I was the first, and yes, now I see that should have caught my attention. But it didn't at the time." He paused as if trying to come up with words. "Please, can't we work out *something* between us?"

"No. You're a married man. I'll take my share of blame for what happened that night, but my defense is naiveté. What's yours?"

He had the grace to hang his head, chagrined. "I can't divorce—"

"I'm not asking you to," Leigh tossed at him. "*I* didn't come looking for *you*, did I? And you don't have to worry about a paternity suit. I want nothing from you." Fearing she might burst into tears or start screaming, she whirled away. "Good-bye."

"Leigh!" He called her name once and then subsided.

She ran from him to the subway steps. As she hurried down the stairs, her heart felt as if it would burst with the pain, the guilt. *God, forgive me. Help me. Don't let any of this hurt my sweet child.*

Part Two

CHAPTER FIFTEEN

New York City, November 12, 1983

Leigh didn't like visiting police stations. Ever since Chicago in '68, she'd despised the decaying institutional decor and the sweaty, musty smell, which could have been bottled as "Old Police Station" to men with very odd taste in cologne. But now she had pinned a bright and engaging smile on her face and not even the old dinosaur in uniform sitting across from her would wipe it from her face.

She was here to get what she needed for a story, and she wouldn't let anything stop her. "But Captain Dorsey," she said, not betraying her frustration, "I'm not doing an exposé on the NYPD. I just want some leads on the new trend of girls joining gangs or forming their own."

He snorted. "And I keep tellin' ya. It isn't new, and we don't want you encouraging gang activity of any kind."

"I'm not encouraging it. I just want to write about it and try to stop it."

"You—" He pointed his ballpoint pen at her. "—write

about it and it gets publicized, and you'll end up making it even more popular."

She felt like hitting him in the head with a two-by-four. But it would probably take more than that to get through to this man. "Well," she said, rising and holding out her hand, her false smile holding, "I won't take up any more of your time then. Thank you for your help." *Or lack thereof.*

He stood and shook her hand with his large paw. "You be careful. A pretty woman like you shouldn't be messin' around with gangs. It could be very dangerous. You're out of your league, lady."

Now in her mid-thirties, Leigh was inured to the compliment he paid her. For once, she wished a man wouldn't feel he had to tell her how pretty he thought she was. To be honest, she had traded on her good looks to get information—but only when no other way was open to her. And today she'd dressed in a stylish black suit with a flared skirt and had left her hair down, knowing she would be trying to get what she needed from a man.

After expressing her empty gratitude, she flashed a charming smile at him—who knew when she might need him or someone he knew to help her on another story—and then exited. As she walked down the narrow hallway back to the entrance, a broad-shouldered man brushed against her. She got a tantalizing whiff of his English Leather. She leaned away from him, unaccountably irritated.

But then she felt him slip something into the outside pocket of her suit jacket. She gave him a startled look, and he gave her the slightest shake of the head as if to stop her from speaking. She gave him a nod and went on outside.

A block away, she pulled out the business card he'd slipped into her pocket. It gave his name, his rank as a plainclothes detective, and contact information. She turned it over and in ink, he'd written: "Call me."

Ten-year-old Carly, in a plaid winter coat over her white ballet tights and pink Care Bear boots, was waiting for her. Leigh approached the poorly lit doorway of the dance studio where Carly went with friends after school for tap and ballet. Her expression broadcast that she was vexed with her mother again.

"Don't look so growly at me. I just proved I *can* get here on time," Leigh said as she smoothed wisps of her daughter's long black hair away from her pretty, oval face.

Carly looked up, her gray eyes serious as always. "I was afraid you weren't going to be, and I don't like it when I'm the last one picked up."

Yes, lay the guilt trip on me. "I know, but today you weren't. I really try to get here early, but sometimes things happen. You know what to do when I'm delayed, right?"

"Yes, I'm supposed to wait inside the doorway until you come," Carly recited as she walked alongside her mother toward the subway station. "But I don't like being last. Everybody walks by me and asks me why I'm standing there."

Leigh only half listened to her daughter's oft-expressed complaint. The business card in her pocket kept generating questions. Who was Nate Gallagher, beyond the fact that he was a plainclothes detective with a face that looked like it grinned a lot? Why did he want her to call him? Was it professional, or was he just using a unique pickup line? She hoped it wasn't the latter. But if it were, she was experienced in keeping men at a distance. In fact, by now she had perfected rejecting unwelcome advances—or any advances really—to a fine art. She'd decided she was busy enough with work and Carly. Men took up too much of a woman's time.

Now, she leaned down, kissed her daughter's head, and then took her gloved hand. "I won't be late again. Promise."

"When's Grandma Chloe coming?" Carly gave a little skip. "She's still coming to my recital?" Carly always needed reassurance about family visits. It was as if she couldn't trust that family really *was* coming.

"I told you," Leigh admonished her, hurrying against the cutting wind, "Grandma Chloe and Grandma Bette are coming the Friday night before your recital."

"Isn't Aunt Dory coming, too?"

"No, she can't come, honey. She's going to be in Africa with the Peace Corps by then."

"Mama, how come I don't got any uncles?"

Where had that question come from? "Because I only had a sister. And it's 'have,' not 'got.' "

"Didn't my daddy have any brothers?"

Leigh stilled inside. Every once in a while, Carly brought up "her daddy." Her little girl had figured out at the tender age of three that children were supposed to have a mommy and a daddy. And then she'd promptly demanded to know where her daddy was. Had he gotten lost somewhere?

Leigh never knew how to answer these questions. She had never told Carly anything about her father except that he couldn't live with them. She hadn't wanted to lie to her own daughter, but neither could she tell her the nasty truth. So the forbidden topic remained wedged between her and her daughter. At these moments, guilt was a dull blade sawing, gouging her spirit.

Now Leigh did what she always did—she ignored the question. *I do my best for you, my sweet child. But all my choices are second-best. I didn't choose your father well. I'm to blame.*

Carly glanced up at her, studied her, and then wordlessly accepted that Leigh once again was not going to answer her question. She changed topics. "And Aunt Kitty's taking us all out to dinner afterward?"

Leigh was happy to answer this one. "Yes, Aunt Kitty is taking all of us to her favorite French restaurant to celebrate the occasion." Shivering, Leigh tugged Carly's hand, and they both ran the last gloomy block to the subway. When Carly had been around a year old, Aunt Kitty—now in her early eighties just as Grandma Chloe was—had sold her townhouse in San Francisco and bought a two-apartment building near them. The much-loved older woman had become an indispensable part of Leigh and Carly's everyday life.

As they boarded the subway train, her daughter prattled on about her friend Katy and the dance recital. Swaying with the motion of the train, Leigh answered automatically while the focus of her mind remained on why the detective wanted her to call him.

Later that evening, after supper at Kitty's apartment and tucking Carly into bed back at home, Leigh dialed Nate Gallagher's number. She tingled with anticipation while it rang and rang. No answer. Disappointed, Leigh put back the receiver and walked to the kitchen to boil water for a cup of herbal tea. Soon she took her warm mug of cinnamon-apple tea and stood by the window, watching the street below. Had her anticipation as she dialed been from the hope she'd get help with the article or because of her memory of his enticing masculinity?

Below her window by the light of the streetlamps, a

young couple was walking down the street holding hands. She sipped the hot tea, trying to deny the restlessness that sometimes stirred inside her. Another evening home alone. Would she ever meet someone she trusted enough to love, or would she end up like Kitty and live alone for most of her life?

From there her mind went back to the day's question: What did Nate Gallagher want? But his face lingered longer in her mind than her question.

Two days later, around three in the afternoon of another chilly day, Leigh shifted from one cold foot to the other at the corner of a street of small stores with caged fronts. She was waiting for Gallagher as arranged. He'd said the meeting had to do with her article, but had hung up before she could ask him how he even knew about the piece. She hoped he was going to offer her help, and she'd find out soon enough. That's all she wanted from him.

The scarred and dirty street where she waited was near a rough area of Brooklyn, Bedford-Stuyvesant. Pulling her scarf up around her freezing ears, Leigh kept a wary eye out for trouble and gripped a can of Mace in her pocket. A dark-blue sedan slowed and stopped in front of her. From the driver's side, Gallagher leaned over and pushed open the passenger's side door and motioned for her to get in.

Studying him swiftly, Leigh slid inside and hooked her seat belt. "Hi." She'd remembered Nate Gallagher accurately. With a head of auburn hair, he looked to be of medium height and was solidly built. He was a man you'd like at your side in a fight. But his clean, blue eyes had laugh crinkles around them and that reassured her.

"Hi." He kept his eyes on the tricky traffic on the narrow

street. "I thought we'd drive around in Bedford-Sty to give you a firsthand look at some gang territory. And while I drive, you tell me exactly what you're looking for on your article about girls and gangs."

She considered this, still guarded. "May I ask you two questions first?"

He gave her a sidelong glance. "Sure."

"How did you know what I was working on? And what's in this for you?"

He grinned. "Easy answers. Someone at the station let me know who you were and why you were talking to Dorsey. Second, I'm directly concerned about gang activity, especially recruitment. I've volunteered to work with city agencies to try to come up with coordinated strategies to fight this. I wondered why the department didn't refer you to me instead of Dorsey."

She liked his grin, but kept herself on task. She could think of one reason for her being handed to Dorsey. The city didn't want a reporter horning in on what it considered *its* territory; municipal bureaucrats always feared uncomplimentary news coverage, and misdirection was a popular tactic. But she didn't voice this. She merely shrugged as she noted pinpoint snowflakes floating onto the windshield.

"I figured we're on the same side," Gallagher continued, "and an article by Leigh Sinclair could go a long way in convincing the city fathers to allocate more funds for this type of prevention program."

"Well . . ." She was a little taken aback at his reference to her name, as if he were aware of her writing. *Probably not.* "I'm glad to find an ally."

"Same here. Now I'm going to point out some hot spots of gang life. But first you must promise me—*on your honor*—that you will not ever—never—come here as a lone pedestrian and walk these streets without me." He gave her a long look and then turned right at another corner.

The way he said this warning sent a chill through her. This was a man who would not make light of danger, so if he put it that way, he meant business. But she was already aware of how dangerous gangs could be. *I read the newspapers, Gallagher*. But he didn't know her. "I'm not a daredevil. I have a daughter I'm raising alone, and I don't take chances with my safety. That's why I sought NYPD assistance in the first place."

"Great. I thought you looked smart." He grinned again.

She ignored its effect on her as best she could and thought it was a nice change that he'd referred to her intelligence not her looks.

After a brief tour of the area's hot spots, Nate drove her out of Bedford-Sty and took her to a small café beside a large Roman Catholic Church in whose small lot he parked. The snow was falling faster now. In the homey café, he waved to the waitress behind the counter. "Two coffees, please." Stopping at the rear booth, he motioned Leigh to take a seat.

He'd acted like he knew the waitress, and she'd given him a very flirty smile. Leigh was irritated with herself for noticing all this. Distancing herself, she shook the snow off her black muffler, sat down, and took out the steno pad and fine-line blue marker she always carried. "Okay. Tell me what your observations have been about girls and gangs."

He grinned. "I do like a woman who knows what she wants."

I'll bet you do. But what if the woman doesn't know what she wants?

*   *   *

Two days later, Leigh sat in a nondescript yet grim-looking visiting room at "Juvey" or Juvenile Hall. She was nervous, but it was a good type of nervousness. She was ready for the group interview she was about to do, and her article was shaping up nicely.

As she watched, a forbidding uniformed matron ushered three teenaged Latino girls into the room. A tall, slender girl led them to the table, followed by a plump girl with teased hair and a petite girl with curly hair. They sat down in that order facing her.

She was visible to them, but Nate, who stood on the other side of a one-way mirror behind her, wasn't. Feeling his gaze on her, she resisted the urge to turn around and look at him.

None of the three girls would meet her eyes. The sound of voices from the floor above them filled the silence. "Hello," she began, trying to put them at ease. "Thank you for agreeing to talk to me."

"What you give us for talkin' to you, lady?" the tallest girl challenged her. She pronounced "you" like "chew."

"I'm giving you the chance to have your opinions printed in a magazine."

"What ma-ga-zine?" the petite girl with short, curly hair taunted, looking pouty.

"I write for *Women Today*."

The three girls exchanged looks. "We never heard of it."

Leigh hid a smile. She was used to this kind of sparring with some of her interview subjects. "If you don't want to talk to me," she said without inflection, "I'll ring for the matron, and you can go back to whatever exciting activity you three were enjoying."

That did the trick. The three girls began telling Leigh how and why they had joined a new gang that would take girls. "We thought it would be kind of cool, you know?" the tall girl said. "But then we find out the guys don't let any of the girls call the shots, you know?"

Leigh was finding the girl's repetition of "chew know?" annoying but she went on taking notes. "So what you're saying is that it was the same old male-dominance thing?"

"Male what?" Once Leigh explained the term, the girl agreed. "Yeah, but once you're in, it's scary to get out, you know?"

"Yeah, we know stuff and how do they know we don't tell," the petite girl explained, one palm up.

"So we're stuck," the plump girl finished and snapped her chewing gum.

"What would it take for you to get out of the gang?" Leigh asked, jotting notes.

"No way, lady." The tall girl spoke, but all three shook their heads. "No can do." The matron appeared at the door and cleared her throat authoritatively.

"How long will you three be in Juvenile Hall?" Leigh asked.

Each of them shrugged. "Talk to our lawyer," the tall girl said. Then the three stood and shuffled out without another word.

When they were gone, Nate opened a door and joined her. "How about tomorrow we go and cruise their neighborhood?"

Leigh frowned, irritated that the interview was over so soon, more irritated that when Nate walked in, her whole body hummed with awareness. *I have to get done with this article fast.* "Where would you like me to meet you?" she asked coolly.

"I'll pick you up in front of your apartment."

No, I don't think so. She kept men away from her apartment, away from her private life. "I don't know—"

"I know where you live so I might as well." He had the nerve to grin at her.

She gave him a miffed look. "Did you have me investigated?"

"No, I did it myself. You're thirty-six, originally from Arlington, Virginia," he recited, his blue eyes, crinkling, gleaming with amusement. "Your stepfather was FBI, and your mother was CIA. You have a daughter named Carly—"

She didn't trust his obvious interest in her. "I know all about myself," she interrupted, halting him. "Thank you," she added repressively.

Still smiling, he led her to the door and opened it. "And try not to look like a reporter tomorrow, okay?"

She made a face and walked from the room. But his honest, teasing grin lingered in her mind, tantalizing.

The next afternoon, Leigh and Nate walked through the neighborhood where the girls she'd interviewed had lived. And Leigh was more than glad she had Nate at her side. In fact, she had to fight the urge to grip his arm.

On a personal level, the sights depressed her. Garbage dribbled out of alleys. Ripped-up newspaper and candy wrappers clogged the bottom of every fence. Windows were boarded up, and starved-looking dogs sniffed crumpled fast-food bags along the sidewalk.

Large, white-haired women who reminded her of Jerusha looked out through cracked, patched windows, and old men like shriveled tobacco leaves sat on the curb drinking from paper bags. Idle men slouched, smoking in doorways of buildings old and scarred. The leering looks they gave her made her feel dirty, slimy.

Elsewhere, gang members congregated around the entrances to pool halls or bars, strutting and preening like prides of young lions. They gave Leigh "the eye," and again she was glad Nate was with her. Men often were a nuisance to her, but she had a feeling that these could become more than a mere nuisance.

On a professional level, Leigh was at her best, her mind acting like a camera, recording every sight and every sound. Words and phrases mushroomed in her mind, and she filed them all away for later use.

One pride of gang members followed her and Nate for several blocks, probably indulging in aimless intimidation. The hair on the back of her neck prickling, she tensed, but Nate acted as if nothing were happening. After a while, they drifted off into an alley, and she breathed easy again.

Finally, they returned to civilization. As she and Nate were getting out of the subway near her apartment, Leigh caught herself just as she was about to say, "Nate, why don't you come in for coffee?" That surprised her. She'd never invited a man inside before. *And I won't start now.*

But unable to force herself to bring their conversation to an end, she stood talking to him about what they'd seen. Before she knew it, Carly was coming home with her best friend—red-haired and freckled Katy. "Hi," Carly said, looking up at Nate and assessing him. "I'm Carly."

Leigh took her daughter's hand, and even as she introduced the two of them, she was urging her daughter up the steps into their apartment building. Looking thoughtful, Nate took the hint, waved, and left.

Carly looked back as he walked away, tugging against Leigh. "Is that your boyfriend?"

"No." She'd be careful next time and watch her timing better. She didn't need Carly getting the wrong idea. She and Nate were just working on an article together. And had they even discussed a "next time"? This might have been their last meeting.

Carly stopped in the narrow vestibule. "Why don't you ever have boyfriends? Katy says that if I don't have a daddy, you gotta have a boyfriend."

"How was school today?" Leigh asked, totally ignoring her daughter's words and hoping this wasn't the last time she'd see Nate Gallagher. Even though that probably would be best. For one second, she longed to do what wasn't best, but to do what she wanted.

She wanted to kiss Nate Gallagher.

"Was my daddy your boyfriend?" Carly looked up at her intently.

Like icy water splashed down her spine, her daughter's question immediately quenched all thought of kissing Nate.

"And if you and him aren't dating anymore," Carly went on, "why can't you get another boyfriend? Katy says you're pretty. All the girls think I have the prettiest mom—"

"That's nice," Leigh cut in, her heart beating fast. The whole topic of boyfriends had the power to panic Leigh. She was unlucky in love. She'd found that out the hard way. And her daughter was only ten. What did she know about boyfriends? Or need to know? "What do you want for supper?"

Carly looked into Leigh's eyes for a long moment and then subsided. Her shoulders down, she stomped up the steps without looking back. Her body language broadcast her dissatisfaction with her mother's lack of candor.

Leigh's heart split in two for her daughter. *I'm sorry, Carly. I'll explain everything when you're old enough to understand. I can't tell you the truth yet. The truth could damage you more than my silence. I will tell you when the time is right. Promise.*

November 22, 1983

$\mathcal{L}$eigh kept her eye on the wall clock in the dingy office. It was Friday afternoon, and she had to be on time to pick up Carly after dance. But she still had a few minutes to complete this interview. After she'd finished her article into the facts of gang activity in New York City, she'd decided to delve into what was being done to combat it. Nate had given her the names and phone numbers of some community groups that were working with gang members who wanted to get out. This one was funded by churches and supported a live-in shelter for the "lost."

"So you see, we are trying to use the love of Christ," the earnest young black man explained, "to help these young people whose lives are taking them straight toward early graves or life in prison."

"Have you had much success?" Her pen poised over her faithful steno pad.

"Many. Would you like to speak to one whose life this ministry turned around?"

"Sure. When could I—"

"Right now. Here I am." The young man grinned at her. "I've been clean for four years now. I became a heroine addict when I was only fifteen."

Leigh's eyes widened.

"And there's someone who recognized your name when you called for an interview. Would you like to talk to her, too? Her story is quite remarkable."

Something in the young man's tone of voice alerted her to expect something or someone that would surprise her. But after years of interviewing, she was very hard to surprise, as he would find out. "Of course."

He went to the door and opened it. "Ms. Sinclair says

she'd like to talk to you, too." He stepped back and ushered in a plump woman with short brown hair, wire-rim glasses, and a dark skirt and blouse.

The shock of recognition shook Leigh to her core; her pen dropped to the floor. She gawked. "*Mary Beth?*"

Mary Beth closed the distance between them. "Leigh, oh, Leigh, it *is* you."

Quivering, Leigh rose and opened her arms. Mary Beth wrapped hers around Leigh, too. Minutes passed as Leigh hugged and was hugged. Tears flowed and were ignored. It was a time of unadulterated joy, of release, of cleansing.

Finally, Leigh wiped her cheeks with her hands and staggered back onto her chair. "I have to sit down. I feel weak. Why didn't you warn me?"

Mary Beth sat in another straight chair opposite her, beaming at her. "I just couldn't. It was like if I'd let you know I worked here, I'd have chickened out again today. Many times I've almost called your mother to find out where you were living. But I always . . . I couldn't get past the last time I saw you. I was so wasted on drugs and felt so lost—"

"Why did you leave?" Leigh asked, dabbing around her eyes trying to wipe away her smeared mascara. "I wanted to help you."

"I wasn't ready to be helped," Mary Beth said simply. "A drug addict has to be at the point of no return. I was still playing out my 'counterculture, self-destructive, rebel-with-a-cause' premise. Two years later, I woke up from a bad acid trip that must have lasted for days. A woman was sitting beside my bed at a Salvation Army shelter. She was holding my hand and praying out loud.

"I lay there and listened to her praying so urgently, so lovingly, for me—a stranger, a drug addict, a failure. Something snapped into place in my mind. I didn't want to die.

And I wanted to know how a stranger could love me that much."

Mary Beth shrugged and made a wry face. "I'd never even been to church, you know. My parents were agnostics. I'd never heard about the love of God for sinners like me, the chance to be born again."

Leigh tried to put this Mary Beth with the Mary Beth who'd stolen money from her in San Francisco and then with the girl she'd attended high school with and shook her head. "I just can't believe this. How long have you been in New York City?"

"Almost five years now. I stayed at the Salvation Army until I was clean from drugs for over a year. Then as a new Jesus freak—" Mary Beth gave one of her puppy-dog grins. "—I signed up with Campus Crusade for Christ and began working on campuses in California, one-on-one with kids starting to make the same mistake I did. I met another CCC staff member at a conference." Mary Beth blushed. "We fell in love, and we married."

"I'm so happy for you, Mary Beth." Leigh had given up on ever seeing her friend again. Kitty would be thrilled and so would Cherise. "When can you come—" Then she glanced at the clock. And felt her stomach contract with guilt pangs. *Oh, no.* "Mary Beth, I've got to run. I'm going to be late picking up my daughter from her dance lessons. I promised I wouldn't be late." Leigh leaped up. "Call me. I gave the young man my card."

Outside, Leigh grabbed the first taxi and rode it to the nearest subway, and then she was on her way to the dance studio. She fretted as her watch ticked away the minutes, and she began preparing her excuse and how to repay her daughter for being later than she ever had before. She ran all the way from the subway station and reached the dance studio.

The silent, dark, locked-up studio where Carly was nowhere to be seen.

It was like a nightmare. She tried the door. It was locked up tight. She called her daughter's name. She ran along the block looking into doorways. She finally stopped at the phone booth on the corner and dialed Katy's number. *Dear God, let her have gone home with Katy's mom.* "Hi, this is Leigh. I'm sorry I was late again. Is Carly with you?"

"No," Katy's mom said, "Katy was sick today and didn't go to school or dance. Is something wrong?"

Leigh's heart thundered, and she hung up. Faintness made her sway.

Chapter Sixteen

*L*eigh stood petrified, insensate. Finally, her mind eased back to consciousness. *What do I do now? What do I do now?*

She left the phone booth and wandered down the block again, directionless. *This can't be happening. No.* "Carly," she called again and then more urgently, *"Carly!"* It was dark now and cold. Shivering, Leigh felt hysteria lurking just behind her throat. In a moment, she'd be screaming and screaming—panicked—out of control . . .

Then Nate's face came to mind. She ran back to the phone. Within seconds, the line was ringing. *Please pick up. Please pick up. Please—*

"Gallagher here."

"Nate," she gasped, shuddering, "it's . . . Leigh."

"What's wrong?" he demanded.

"I . . . can't find Carly."

"Your little girl?"

"Yes," she replied and began weeping, cold tears sliding down her face. "I'm so frightened," she wailed, "I can't think—"

"Where are you?"

She had to pause to remember, and then she gave him the dance studio's address.

"Could your daughter have gone home with a friend?"

"Her friend didn't go to dance today." His calm businesslike manner and questions were helping her focus. "She's home sick."

"Is there any chance that she might have gone home with someone else or the dance teacher?"

"I don't know. That wouldn't be normal. I don't know."

"Wait at the entrance of the dance studio. I'll come and look over the situation, and we'll go from there."

"*Thank you.*" She hung up and stood, clinging to the telephone, gasping as if she'd been running. People passed by, bundled up, hurrying home. She watched them, envying them. Finally, she pulled herself together enough to return to the entrance. Alone on the bleak and windy street, she began silently reciting the Twenty-third Psalm.

If someone had asked her this morning, she would have said she didn't even remember more than its beginning, "The Lord is my shepherd." But now the words came to her, lifting her onto their strong, comforting shoulders. God would help her. Grandma Chloe had always said so. And she needed to believe that now, to believe in Him *now.* "Though I walk through the valley of the shadow of death, I will fear no evil."

Carly, please, I hope you've just been disobedient and have gone home with a friend without telling me. Please. Please, God, let this just be naughtiness.

It was past midnight. Leigh sat at her kitchen table, a cold mug of tea untouched in front of her. In the living room, Aunt Kitty had finally fallen asleep in a recliner under a crocheted afghan. Nate was on the phone again. The three of them had spent the evening calling all of Carly's friends, the owner of the dance studio, the dance teacher, Carly's principal. And they'd found out nothing except that the dance teacher had left before Carly was picked up. She'd had a doctor's appointment. So Carly had been left waiting for Leigh, not in the studio vestibule, but outside, on the street.

Nate hung up at the end of another long phone call and then stretched his shoulders. "I've done all I can." He gripped the back of the chair across from her. "Unfortunately, the law says that Carly isn't missing until she's been gone for twenty-four hours."

"She could be taken to another country in twenty-four hours," Leigh railed, sour and aching. "What's wrong with people? This isn't the horse-and-buggy days. If she was taken and put on a plane, she could be in *China* by then." Her self-control was spinning . . . lurching.

Nate came to her and squeezed her shoulder, steadying her. "I know. The law needs to be changed in the case of children. But right now we're stuck with it. Fortunately, my family has been part of the NYPD for three generations, and I have a lot of friends. I've called in favors, and tonight *unofficially* almost every cop who's cruising is looking for Carly. An unofficial APB. My dad called a friend in the New York State Police and did the same thing. On the Q-T, every state cop is watching for a little girl with long, dark hair named Carly. We have to have faith that she'll be found."

Gratitude to Nate gushed up like a geyser inside her. She sprang up and threw her arms around his neck, the weeping she'd held back for hours bursting forth. Rock steady, he held her as she cried until she couldn't weep another tear.

When she could speak again, she couldn't stop herself from repeating the same phrases she'd said all evening, "It's not a bad neighborhood. It wasn't dark yet. She should have been fine. I was only ten minutes late."

"Stop torturing yourself." Nate held her close. She felt the stubble of new beard growth against her forehead. "You didn't cause this. Kids are snatched sometimes right off their front steps with their mothers watching from a window."

"What do you think has happened to my daughter?" she whispered her deepest fear. As she rested her head on his shoulder, she found it was just the right height for her to lean on. And she, the single mother, the liberated woman, needed a man to lean on right now. Not any man, but this man. Nate Gallagher.

"I don't know. There are many possibilities. I'm still hoping that she's just lost—that she thought she could get home by herself or was mad at you for being late and started off and got lost." He kissed her hair once, twice. "Kids do stupid stuff like that all the time. It's what causes gray hair in parents."

Leigh nestled her face into the crook of his shoulder. She wished she could put stock in this theory, but she didn't. Carly wouldn't have left the dance-studio entrance. That wasn't like her. And even if she had, too many things could happen to a lost child that strayed into certain parts of New York City. But Leigh didn't voice this. Nate hadn't, and maybe he wasn't just being kind—maybe he'd be right.

"You know, I've been thinking all night what feels familiar about this place, and I've finally put it together. Did you have your daughter here in this apartment?"

"Yes." She gazed up at him, wondering what his point was.

"I was here that night. Didn't a policeman bring your sister or cousin here from the bus station?"

Leigh stared at him. "That was you?"

He nodded. "Life's strange sometimes, isn't it?"

Too strange. Not knowing what to say in response, she glanced over his shoulder and glimpsed the clock. *I can't think about the past right now, only Carly.* "I didn't realize the hour," she apologized. "You should go home. You're on duty tomorrow, aren't you?" *Please don't leave me. I need you.*

"I'll rest on your couch," he said without hesitation. "I gave this number in case anyone gets a lead. And I don't want you here without me."

She gazed up into his honest blue eyes. What would she be doing now if he hadn't come? He was the answer to the prayers she'd uttered. She wrapped her arms around his neck and pressed herself closer to him. "Thank you," she murmured, "thank you." *Thank you, God, for sending Nate.*

The long, sleepless night finally ended. Leigh paced the apartment, feeling like the living dead. Blinking herself awake, Kitty got up from the recliner and made a fresh pot of coffee. Breathing in its aroma, hoping it would lift her, Leigh carried a cup to the front window that looked out over the street she'd come to love. She thought of Nancy, who now lived in Colorado. Of how ten years ago, Leigh had run *here* to Nancy's apartment building and away from Maryland, from Trent Kinnard.

She'd prayed all night long, but God wasn't under any obligation to her. She'd ignored him for the last twenty years. She recalled the morning after Carly had been conceived, recalled wandering among the gravestones, seeking forgiveness. She didn't feel like she'd found any that day. Was that God's fault or hers?

*   *   *

Nate watched Carly standing at the window, her spine straight, but her head bowed. Would they find her daughter in time? He didn't want to think of the terror her little girl could be enduring right now, didn't let himself think of what someone might be doing to her. He always understood that he walked in a fallen, wicked world, but he never got used to it. Evil swept into a person's life, and nothing was ever the same. *God, protect this good woman and her child.*

He walked up behind Leigh. His hands claimed her shoulders. "Don't give up hope. I haven't."

She reached up and placed one of her soft hands over his. "I'm trying. But I just don't feel like I deserve . . . anything."

"You haven't mentioned much of Carly's father," Nate said cautiously, sensing he was tiptoeing into forbidden territory, "just that he couldn't be involved. But are you sure he couldn't have kidnapped her?"

"Carly was conceived in a one-night stand with a married man ten years ago. We have not kept in touch."

He winced inside at her flat recital. How much pain did that emotionless tone hide? It was as if she were saying to him, "You might as well know what kind of tramp I am."

"He must have had," Nate said evenly, "a really good line to get you into bed."

She glanced over her shoulder at him. "What?"

"You're not the kind of woman who does one-night stands. I knew that the first time I met you."

"You're that good a judge of character?" She lifted one brow. Mocking him or herself?

"Yes, I am. A cop learns to size people up in an instant. And I've been a cop for over twenty years. I wouldn't have lasted that long if I hadn't learned how."

She stared down into her mug. "He did have a good line, and I didn't know he was married."

"And you've never made a mistake like that again."

She nodded with a sober chin and turned back to the window.

"I'm not married." He massaged her shoulders. "And I don't do one-night stands. Just so you know."

She made no response.

"I'll do everything I can to find her." He squeezed her shoulders tight, letting her feel his resolve through the strength of his grip. *God, let us find Carly. Soon.*

Leigh stiffened.

He wondered why.

Then she stepped away from him and turned to the kitchen. "Aunt Kitty, Grandma Chloe, and my mother are down front. It looks like Uncle Thompson drove them. I think it's his car."

"I'm glad your family has come," Nate said, but he wondered why she'd stiffened when she'd realized her family had come and why her voice had changed subtly. How, he couldn't say, but he'd heard it. Why wasn't she happy to see them? Had they rejected her for having an illegitimate child?

"I have to go on duty today," he said. "I should be leaving now."

She looked up into his face as if she was foundering at sea, and he'd just yanked a life preserver out of her reach.

Again, he gripped her shoulder. "I won't stop the search for Carly. And unless she's found earlier, at 4:00 p.m. you need to come in to the precinct and fill out the missing person's report. Or we still might get a ransom note."

Nodding, Leigh wondered if he'd noticed that her already low spirits had nosedived when her mother had come. The buzzer from below sounded, and Kitty spoke into the intercom in the kitchen. With a heart of concrete, Leigh went to the apartment door and opened it.

Regal with a crown of silver hair, Grandma Chloe was the first through the door, and she threw her arms around Leigh. Over her grandmother's shoulder, Leigh saw her mother and then Uncle Thompson enter. Leigh braced herself for her mother's words. She'd blame this on Leigh's poor mothering, her irresponsibility.

But the condemnation didn't come. When Chloe released Leigh, Bette folded her into an embrace. "I'm so very sorry, honey. Is there any word?"

Leigh couldn't speak. It struck her that her mother was in her mid-sixties now. But it still surprised Leigh to see her striking mother with salt-and-pepper hair and faint lines around her eyes. And as Leigh lingered with her arms around Bette, her mother felt a bit too thin to her. And frail, frailer than Chloe. Dory was overseas with the Peace Corps. Bette was alone.

"What's being done?" Uncle Thompson, now in his early fifties, kissed Leigh and then went to kiss Kitty's cheek.

"This is Nate Gallagher." Leigh stepped back from her mother, fighting an onrush of tears. Having family come tapped into a deep well of emotion.

Over the past decade—in spite of her grandmother's repeated invitations—she and Carly had stayed away from Ivy Manor for so long, not wanting to "bring shame" on the McCaslins and the Sinclairs. *I allowed that to keep Carly from knowing Ivy Manor. God, please give me another chance to be a better mother.* Gooseflesh rose on her arms and she folded them around herself. "Nate's been working on a story with me. He's a NYPD detective."

"I've talked to all your stepfather's old contacts at the Bureau," Bette said, looking Nate over in detail. "Have you received a ransom note?"

"No," Nate answered for Leigh, "I'm glad to hear you're using your contacts. I've had my friends in the NYPD and state police working on this *unofficially* since last night." He glanced at his wristwatch. "I've got to run. I'll just have time to shower at home and change for work." He patted Leigh's arm and hurried out with a wave of his hand.

Leigh wanted to stop him, but she remained silent. *What would I have done without him?*

Smiling, Kitty took Thompson's arm. "Why don't you walk me home so I can do the same?"

"Sure, Kitty." Thompson led her toward the door. He turned back. "Call us if anything develops."

Leigh hadn't seen them together very often, but when Thompson came, Kitty always wore the same special smile, one that was hard to analyze. But it reminded Leigh of how a person looked when she opened a lavish and completely unexpected gift. *Oh, God, give me back my daughter.*

When the door closed, Leigh faced her mother and grandmother. "Thanks for coming so quickly. It's . . . been awful."

Both of them put their arms around her in a three-way hug. "God is still in control," Chloe said. "We'll have to trust Him to keep our little Carly safe."

Bette nodded but didn't look very convinced. Her expression said, "Praise the Lord and pass the ammunition." But aloud, she said, "I'll pour us some coffee."

Watching her mother head toward the kitchen, Leigh realized that she was already holding a mug and took a sip of the lukewarm brew. "Sit down, Grandma."

"I've been sitting for hours." Chloe took off her scarf and coat and hung them on the crowded hooks by the door. Leigh looked at the assortment of mufflers and jackets hanging there—many of them Carly's—and nearly burst into a fresh round of tears. She breathed deeply and sipped her coffee instead.

Bette handed Chloe a mug and then sat down on the sofa with her own. "Tell us," she said in a completely businesslike tone, "how this happened."

Pacing, Leigh went over the story of how she'd been delayed in picking Carly up from dance.

"You saw Mary Beth again?" Bette looked surprised. "And she's working at a mission for drug addicts?"

Leigh finally perched on the arm of the chair across from the sofa. "I know what you mean. I was so shocked. That's why time got away from me."

"That's very understandable." Chloe paused, still standing behind the sofa. "You must not feel guilty. Carly should have been perfectly safe—"

The downstairs buzzer sounded again. Leigh hurried to the intercom. The voice she heard surprised her. She pushed the button to unlock the door downstairs. "It's Minnie and Cherise."

"Oh, yes," Chloe said, "I called them last night so they could be praying. Drake and Ilsa are away in California at Sarah's grandson's bar mitzvah."

Bette opened the door and the two women plus Cherise's youngest son, a toddler, came in and were greeted with hugs and kisses. "Cherise arrived yesterday for a visit to do some shopping and to let me have some time with my youngest great-grandbaby," Minnie explained. "My husband and Frank Three are in Georgia helping take care of the house and kids while Cherise is here. Now tell us what's happening and what we can do."

Before Leigh had a chance to reply, the buzzer sounded

again. Within moments, Mary Beth was there, introducing her husband, Chet. Cherise clung to Mary Beth, weeping tears of joy. Leigh watched her two oldest friends—Cherise, whom she saw rarely but who called often, and Mary Beth, who'd disappeared over fifteen years ago. She contrasted Mary Beth the 1968 hippie with the woman here now. In spite of her grieved manner this morning, Mary Beth had never looked more content. Her husband, Chet, was tall and thin and had kind brown eyes.

Why did this reunion have to happen now when her heart was so choked by Carly's disappearance she could feel nothing else? Friends and family had gathered around Leigh even if they couldn't do anything. Why had it happened like this—the joy and the heartbreak at the same time?

Leigh glanced at the clock. It was just after 8:00 a.m. Mentally, she counted out the hours that still had to pass before she could file an official missing person's report. Eight hours. Eight more grueling hours.

She gazed at her mother, who was holding Cherise's youngest on her lap. She'd expected recriminations and blame from her mother, but she'd received none. Was it possible this might finally bridge the chasm that had opened up between her mother and her ten years ago when Leigh had insisted on keeping Carly instead of giving her up? Did she have to lose her daughter to regain her mother?

The phone rang much later that night, sending a shock wave through her. In Leigh's dimly lit living room, Nate was asleep in the recliner. Chloe and Bette were asleep in the bedrooms, and Leigh was lying on the sofa trying to rest her body if not her mind. She picked up the phone on the end table on the second ring. "Hello," she gasped.

"Leigh, it's Frank."

"Frank." Her heart thumped and then slowed again. How long had it been since she'd heard his voice on the phone? That November day in 1963 flashed in her mind—the day he'd said that she attracted him like no other. "Hi," she said, gripping the receiver.

"I waited to call you until everyone here was asleep, and I hoped you'd be alone . . ."

"Everyone here is asleep, too," she whispered.

"Leigh, I can't tell you how I wish this hadn't happened. We're all praying for Carly along with our church here. I wish I could be there with you. But I can't leave . . ."

"I know." He was stationed in Georgia and had three children.

"Cherise says there's a NYPD detective helping out. She thinks he's . . . he might be interested in you."

Leigh didn't know where this conversation was going. What did Frank want her to say?

"I hope he is," Frank murmured in that velvet voice of his that she'd never forgotten. "You've been alone too long, Leigh. I want you to find someone good who will love you like you ought to be loved."

Because you couldn't let yourself love me? "I'm not think-ing about that now," she said, speaking close to the receiver. "I can't think of anything except my little girl."

"I know. I just wanted to speak to you, to tell you . . ."

Tell me what, Frank?

"You've always been a special friend to me . . . and Cherise. If you need me, I'll find someone to take over the kids—"

"No, Frank, Nate's here, and he has the connections I need. And my Uncle Thompson is here, too."

"All right. But if you decide I can do anything, just call. I'll come."

"I will, Frank." His concern did shore her up. "Thanks for calling."

They both said their soft good-byes and hung up. Leigh kept her hand on the receiver. Did anyone ever forget a first love?

But would there be a last love in her life? Unable to help herself, the tears started again.

In one swift motion, Nate got up from the recliner and came to her. Wordlessly, he urged her back down on the sofa and then lay down by her side, facing her. With a gentle look, he put his arm around her and squeezed before laying his head down and closing his eyes.

She nearly sighed aloud with the relief of feeling his body alongside hers. She didn't take time to ponder it, but Nate had become intensely, intimately important to her over the tense hours since Carly had disappeared.

"Nobody important?" he mumbled, already falling back asleep.

"Not now." She let herself relax against him. She didn't have to stay alert. Nate was here.

November 24, 1983

The crucial phone call came late the next night. Carly had been missing two days, officially for a day. Leigh stood holding the phone to her ear, stunned. "My little girl's where?"

"She wandered in a few minutes ago and told us her name and phone number. Will you come and pick her up?"

"Yes." Feeling like a mechanical doll, she turned to Nate

and her mother, who'd planned to spend the night with her waiting for any word of Carly. Chloe and Thompson had gone to Kitty's. "Carly just walked into St. Vincent's emergency room," Leigh announced, hardly believing her own ears, "and they want me to come and get her."

Nate surged to his feet and lifted the receiver out of her nerveless hand. "This is Detective Gallagher, NYPD. Haven't you watched the news tonight? Carly Sinclair is a missing person, believed to have been abducted. Make sure you keep her under close supervision. Call security to guard her, and don't let *anyone* speak to her. I'll bring her mother and grandmother right now." Nate shepherded the two of them out to his car and they sped down the lamp-lit streets.

"I can't believe it. It doesn't make sense," Leigh, slumped beside Nate in the front seat, repeated. The suddenness of Carly's return made her feel still trapped in a dream. What would they find out at the hospital about her baby? "Why would someone take her and then drop her at an emergency room?"

From the backseat, Bette squeezed Leigh's shoulder and held it, but said nothing.

Nate also remained quiet, driving swift and sure through the light night traffic. Outside the emergency room, he screeched to a halt. The three of them—Nate holding Leigh's hand—ran into the reception area. Behind the desk, Carly sat too still and too quiet.

"Carly!" Leigh dodged around the counter and pulled her child to her. It wasn't a dream. Tears poured down her face in sheets. *Thank God. Thank God. Thank God.*

Showing his badge and ID to the triage nurse, Nate ordered, "This is a police matter. We need to have her examined immediately, so we can get her home."

Leigh squeezed her eyes shut and wished she hadn't

heard Nate's order, vibrating with the horror of what the doctor might find. *Don't let anything bad have happened to her. Please. Please.*

The next minutes went by in excruciating slow motion for Leigh, who kept her hand pressed over her quivering lips and paced and paced. After Carly had been examined by a doctor with Nate at his side, Leigh was allowed back in and watched the doctor give her child a sedative. "She needs sleep more than anything," he murmured. "And I suggest she see a child psychologist as soon as possible. Though I have not found any evidence of abuse, being abducted can have serious emotional consequences."

Leigh wanted to shout at him, "Do you think I'm an idiot! I know that!" But she only nodded.

Her mother had stood at her side through it all, giving Leigh silent support. Now Bette began to weep quietly.

"Don't cry, Grandma Bette," Carly said with genuine concern. "I'm home now. They got me away from the bad men."

Who were "they" and who were "the bad men?" Nate and Leigh exchanged looks laden with meaning. She knew without a word that he was going to see this through with her. She didn't want to depend on him, but this was beyond anything she could handle alone.

As they left the hospital, a few reporters and a TV van with a cameraman had gathered. Someone must have called the media about Carly's reappearance. The night lit up with flashing cameras and TV lights on poles. Protecting her and Carly, Nate shouldered his way through the reporters, telling them to contact the NYPD for all the information.

Nate had come through for her during the long hours of Carly's abduction. He would guide her through the maze of recovery, as well as the continuing investigation into why

Carly had been taken and then returned. The feeling of his arm around her shoulders, strong and protective, was balm and hope to her ragged spirits.

Leigh had absolutely no right to expect this of him, but she knew she wouldn't even need to ask. Nate would not desert her. Love for him sprouted, a tiny but brave new shoot in her heart.

Nate drove them home. While she and her mother put Carly to bed, he called Kitty's apartment to give them the good news and to ask them not to come over tonight. Carly needed quiet. At the hospital, he'd contacted the authorities.

Both Leigh and her mother—one on each side—lay on the bed with the little girl, caressing Carly, kissing her, letting her touch their faces with her small, soft hands.

Leigh had never felt closer to her daughter *or* her mother as she did at this moment. She reached over and briefly clasped her mother's hand and then went back to stroking Carly's long, dark hair. Finally, her sweet baby fell asleep, clutching the faded rag doll Aunt Kitty had made for her many years before.

Bette touched Leigh's shoulder. "If you don't mind, dear, *I'd* like to sleep with her tonight."

Leigh had wanted to sleep beside Carly. But something in her mother's eyes stopped her from voicing this. "Won't you be uncomfortable?"

"No, I'll be fine." Bette gave Leigh a nudge. "You go and thank that good man again. I want to be here in case my precious granddaughter wakes up." Her mother appealed to her with a look of remorse and hope.

Was her mother trying to finally close the distance between them? Leigh nodded, kissed both her daughter's and her mother's cheeks and then left, closing the door behind her.

Just outside Carly's door, all her self-control dissolved in an instant, and she started shaking. *I could have lost her. I almost lost my child.*

Leigh was only alone for moments. Nate drew her into the dark living room. He urged her down onto her sofa. Murmuring, he sat down and laid her head against his shoulder. And slowly the trembling ebbed.

Just two weeks ago, Leigh had only known Nate Gallagher, NYPD detective, professionally. He'd made it clear she interested him, but she'd kept him at arm's length as she did every other man. Then she'd needed him and he'd come through for her. Now he stroked her long hair with strong, steady hands, giving her wordless comfort.

"It's all my fault," the words flowed out of Leigh's mouth. Through the crisis, she'd fought voicing this admission—knowing it wouldn't help, knowing that guilt was natural and unavoidable—yet all the while fearful that someone else, *everyone else*, would point accusing fingers at her.

Nate said nothing in reply, just continued stroking her hair. In her weakness, she was very aware of the latent strength in his large, rough hands.

"I've always carried so much guilt about Carly," she whispered. "Not just now. But always." *And I always will.*

Little Carly's face glowed in Leigh's mind. "My Grandma Chloe always says my little girl gets her looks from my grandfather, who died in World War I. But that's because Grandma never saw Carly's father. My daughter's the spitting image of her own father. Carly has never seen her father, either, and she wants to know about her 'daddy.' She keeps asking me, and I never know what to tell her. How can I say I made a horrible mistake and not make her feel that she's one, too?"

Leigh couldn't go on. This riddle never stopped gnawing at her peace, and somehow it had created an invisible barrier between Leigh and Carly. Her daughter's sober little face, her silent little mouth, those somber eyes that hid every thought haunted Leigh.

"Everything will be okay," Nate said at last. "You love her very much, and she knows that. You'll find the strength to tell her the truth."

She gazed up at him, his face in shadow, but the moonlight illuminated the warmth of his auburn hair. She couldn't form words, her mouth paralyzed. *Will I find the courage to tell her what she wants, needs to know?*

I've stood apart from my daughter since she was born. Secrets separate us. Secrets I can't divulge. Will I never break through to her, connect with her heart-to-heart?

She reached up and captured his face between her hands. "Kiss me," she implored.

Enfolding her, Nate lifted her head and shoulders and pressed his mouth to hers. She drowned in his tender care, his persuasive lips, his solid arms. Her tears had left her drained. And he was so very strong. But a tiny voice in the back of her mind cautioned, "This is all very nice, but be careful. You've always been unlucky at love."

CHAPTER SEVENTEEN

*T*hree days later, Minnie brought Cherise and little Tad
over to say good-bye. Cherise and Tad were flying
home to Atlanta in a few hours. Tad, Chloe, Bette, Kitty, and
Minnie were all playing with Carly, who wouldn't be going
back to school until next week. Christmas had come early for
her daughter, and she sat in the middle of an embarrassing
array of new toys—even a Cabbage Patch doll. Leigh couldn't
take her eyes off Carly.

In the aftermath of her abduction, Carly had not been
able to give much information about her kidnapping. A blind-
fold had been taped over her eyes, and she'd been afraid of the
bad men who'd forced her into their car. Understandably, her
daughter didn't like it when Leigh left her sight.

The psychologist had told Leigh not to push Carly to
speak about what had happened, but on the other hand, not
to overreact with extra mothering or show of fear. The question of *why* Carly had been taken had so far been left begging.
Carly hadn't been sexually assaulted, physically abused, or
otherwise threatened with harm. She'd just been taken and returned. Was this the end of it?

Apparently not, since their apartment was still under police surveillance.

Cherise drew Leigh out into the hall and in a voice that communicated, "We need to talk," said, "Let's have a cup of tea before I go."

Wondering what her friend would have to say that the others shouldn't hear, Leigh followed Cherise into her small kitchen, filled the kettle, and set it on the burner.

"Frank said he called you."

Suspicious of Cherise's motive, Leigh nodded and stood across from her friend, who sat down at the small kitchen table. In the past, other married women had distrusted her around their husbands. "Yes," Leigh replied in a very neutral tone, "I appreciated his concern." *Please, Cherise, I have had a rough, very rough week. I can't take any—*

"I know that you were in love with Frank."

Leigh stood stock still. Normally she wouldn't reply to this. She would have ignored it, like Carly's questions about her daddy. But too much had happened over the past week and, too, if this week hadn't happened, Cherise probably wouldn't have said this. Leigh lifted her chin. "I always wondered if you knew."

Cherise nodded. "I gave it a lot of thought back when we were teens together. From what you told me about Frank's parents and from what I guessed that you *didn't* tell me, I decided that he wouldn't make any promises to you. He wouldn't become involved with a white girl."

It's just what Leigh had thought, but that didn't absolve Cherise. *You were my friend.* "So he was fair game?" Leigh couldn't hold back the mocking tone.

"Yes." Cherise's eyes never left Leigh's. "As we three girls wrote him those letters, I began to see that he was the kind of man I was looking for, and when we met, I fell for him."

"This is all ancient history." Leigh threw a piece of crumpled paper from the countertop to the waste basket. "Why are you telling me this?"

"Because I've always wanted to tell you, to try to explain that I felt bad for you, but that I wasn't what was keeping you and Frank apart."

"I knew that. But it still hurt." Leigh looked back at the kettle, which was bubbling.

"I know. I just wish . . . Dane hadn't died."

"You're not alone there." Did Cherise have any idea of how tired Leigh was?

"Sometimes I feel funny calling you like I do—knowing that you had, maybe still have, feelings for Frank. But the truth is that I've found you to be one of the most honest, most vital friends I've ever had." Cherise's voice begged for understanding. "I know it probably stings you to hear from me, but I can't break with you. Not you. You were the one who introduced me to the man who's given me everything I've ever wanted."

The kettle began to whistle in earnest, giving Leigh a chance to think of what she wanted to say. She turned and lifted it from the burner . . . but nothing came to mind. So she said, "I wouldn't want to lose you, either, Cherise."

The words were automatic, had come out of their own will. Still, they connected with deep truth inside her. She loved them both, and she always would. Cherise and Frank had made a good family together. It was right. And she wouldn't begrudge them anymore. "And I'm happy for you and Frank, truly I am."

"I believe you—"

Tad ran to his mother, resting his outstretched arms on her lap. "What was that whistle?"

Cherise stroked the little guy's face, a face that said, "This is Frank's son." "Aunt Leigh is making me tea. Do you want some?"

"If it gots honey in it."

Leigh went about making the tea and getting down the honey. Then she turned with the tray and said in a sassy tone, "Cherise, I know you've used up your vacation time with this trip. But girlfriend, you and Mary Beth and I have got to have a girls' weekend soon!"

Cherise smiled. "Soonest."

It was Monday, a bright, shiny-as-a-new-penny, crisp November day. Thanksgiving was just around the corner. A grisly murder in Boston had overshadowed the news of a local girl's kidnapping, so Carly was back in school without TV cameras following her and Leigh was going back to work. Wearing her royal-blue parka unbuttoned, she walked briskly toward her office building in Manhattan, feeling a wonderful joy at the normalcy of the day.

A black limousine with tinted windows glided to a stop at the curb right beside her. The rear passenger window slid down.

"Miss Sinclair!"

Leigh froze.

"Miss Sinclair, may I speak with you?" The voice was old, deep, and rough like heavy-duty sandpaper.

She approached the limo cautiously and glanced inside the dim interior. A lone older man, well-dressed and with white hair, looked back at her. "I need to talk to you, Miss Sinclair."

It was too much like a setup. "They'd" taken Carly. Did "they" want her now? "I . . ." Heart racing, she began backing away.

"I'm here to tell you why your daughter was kidnapped."

Halting, Leigh couldn't draw breath. People hurried around her, barely glancing her way. She opened her mouth to what—scream for help? She couldn't think.

"I'm Dane's grandfather, Roman."

Something told her this was true. But why was he here? Leigh reached to open the door, paused, and then she squeezed the handle and slipped inside. She stared at the man as the window beside her slowly went up. She saw Dane in his face. Or was it just her willing imagination?

"If it's okay with you, I'll have my driver take us 'round while we talk and then he'll drop you back here."

She studied the man. He was Dane's grandfather. He had Dane's eyes and brows. Or vice versa. She nodded.

The car purred away, and they rode in silence for a block. Roman gazed out the window, not looking toward her. "I know all 'bout you. I know my grandson intended you to be his wife. When he died, I made it my job to watch over you. I kept track of you all these years."

The idea surprised her. She turned a little more toward him. This man had been watching over her? Like a fairy god-mother?

"I know your little girl isn't Dane's." He grimaced as if this bothered him. "It was too many months later that she was born. But Dane loved you, and I failed him. I had to make that right."

Leigh felt like this was an improvisation that she'd been sucked into without warning. But all she really cared about was simple. "Who took my baby?"

"Funny you should ask," Roman said dryly.

The car slowed; the door opened, and Trent Kinnard slid into the backseat.

"You!" Leigh gasped and made a move to get out past Trent. But he caught her arm.

"Don't, Leigh. We need to talk."

"I said all I needed to say to you ten years ago," Leigh blazed. "What does this mean?" A horrifying thought nearly gagged her. "You? *You* took Carly?"

"Miss Sinclair, calm down." The older man touched her arm. "Take it slow. There are things you need to hear, to understand. I won't stretch this out a minute longer than I need to. I understand you not wanting to talk to this jerk. I don't like him, either."

Leigh sat back, moving closer to Roman. Trent was as handsome and well-dressed as ever, though he was completely silver now, looking like an aging aristocrat.

"What have you told her?" Trent asked, rubbing his hands together like Lady Macbeth.

"Not much. She just asked me who kidnapped her baby. And I'm going to tell her." Roman directed his attention to Leigh. "Now this is a twisted story. I know all about this father—" He nodded toward Trent. "—of your child. When you come up pregnant, I had someone look into it. Trent Kinnard was the only man you were close to that year after Dane—"

"I made a mistake, a bad one." She cast a glare at Trent.

"Yeah, you did, but when your heart is broken, you do dumb things." He shrugged. "And you didn't understand that every man wasn't like Dane or your stepfather, that FBI agent that rescued my grandson all those years ago. Another debt I owed and needed to repay."

"*And I* didn't understand that there were women who actually gave their hearts instead of selling them," Trent muttered, looking down, still rubbing his hands together.

Leigh began to feel as if she'd been tricked into doing a

scene for a *Godfather* sequel—the car, the way the man talked, the way he dressed. Was this for real? Trent was real. And she remembered Dane saying that she didn't know about his family. Now that statement made sense. But Dane had been gone a decade. "Who took Carly?"

Roman pointed a thumb at Trent. "A guy that didn't like Trent Kinnard digging into his business."

"I'm sorry, Leigh," Trent insisted, pleaded, "I've never told anyone about Carly being my child—"

"But Kinnard set up a half-million-dollar trust fund for your little girl, his only daughter." Roman grinned. "It was the right thing to do. But that guy—the one who didn't like Kinnard—was digging for a way to stop Kinnard, and he found out about the trust fund. He put two and two together and decided kidnapping Carly would clip Kinnard's 'Attorney General of Maryland' wings, force an end to the investigation into his dirty business."

"How did you find that out?" she asked, staring at Roman, her mouth open.

"I told you I keep tabs on you, and when Carly came up missing, I did my own digging. I found the man responsible for taking your girl. And I made him give her back."

The satisfied tone made her tremble for the man who'd taken Carly. What kind of man was Roman? Was he really what he appeared to be, a ruthless and powerful man?

"That guy won't be bothering you again. I took care of him," Roman said offhandedly. "I wasn't able to rescue my grandson all those years ago. But I was able to get your little girl back for you."

Leigh sat back, stunned by all the information that had just poured forth from Roman's lips. Had it really happened the way he'd just told her? A trust fund for Carly? A man trying to get at Trent?

"It's the truth, Leigh," Trent said, leaning forward. "I'm sorry I put Carly in danger. I thought I'd buried that trust fund deep enough that no one but my lawyer knew about it."

"There's always somebody who'll talk if the pot's sweet enough," Roman said, rubbing his thumb and forefinger together. "But neither of you has to worry about the future. No one is going to make the same mistake twice. I made sure of that."

His tone chilled Leigh. She didn't want to know how he'd made sure of it. Still, he'd rescued Carly. She laid her hand over his. "Thank you. I can never—"

He waved his hand, dislodging hers. "You don't need to thank me. I owed Dane, and I was finally able to pay my debt. I let his mother marry a zero with a gambling habit. He nearly got Dane killed. If it hadn't been for your stepdad, he would have. And see, now I paid that debt off, too. So I'm sorry your little girl had to go through that, but now my conscience is clear. I'm an old man, and I thought I might die before I could pay what I owed. Now everything's settled." He sounded completely satisfied.

Leigh touched his hand again. Here was someone who'd known and loved Dane, too. "I loved Dane with all my heart. I wish that Carly were his child, and then I would have kept part of him with me. I still grieve for him at times."

Roman squeezed her hand. "I know," he said gruffly. "You're a good woman—too good for this jerk." He nodded toward Trent. "You just made a mistake. Everyone gets to make a mistake. I've made a lotta them."

"And so have I," Trent agreed. "Leigh, isn't there any chance for us? I found out that a marriage based on a business arrangement is doomed. I'm a free man now. We could start fresh."

*   *   *

After Roman dropped Leigh back at the curb, she headed down the remaining few blocks to work. Mary Beth was waiting for Leigh in her office at *Women Today*. Leigh plopped down on the chair behind her desk and stared at Mary Beth, who looked very much out of place in her simple skirt and blouse. Was today going to be like that—just one surprise after another? Was her life never going to get back to normal?

"I won't stay long," Mary Beth stated. Telephones rang in and indistinct voices chattered in the background. "I just wanted to see you today. Everything happened so fast after we met again. I wanted to tell you again how much I regret how we parted—"

Leigh waved her hand. "Mary Beth, I've forgotten all about it. I just wished you'd contacted me years ago. You don't know how many times I've wondered where you were. If you were even still alive—"

"I know." Her friend gazed down at her ample lap. "I was ashamed of myself. I'd done things . . . well, I don't mean to burden you with how low I went before I was willing to surrender my will to God. But I'd sunk about as low as a person can and still be recognized as human." She looked up. "Maybe that's why I sense your guilt over Carly. Things aren't right between you and your daughter. Make it right, Leigh. Tell her the truth. And then forgiveness can begin."

Leigh's throat tightened, and she couldn't speak.

"The truth will set you both free." Mary Beth got up, kissed Leigh's cheek, and left the office without another word.

"I can't believe you got into a limo with a strange man," Nate repeated, looking at her as if she had soft macaroni for brains. It was late at night, though the scent of Carly's favorite pizza they'd eaten for supper still hung in the air. After her first day back at school, Carly was sound asleep, and he and Leigh were side by side on her sofa. He was going to get all the facts, and then Leigh was going to get the scolding of her life—even though being here with her was the nearest thing to heaven he'd ever felt. "Carly gets snatched, and you don't see that—"

Leigh's delicate hand covered Nate's mouth for a few moments. "I recognized him as Dane's grandfather."

"That doesn't mean—"

She put her hand over his mouth again. "Nothing happened to me."

Nate grumbled to himself. He had a pretty good idea of who Roman was, but he wasn't going to tell Leigh what he knew. Some things were better left unsaid. But who would have thought that a straight arrow like Dane Hanley had come from a crime family?

He kissed Leigh's palm, and she lifted it from his mouth. "Well, at least, now we know what happened and why."

Leigh nodded. "There was another man in the car."

He moved a few inches closer to her, his desire to scold her melting. "A bodyguard?"

"No," Leigh said, looking him directly in the eye, "Carly's father."

He felt his mouth go dry. "He was there. Why?"

Leigh shrugged. "I think Roman brought him because he wanted to see him humiliated."

Nate sat up straighter. "I don't get you."

"Dane's grandfather has evidently been keeping tabs on me for over a decade. He knew or guessed that if he brought Carly's father along, he would take this opportunity to try to get me to come back to him and Roman bet that I would refuse. I don't make the same mistake twice. He wanted to see the attorney general of Maryland shot down—"

"Carly's father is the attorney general of Maryland?" Nate asked in total disbelief.

She nodded. "Please keep that in confidence." She folded her fingers over his. "Anyway, I think Roman wanted to see Dane's fiancée put Trent Kinnard down, prove that his grandson was the better man."

"That sounds way too convoluted—"

"I was there. I saw the body language and heard the tones, the inflections of his voice. I'm sure of it."

"So you turned Kinnard down?" His spirit lightened.

She nodded.

"Going to turn me down?"

Her head swung around and her eyes met his.

"I'm here for good, you know." He traced her lips with his forefinger. "I keep thinking about the fact that I came here the night Carly was born. That I saw her before she was even an hour old. I feel attached to her already. It feels like I've just been marking time until I found you and her again. And I'm not bowing out of your lives unless you get a court order."

Unwilling to be swayed by his words, she still pressed her lips together and tugged away. "I'm not good . . . with men—"

"You've had a rough time, but that time is over." With his right hand, he lifted her golden hair over one ear and watched it flutter down again like spun gold. "I've fallen in love with you, Leigh Sinclair. And that's that."

"I can't give you what you want, Nate." She sounded tight inside.

"And what do I want—" He lifted her hair again. As it drifted back to her shoulders, he watched it gleam in the low light. "—except for you?"

"I'm just not the loving-wife type." She turned her profile to him and tried to move away from his hand sifting her hair.

"You're fooling yourself if you believe that. And what's a loving-wife type?" He moved closer, his mouth hovering over hers. "Do you think I expect to come home to fresh-baked bread and slippers? Get real. I love you, Leigh. Deal with it." Then he bent his head and claimed her soft lips, marking her as his own.

Feeling the warmth spread through her, Leigh wanted to believe him, wanted to be persuaded, but it didn't feel real. *I'm thirty-six years old, and I've never won at love before. How can I believe it would ever happen now? Don't love me, Nate. I'm bad with men—either they leave me or they die.*

CHAPTER EIGHTEEN

December 10, 1983

At the centuries-old cemetery, Leigh stood in bitter, blustery wind. Icy sunlight dazzling her, she'd slipped on her sunglasses. Nate had his arm around her, keeping her close. The priest was pronouncing the final benediction at the graveside of Nate's grandfather. It was a policeman's funeral. Legions of retired and active policemen in blue and braid had come out to honor this ex-cop who'd walked his beat back through the Roaring Twenties, the Depression, World War II, and on past Korea.

Then bagpipes began to play "Amazing Grace." The plaintive melody caught Leigh around the heart and she couldn't have moved if she'd tried. Had Nate's grandfather requested it just as her grandfather had?

In 1972, Minnie had sung this at both funerals, her grandfather's and the double one for Ted and Dane. But it was as if Leigh were hearing the words for the first time. In her mind, she heard once more Minnie lifting her rich contralto voice, "*. . . that saved a wretch like me. I once was lost but now I'm* *found. Was blind but now I see.*" And then it was as if Grandpa Roarke, Ted, and Dane were there, hovering close, enfolding her in their love—their abiding love for her that hadn't ended with their deaths.

Remorse, gratitude, hope swelled inside her. She clung to Nate, fearing that the power of these surging emotions would sweep her from her feet. Something hovered at the back of her consciousness. What had Grandma Chloe said to her after Dane's death—something that Leigh should never forget?

She closed her eyes, and it started to return. Chloe had told Leigh that God loved her just she was, an imperfect human. That sounded good, but how did one make up for being fallible? Her life hadn't gone the way she'd planned. And after committing adultery and in effect cursing her child, how could Leigh ever make things right? Carly was back with her, but only in body, not spirit. How could she close that hollow space between them?

In her suddenly sharpened memory, Minnie continued to sing along with the bagpipes, *"Through many trials, toils, and fears, I have already come. 'Twas grace that brought me safe this far, and grace will lead me home."*

God, I've sought Your forgiveness, Your grace all these years without realizing it. What do I have to do to get it? I can't begin again until I put the past, my sin behind me. I can't reach Carly until I've made things right.

Sudden warmth filled her, driving away the chill. Her mind had never been clearer. Grandma Chloe's voice whispered in her mind, *"Lay down your pride that insists you can do this life without God's forgiveness."*

Mary Beth's voice whispered, *"Just tell the truth. It will set you free."*

Nate's defiant words came back, *"I love you, Leigh. Deal with it."*

Leigh couldn't hold out any longer. Suddenly she realized that *she* was the stumbling block, the dam that was holding everything back. *I give up, God,* she acknowledged silently. *I accept that I can't make You forgive me; I can only accept Your grace. I'll tell Carly the truth about her father.*

Then she turned into Nate's embrace and hugged him so tightly she felt his uniform's buttons pressing into her. The crescendo of the song lifted above her, "When we've been there ten thousand years, bright shining as the sun, we've no less days to sing God's praise than when we first begun."

"I love you, Nate Gallagher," she whispered into his ear, relief washing through her like a baptism.

He looked down and kissed her cheek. "I know." And then he grinned.

HISTORICAL NOTE

Writing *Leigh* was difficult for me. Leigh Sinclair was only a few years older than I, so her youth and coming of age was mine too. The thought of writing a "historical" novel around my own generation jarred me. But once I got into it, I found that bringing up realistic details from my own past instead of from history books paid an unexpected dividend. I recalled things I had forgotten. And *Leigh* gave me a chance to revisit the turbulent times of my youth.

I recalled the Cold War, the fearful days of the Cuban Missile Crisis and the very real anxiety of a nuclear holocaust, so very different from today's worries of "dirty" bombs and terrorism. I recalled awakening to the news that Robert Kennedy had been killed and wondering when the assassinations would stop—or if they ever would. I recalled the violent transition from segregation to racial integration, the trauma of Viet Nam and of Watergate.

I remember ladies wearing hats and gloves to church on Sundays when all the stores were closed and families got together over "Sunday dinner" and a quiet afternoon. I remember wearing a skirt every day—not just for special occasions—and wearing a girdle with hooks to hold up nylon hose with seams. I remember the advent of pantyhose and bra-burning and much, much more. My generation rebelled against the World War II generation, very much matching the "Lost Generation" of the Roaring Twenties. Chloe said it best: "It seems like in America, we have these times that come through like gangbusters, ripping things apart, and what's been accepted for decades and decades changes overnight." That was the sixties and seventies. Those were the days, my friends.

READING GROUP GUIDE

1. What historic events, if any, have impacted your life? In what way? And what were the consequences?

2. How have the years changed popular opinion about the Viet Nam War? Or have they?

3. Leigh makes a life-altering choice the night of Mc-Govern's defeat. Can you find parallels to this in the Bible? In history or your own life?

4. What do you think are the causes of the conflict between Leigh and Bette? What advice would you have given Leigh? Bette? Does heredity play any part in their personalities? If so, how?

5. Leigh's response to her little daughter's questions about her daddy was pained silence. Was she right or wrong? How would you have handled it?

6. Did Kitty's story surprise you? What led her into an affair and out of it?

7. Do you see any parallels among the lives of Chloe, Bette, and Leigh? Explain.

8. Of the three generations of women, who seems to have found the greatest peace? Why do you think this is so?

9. Nate visited Leigh's apartment the night Carly was born. Have you ever experienced a similar "coincidence" in your life? Or do you know of a real-life example that happened to someone you know?

10. Compare and contrast how each generation handles universal experiences, such as births, deaths, weddings, et cetera. Show how each is somewhat the same and different for each generation.

ᴳTHE WOMEN OF IVY MANORᴼ

Meet the women of Ivy Manor—four strong and independent ladies who live and love throughout the decades of the twentieth century. Each has experiences unique to herself; each must learn to grow and succeed on her own terms.

Chloe

Born in the early days of the new century, she gives up her old life for a new one—before realizing that perhaps what she's always wanted was right in front of her.

Bette

Coming into her own during World War II, Bette learns that dreams and expectations often change, hopefully for the better. Can she give up her childish hopes and embrace real life?

Leigh

A child of the civil rights movement, Leigh lives and breathes the exploration of new ideas and thoughts. But independence isn't always easy, and mistakes are made. Can she learn to accept who she is before it's too late?

Carly

Carly longs for independence, and finds it in the military. But when all that is stripped away, will she realize that her sense of identity comes from within, not from anything and anyone else?